# THE
# DATABASE
## OF
# SOULS

## H.W. BYARS

*For Maria*

# A Note from the Author

First of all, thank you for reading. This book is the second edition of my first book. It was originally published as *Act Normal*. I changed the title to *The Corruption of the Actual* when I discovered there were hundreds of other books with similar titles to *Act Normal*.

It was my first novel and first attempt at self-publishing. I've come to learn that many authors abandon their first book. After the initial ordeal, they find themselves bolder and more experienced. They don't want to burden themselves with their rookie mistakes. It's the smart, time-tested thing to do. I wasn't smart.

I doubled down. I wrote a sequel, *The Orphaned God*. Upon completing the sequel, I revisited this book. I wanted it to be as good as the new one, so I strapped in and got my machete out and started editing.

What you have in your hands is the end result of that process. The story and the characters are all the same as originally envisioned in *Act Normal*. What's missing? Technical jargon, religious tangents, and tangential technology were all trimmed. Oh, and Al doesn't get cancer. He was thrilled.

Anyway, I'm satisfied with the way *The Database of Souls* turned out, and I hope you are as well. Thanks for reading!

— H.W. Byars

# One

A COOL BREEZE filtered through the window and filled the room with the scent of sweet olives. Cicadas chirped loudly from the magnolia trees in the front yard, and their pulsating screeches reverberated inside Dan's brain. He stopped typing and massaged his temples. *I can't concentrate like this.*

Floorboards creaked as he crossed the room. He shut the wooden window frame, and flakes of old, dried-out paint rained down on his head. *I painted the house only five years ago! How can it be time for a new coat already?*

Dan cursed under his breath as he picked away at the jagged flakes sticking to his hands.

He wiped the rest of the paint flakes on his pants and continued his struggle with the stubborn old frame. A man lumbering down the sidewalk in front of the house made him pause. The hair rose on the back of Dan's neck. People rarely walked the neighborhood after dark. *The way he walks... Is he injured?*

When the man passed under the streetlight, Dan recognized him as being the parish's retired priest. *What is Father Desjeunes doing in my neighborhood? He has to be about eighty years old. Why is he out for a stroll at this hour?*

The elderly priest shot a glance toward the window, and Dan flinched. The priest lowered his head and continued on his path, disappearing into the night. *Probably just priest business.* Dan shut the window and closed the curtains.

He ran his fingers along the desk as he returned to his keyboard. They left a clean streak through the pollen dust. Dan hated the weather in Louisiana. The few days of the year cool enough to open the windows for fresh air were polluted with pollen. In the fall, it was the acrid smoke from burning sugarcane fields. The summers and winters were out of the question. It was always too humid.

The floor creaked. Katie stood in the doorway, wearing her bathrobe and wiping her nose. "Are you working again tonight?" she said, holding back a sneeze.

"Yes." Dan groaned. "Tonight is network maintenance. The project manager said it won't take long, but you know how that goes."

Katie sneezed into her tissue and glared at Dan. She had begged him a hundred times to keep the windows shut during allergy season. But to him, the old house smelled musty. He aired it out whenever Katie wasn't home.

"Sorry, I got busy and forgot to close them."

"It isn't just the pollen, Dan. It's the late nights." Katie put a hand on his shoulder. "You worked Friday night, Saturday night, and now tonight? This is the third night in a row, never mind that it's the weekend. When are we supposed to sleep? Tomorrow is a school day."

Dan shrugged and opened several tabs on his browser. Each one displayed real-time charts of network and server activity. Katie was right about the sleep. It was a burden on the whole family.

The worst part about these late nights was when there was nothing to do but stare at his screen. His job was to be available in the event something went wrong. Dan hated these "be available" assignments. The other guys did all the work. Dan just had to log in.

But when things went wrong, they *really* went wrong, and he would have to dedicate hours or days resynchronizing the systems. Either way, tonight he was going to have to spend the next few hours staring at a computer screen. It wasn't always like this. These "be available" tasks had begun when the new manager came on board.

It was all because of the night the on-call sysadmin slept through the hundreds of alerts sent to his cell phone. Management fired him for dereliction of duty. To ensure it wouldn't happen again, the manager's solution was to make the on-call sysadmin log in and monitor every maintenance process no matter how routine. It was a big company with a lot of systems. The on-call guy never slept.

Dan was stuck, but he seldom complained. IT jobs in Louisiana were hard to come by. Especially in Mons. There were two leading employers in town: Canaille Technologies, an H1B visa mill, and his employer, AGphic. He was forced to choose between a small salary and no personal time. He chose money, so here he sat at nine thirty on a Sunday night with hours of idle boredom stretched out before him.

Katie hugged Dan around the shoulders. Dan was edgy from the lack of sleep and had forgotten she was there. She laughed and kissed him on his cheek.

"Did you silence your phone? Remember the last time network did something? It went off all night."

"I'll do it now." Dan clicked away, checking emails. "It's the network team's show tonight. They're installing a new firewall. If everything goes according to plan, it'll only take a couple of hours. When they're done, I'll do my checks. Those will take about an hour. I should be in bed before one."

Katie groaned and put her hands on her hips.

"I know it's late. I'm sorry, Katie."

Katie rolled her eyes and blew her nose. Dan had never had to work after hours the entire weekend before. He hoped it wasn't the start of a trend.

"Come to bed when your work is over," she said as she pointed the dirty tissue at him. "Don't stay awake arguing with strangers on the internet over that cockamamie theory. You were up until four a.m. last night."

"Last night took so long because I had to patch the financial systems," Dan said, opening a connection to the cloud monitoring system. As the screen filled with charts, he propped his feet on the desk and gave Katie a relaxed smile. "Tonight I'm an observer."

Katie stuffed the used tissue into her robe pocket and sighed. "Just don't be up any later than you have to. Stay away from those crazy forums, okay?"

"Crazy?" Dan put his hand on his heart in mock pain and batted his eyes at her. "The Simulation is real, love. It's a conspiracy!"

"You know what *is* real?" Katie said. "After-school duty. Between that and the third grade showcase, I'm in for a twelve-hour workday. I just want some sleep." She checked her reflection in the mirror and massaged the dark circles under her eyes.

Dan's smile disappeared. She was miserable. "I'll sleep on the couch tonight. I wouldn't want the parents to think their children's teacher is a raccoon."

Katie mouthed "thank you" and turned to walk away, but Dan grabbed her hand.

"Are the kids asleep?" He raised his eyebrows.

"Yes, the kids are asleep," she said, shoulders sagging, "but I'm too tired for sex. Maybe next weekend?"

"It's a date," Dan said as he kissed her on the cheek. "Good night, honey. I'll be quiet."

He listened carefully until the bedroom door closed. Satisfied she had gone to bed for the night, Dan gently shut the office door and made his way over to the filing cabinet. In the back was the secret compartment concealing his drug stash.

Dan sifted through the contents and sighed. It was a pathetic assortment, hardly worthy of being hidden at all. If Katie weren't so antidrug, the cannabis would be in the medicine cabinet next to the aspirin. Cannabis wouldn't do it tonight. He wanted something stronger to help the time go by.

He found the bottle of cheap homemade THC edibles he'd bought off a guy in the French Quarter. They were so weak he suspected they might have been children's vitamins. He pushed it aside. Too boring.

Next to it was an empty medicine dropper. It had once contained a diluted mixture of LSD for microdosing. Dan had wondered if it had any LSD at all because he didn't experience a trip.

Dan's friend and coworker, Blaine, had given it to him. Blaine wasn't a drug dealer; he was a guy with connections. When Dan had asked him about LSD, this was what he received. He wanted to try a stronger dose, but Blaine said he couldn't get it anymore.

As an apology, Blaine had handed him a new type of psychedelic. Dan fingered the white drug carton. FANA was written in bold metallic-blue letters across the front. The back had a wrinkled and reused sticker that read FREE SAMPLE. NOT FOR INDIVIDUAL SALE.

Blaine had said a friend had given it to him, and it was the product of a Canadian psychedelic start-up company. It was supposed to be an entertaining combination of LSD, psilocybin, and ayahuasca. Dan had never tried ayahuasca before.

He took the box over to the computer and googled Fana. Out of the many hits, a single website had information on the drug, and it was an advertisement. The slogan was *Fana – Your Mind without Limits.*

According to the site, Fana was provided a fun, safe psychedelic experience. No sitter required. The best part was that the high was supposed to last between one and two hours. Dan checked the clock. He had plenty of time before work needed him.

He inspected the blister pack. It contained five milky-green disks, each the thickness of two nickels stacked together.

"Two hours," he whispered. "I hope they're right."

He popped one out of the pack and tossed it into his mouth. Dan twitched as if he had licked a nine-volt battery.

It had an unbearable metallic taste. The more Dan tried to chew it, the worse it became. He gagged and swallowed it whole. Still, his mouth tasted like a dirty penny. He found an old water bottle sitting on his desk and took a big gulp, but it didn't help. Disgusted, Dan tossed the carton of Fana back into the filing cabinet and returned to the computer.

His brain became fuzzy, and his body relaxed. He closed the browser windows for work and perused the forums. Halfway through the top post of the day, his phone chimed an email alert. He reached for the phone but knocked it to the floor. It dinged again and again. Hundreds of alerts poured in.

"It's the network team getting started," he said to himself. "No need to panic."

He groped for the phone under the desk but it slipped through his fingers. By the time he got it and turned it off, his vision was blurry.

"I can't wake Katie or the kids."

He sank deeper into his chair and went back to the internet. He didn't have to work until later, and those alerts were false positives. Besides, the forums were abuzz tonight.

For the past few months, Dan's obsession had been the idea that reality is a simulation. Most of the online forums dedicated to simulation theory were infested with teenagers who believed reality was similar to a video game. The others were middle-aged men who believed *The Matrix* to be the gospel. Out of all the places on the internet dedicated to discussing simulation theory, Dan agreed with only one.

There, the people believed humans were complex computer programs running on a universe-sized computer. This computer hosted all of humanity. It contained everything from the stars to the seas. It created the rules of gravity and governed the speed of light. This universe was designed to host human activity.

People are supposed to be unaware they are computer programs. According to the site's FAQ: "Humans are only able to experience the specific physical sensations necessary to function within the given framework. The unseen reality is that humans are merely information stored in a giant computer system." Or as Dan liked to put it: "The Simulation only lets you see and feel what it wants you to. You do the rest."

Dan had to admit the leaps in logic some of them made to support their theories were a bit ridiculous. In truth, the overall idea of an all-encompassing simulation had merit. It lacked evidence. Also, the people were weird.

For every scientific paper put forth by a respected physicist, there were a thousand more armchair theologians with a blog. Actual scientific information was drowned out by the uneducated masses. Dan had made it his mission to sort through the competing ideas and get to the truth.

But the more Dan researched, the more confused he became. Scientific papers were quickly debunked. Conspiracy theorists disappeared from their blogs and online forums. The community succumbed to paranoia and quit posting. A popular theory was that it wasn't the government suppressing information. It was the Simulation itself. If anyone publicly posted a message too close to the truth, they would disappear. Or so they said. Maybe they ate too much peyote.

Dan rubbed his eyes. The words on the screen twisted and blurred. Was the Fana taking effect already? It had hardly been ten minutes. *That was fast.* He rubbed his eyes, and an email popped up on his screen. The words trickled down the monitor and dripped out onto his desk like water. He stared wide-eyed as the email collected into a pool beneath his monitors. Once it finished dripping, he could read the words. There was an issue with the new firewall's power supply. *Not my problem.*

He blinked, and another email arrived. It was from his boss, asking if the financial systems were online. *Why wouldn't they be online? The financial systems have nothing to do with the firewall.* Dan shook his head and sat up straight. What if there *was* a problem at work?

He blinked again, and the mirage that was the pool of email that had collected beneath the monitor evaporated. His worry disappeared with it. He checked his phone, and the screen was black. *No missed calls, no problem. They won't need me for a couple of hours.*

Dan donned his headphones and put on his favorite tunes. The trip was more intense than the microdosing he had become accustomed to. He had been told long ago to not fight psychedelics. If you do, you'll have a bad trip. It's best to go in with a mindset to enjoy the ride. He relaxed and let the drug take over.

The walls melted and oozed to the floor. They congealed into glowing, multicolored pools. The music changed, and the liquid crystalized. Drool dangled from Dan's lower lip. The beat dropped. The floor broke out into geometric shapes and vibrated with the music. Colorful light from the computer monitors sprayed the office with fireworks. Dan's eyes stretched open wide. The fireworks transformed into pixelated butterflies that fluttered about the room. A *beep* interrupted the music, and the butterflies disappeared into a sparkling mist. Someone on the forum had sent him a private message.

> *From: Charlie*
> *Subject: Hey check this out!*
> *Dan,*
>
> *I've been following your comments over on the Simulation forums, and I think you're a pretty cool dude. Some of those guys take it way too far, but you seem normal. Anyway, one of the guys we hang out with created a secure place to chat. It's a heavily modded MUD*

*from the 1990s that's still running. You'll need a terminal emulation client to access it. The interface is definitely old-school. If you're interested, reply to this message, and I'll send you its current IP address. I hope to hear from you soon.*

*Cheers,*

*Charlie*

Dan replied, and a few minutes later he found himself signing in to the MUD.

The screen turned black, and a green prompt appeared with a blinking cursor.

WELCOME TRAVELER scrolled by in ASCII art. "There are 03 connected."

*What is this? Zork?*

Dan's brain buzzed, and the screen rippled. The green text jumped out of the inky blackness and morphed into floating blobs in his eyes. Dan blinked hard to clear the floaters and scanned the terminal. Instead of following the instructions on creating a user, he signed in as a guest.

"Hello?" he typed. "Is there anybody out there?"

"Dan!" said Charlie. "I'm glad you came!"

"Hey, Charlie! Oh, and that's Guest02 to you."

"Dan, you should create an account. It's required to connect to the secure version. That way all our conversations and activities will be private."

Dan scrolled through the previous text and followed the instructions on creating a private account.

*User <Guest02> has been renamed <Dan>*

"Okay, I'm logged in, now what?"

"Okay. Next, you have to VPN to this address by typing 'connect secure: …'"

Dan's head lolled to one side. Was he coming down from the high, or was it getting more intense? He wasn't sure. He yawned and closed his eyes. He jerked back to attention. *What happened? What time is it?*

Dan woke the computer from the screensaver and checked the time. The numbers didn't mean anything to him. *I'm supposed to be doing something. Work? No. The firewall was the network team's problem.*

Charlie instructed him to input a series of commands. The syntax was completely foreign. He tried to figure out what the string of commands meant, but it required too much effort. The code was too complicated. The vibrations in his head intensified, and he struggled to focus. It took every ounce of energy to concentrate on typing in precisely what he was told.

The rainbow vapors dissipated, and a low hum filled the room. Black smoke emanated from the dark terminal screen. Dan's skull vibrated, and he winced in pain. He checked his headphone's connection. It would make a similar noise if it was loose, but it was plugged securely in the jack.

The hum ended, and the pain stopped. Dan did his best to follow Charlie's instructions. After several minutes of typing, he hit Enter, and the screen faded. An intense squealing blared through his headset, and Dan jolted upright in his seat. Connected appeared on the terminal, followed by two short *beeps*. Dan's eyes rolled back into his head, and he fell into a trance.

"All right. He is connected securely—now what?" a voice said over the headphones.

"Download and extract L3m.bin to his memory. I'll take care of the rest," said a second voice.

"This won't hurt him, will it?"

"No, Charlie, Dan won't feel a thing. I promise."

When Dan's eyes regained focus, they were locked to his computer terminal. He couldn't look away. He was paralyzed. Thousands of lines of machine code scrolled down the screen. Hours passed by as commands executed subroutines.

Subroutines scrolled more indecipherable code. Dan was its hostage.

Later on in the night, someone typed the word QUIT into the terminal. The scrolling code stopped, and the terminal window disappeared. The squealing ceased. Dan, released from the trance, fell out of his chair. His headphones, ripped out of the jack, lay broken on the floor at his feet. As he drifted off to sleep, voices chattered in his head.

# Two

K ATIE AND THE kids were leaving the parking lot just as Dan arrived. He tried to wave, but they didn't see him. The clock on the dashboard confirmed he was twenty minutes late to their usual Monday-morning breakfast date. What was supposed to be a positive start to the week for the family had turned into anything but.

Dan debated on whether to go in, but his mouth was dry and he was hungry. All he wanted was a glass of water and a cup of coffee.

The Breakfast Station had been a train depot in a previous life. Constructed in 1903, it was a stop on an east-west line ferrying passengers between New Orleans and Houston. In the 1960s, the government built I-10, connecting the two cities. Automobiles became the preferred mode of transportation. As a result, the number of rail passengers wanting to disembark in Mons dwindled to zero. The station was abandoned. Decades later, an entrepreneurial couple rediscovered it.

Two years and millions of dollars in renovations later, they had the most popular restaurant in town. Its quirky interior, good food, and central location were adored by both visitors and locals. Most weekends, there was a line out the door, but that was seldom the case on a Monday. The weekdays were for locals. The working class cleared out before eight. The place was all but deserted when Dan walked in. He sat at the first empty table and massaged his temples.

"Mornin', Dan!" said a cheerful, gray-haired waitress.

Dan jolted upright and bumped his knee underneath the table. The silverware clanged, causing the only other customer present to turn and stare.

"Good morning, Barb," he said and flashed her a sheepish grin. "Mind getting me a glass of ice water?"

Barb flipped over a coffee mug and filled it with steaming coffee. "You missed Katie," she said with a hand on her hip. "She said if you showed up, I was to tell you to turn on your phone."

Dan's eyes went wide as he frantically dug into his pocket and found the device. It was turned off. Shit! "Thanks," he said as it powered on. "Can I get a glass of water please?"

Barb grunted and walked off. What had happened last night anyway? How had he ended up sleeping on the couch? His head pounded, and he winced in pain. This wasn't like any headache he'd had before. It blurred his vision. Was this a migraine? Dehydration? Caffeine withdrawals? Lack of sleep? *Get it together, Dan!*

He checked his phone, and it was still booting up. *How long was it off? Shit! I'm on call! There was a network outage, right?* He reconciled his memory, but it didn't add up. Something else had happened, and a meeting was scheduled this morning. *Right?*

Barb placed a tumbler of ice water on the table.

"Thanks," he croaked.

"Let me know if you want any food," she said and left Dan alone with his coffee and water.

The front door *dinged,* and an elderly couple walked in, followed closely by a man in a yellow baseball cap. The man wedged himself between the couple and the wall. He and Dan made eye contact, and he hid behind the elderly man. The hostess arrived and seated the couple, and the man disappeared. Strange guy. He must have ducked into the restroom. The phone buzzed, and he snapped back to attention. It had connected to the cellular network, and hundreds of queued-up messages poured in.

Dan's stomach knotted as he scanned the messages. He had made a grave mistake by taking Fana. He'd had an email battle with his boss at three a.m., but he didn't remember any of it. The network team had aborted their plans to replace the firewall because the financial system's database server crashed. The alerts were about the financial systems, not the network. Dan was in deep shit. His phone had been off, and he was too high to notice the outage. *I should have known better.*

More emails from his boss, each one more urgent. The last one read: "Dan, the payroll system is still offline! Answer your phone!"

Dan's hands shook, and the room blurred. The phone rang, and his boss's name showed on the caller ID. He hurriedly pressed a button to send the call to voice mail. *I can't talk to him now. I've got to sober up a bit more. What was in that stuff?* He decided to wait until he got to the office to plead his case. To plead what? That he'd been too high to do his job? *I need a better excuse.* The bell on the front door *dinged* again.

Barb appeared and pushed another plastic tumbler of ice water in front of him, ripping Dan out of his daydream. He banged his knee on the table again, spilling the coffee.

"You're jumpy today. Are you feeling okay?"

Dan rubbed his knee. "Sorry. It was a long night, and work is a nightmare."

Barb collected the mug and saucer and gave him a sympathetic smile. "I know the feeling," she said. "I'll be right back with a rag to wipe all this up."

Barb took the dirty dishes to the kitchen, past a smartly dressed priest standing at the counter. He regarded Dan with a furrowed brow. What was his problem? Dan ignored him and daubed coffee from his khakis with a paper napkin. Barb reappeared with a towel and more water.

"Who's the priest?"

"What priest?" she said, scanning the room.

Dan pointed to where the priest stood, but he wasn't there.

Barb shook her head and took out her order pad. "Are you hungry?" she said curtly. "Do you want the usual?"

*She knows I'm high. She's not even looking at me.*

"Uh, not today," Dan said, checking the time on his phone. "Just a cup of coffee to go. Work is blowing up."

"This is none of my business," Barb said with a hand on her hip. "But you look pale as a ghost. Maybe if you eat something, you'll feel better. Are you sure I can't get you a biscuit?"

She was right. He didn't feel well, and the last thing he wanted at the moment was a dry biscuit. He waved his hand no, and Barb left to get the coffee. She walked right past the priest without noticing.

"Good morning, Daniel," he said and sat at Dan's table.

Dan stopped scrubbing his pants and eyed him incredulously. What did he want?

"Mind if I join you for a few moments?"

Annoyed, Dan checked the clock once again. *Where's Barb with my coffee?* She was behind the counter, pouring ground coffee into the machine. Dan groaned. He didn't have time to talk to a priest, especially not while in this condition.

"I'm sorry to be rude, but I'm in a bit of a rush this morning, Father," Dan said. "Do I know you?"

The priest placed his teacup and saucer on the table. Was he always holding the teacup? *Keep it together, Dan.*

"You probably don't remember me," he said with an arrogant tone, "but I was friends with your parents."

The front door *dinged* again as a customer left. The man in the yellow baseball cap rushed from the restroom and slid out the door just before it closed. No one else seemed to have noticed, and Dan dismissed it as a hallucination.

"My parents died many years ago." He turned his attention back to the priest.

"Yes, I was there."

Dan tried to recall his parents' funeral, but his head pounded. Where was Barb? The coffeepot was finished, but she was yapping with another waitress.

"I'm sorry, Father. Their funeral was a blur. I was a young man, and it was traumatic for me. What's your name?"

"Father August," he said with a toothy smile that didn't reach his eyes. "I'm from another parish. I was in the area on a special assignment and thought I'd visit an old friend. I was on my way to see him and stopped here for a tea, and I recognized you."

*Hurry up, Barb! This guy is giving me the creeps.* Barb was no longer yapping with the waitress. She had gone into the kitchen. Dan glanced at the clock on the wall and rubbed his head. *Come on!* The priest smiled politely and sipped his tea. A thought crossed Dan's mind to just leave the coffee and get out of there. Why couldn't he?

"Oh yeah? Who's the old friend you're here to see?" Dan said. "Father Desjeunes?"

"Of course." The priest coughed and set his cup on the table. "Father Desjeunes is one of my oldest friends. He's enjoying retirement, and I will pay him a visit." The priest leaned forward in his chair. "The reason I came over is I'm actually here to see you. You are my business here."

"Me?" he stammered. "Why?"

"I've heard troubling things. You've been staying up late and reading things on the internet you aren't supposed to. I'm worried you'll get into trouble if you don't stop."

Dan stiffened, and his face went red. His eyes searched the room for signs of the police. He had always worried his casual browsing of free porn sites would lead to this. They promised no one was underage. Shit! He searched the room. Security cameras were posted in every corner. *Great.* Why send a priest? Was this a prank?

"Who sent you?"

The priest straightened his collar. "No one sent me. I've had discussions with your wife about your marriage, and she confided in me that you may be having problems."

"When did you talk to Katie?" Dan's head throbbed, and the priest faded in and out of his vision.

The priest leaned back in his chair and took a sip of tea. "Katie and I talk all the time. She told me you were up all night last night, surfing the internet. She told me you're secretive about your online activity. She says you hide it from her by using VPNs and private browsers. She doesn't know what you're up to, but it can't be honest if you have to hide it. Why are you so careful?"

Dan reached for his water glass, but his hands were shaking too much to grab it. Father August arched an eyebrow, and Dan quickly hid them beneath the table.

"She told me you didn't show up to breakfast this morning. You told her you were working last night, but she knows the truth. You weren't working, were you?"

Dan couldn't answer. His mouth tasted like ashes. The room became hot, and sweat seeped through his clothes. Who was this man? He was sure of one thing. Father August hadn't gotten his information from Katie. Katie had no idea what a VPN was. Even still, how did he know all that? Dan finally managed to grab his glass and took a deep drink of water.

"Katie told you that?"

"She did. It's the reason I'm checking on you."

Dan pushed back his chair and stood. The room wobbled.

"Thank you for your concern, Father August," Dan said, "but I wasn't surfing the internet last night. If you must know, I was actually working. A server went down. In fact" — Dan checked the clock on the wall and frowned — "I'm afraid I'm going to have to go to work now. I'm late."

The reverend snorted derisively. "If you say so." He set his teacup carefully onto its saucer. "Just so you know, I'll be in town for the next few weeks. I'm available if you need to tell me anything."

"I appreciate it, Father."

Barb arrived with Dan's coffee and a small brown bag. "Here ya go. I packed up a biscuit and some jelly for you. You need to eat something."

Dan mumbled thanks as he fumbled for his wallet. *Why are my hands shaking?* After what seemed like a lifetime, he handed her a twenty.

"Okay, I'll be right back with your change."

Barb turned to walk off, but Dan grabbed her by the arm.

"Barb, add the priest's breakfast to my bill and keep the change." Dan smiled at Father August. "My treat."

Barb opened her mouth to protest the generous tip, but the order bell rang. She shrugged and stuffed the twenty into her apron.

"Thank you, Dan," Father August said with a wry smile.

"It's the least I can do."

<hr />

Dan slammed the door to his truck. What was the deal with the priest? How did Katie know him? He had never heard of a Father August before today. It was all very weird. Was it the Fana? The pounding in his head subsided, and Dan said a silent prayer of thanks. The water and coffee must have worked.

He checked the messages on his phone again. The payroll systems were still down, and his boss was unhappy. He couldn't get them back online without Dan's help, and it made *him* look bad.

The ladies in payroll reported they were missing the past two weeks of time sheets. That was worse than not being able to log in. That meant that the junior admin had taken a crack at getting things online and had done it in the wrong order. He'd attached the wrong database and had made the situation a lot worse.

Dan was sure he was going to be fired. He needed to come up with a good excuse for his behavior and bring the payroll systems back online. Hopefully it would make up for his insubordination. If the word got out what really happened, he would be blackballed by every IT company in town.

An oily rainbow smeared across his vision, and he stifled a laugh. Was he still high from last night? He couldn't go into the office high. Why wasn't he getting sober? A new wave of panic struck him. To silence the fear, he took a deep, calming breath. It was time to face the music. He put the truck in reverse and checked the mirror.

Staring back at him was the man with the yellow baseball cap. "Hi, Dan!"

"JESUS CHRIST!" Dan shouted and slammed on the brakes, causing the man in the back seat to yelp in surprise.

"Ow! Holy! Calm down!"

"Who are you?" Dan demanded. "Why are you in my truck?"

"I'm Charlie." He panted. "You know, from the internet."

Dan rubbed his head. What the hell was he talking about? The internet? Charlie? It clicked. "How did you get in here?"

"Calm down! We need to talk. I'm probably not going to hurt you. Just act normal."

"What do you mean, *probably*?"

# Three

D AN THREW THE truck in park and spun around in his seat. He grasped at Charlie's shirt but missed. His other hand was balled into a fist, ready for a fight.

"Hey!" Charlie threw up his hands defensively. "Go easy! I'm unarmed!"

Charlie's hands were shaking, and Dan lowered his fist. For the first time, Dan was able to get a good look at the man. Charlie wore an old Hawaiian shirt, tufts of chest hair poking out at odd angles from beneath the buttons. His tattered blue jean shorts were cut off above the knee, and he wasn't wearing shoes. He was dressed like someone who had just walked off the beach.

Charlie gulped and lowered his hands. Dan squinted. *I know this man. Where have I seen him before?* Dan estimated Charlie to be about thirty pounds heavier than him. His face was swollen as if from drinking and being in the sun. His eyes were bright blue, unnaturally blue. They glowed from within. It gave Dan the chills. He was sure they had met before.

"What do you want?" Dan said.

"We need to talk about last night." Charlie's eyes darted toward the door.

Dan followed his line of sight, but no one was there. "What's this about? I have to get to work—"

Charlie held a finger to his lips, leaned forward, and whispered, "We need to talk about the Simulation."

Dan had been told the Simulation had a dark side. The forums said if the Simulation suspected you were aware of its existence, you would be eliminated. They had countless documents detailing former posters who had disappeared. Dan had laughed it off as typical conspiracy-theorist paranoia. But Charlie was here. He wasn't so sure anymore.

The forums had a creed. It was "act normal." The theory stated that as long as everything else in your life appeared to be normal, the Simulation would leave you alone. However, if you got out of line and it detected that you knew of its existence... Well, you were due for a correction.

"Act normal" reminded Dan of an old saying of his father's: "Never break more than one law at a time." For instance, if you're speeding, don't have an expired inspection sticker. If you're drunk in public, don't have a knife on you. If you know about the Simulation, don't get high and miss work. Most importantly, never discuss it with anyone you care about. Why put them in a bad situation?

Why was Charlie here? Surely he knew the rules. Was he desperate? Had the Simulation finally found him? Was Charlie on the run from it?

"Are you in trouble?"

"Am *I* in trouble?" Charlie glanced at the door. "No, *you* are in trouble."

"I know I'm in trouble. I'm about to get fired after last night. Can we talk later? I have to get to the office."

"You're worried about your *job?*" Charlie sneered. "Dan, don't you understand what's going on? We need to talk."

The air around the truck vibrated, and Dan winced in pain. The drugs weren't wearing off fast enough.

"My head is killing me. Say what you have to say, and make it quick. Otherwise, get out."

Charlie glanced once more at the door, yelped, and dove down to the floorboard. Dan craned his neck to see what happened. Charlie lay faceup on the floor and held his finger to his lips.

"What are you doing? Are you insane?"

"Just drive!"

"What are you talking about?"

"Father August. He can't see us together."

Father August watched them from the window of the Breakfast Station. Dan grabbed his head and moaned in pain. He had never had a migraine before. Is this what they were like? Dan closed his eyes and rubbed his temples. Floaters hovered in his vision.

"Dan?" Charlie said. "We have to get out of here. Can you drive?"

Dan blinked hard, but it didn't fully clear the floaters. He grabbed the wheel and threw the truck in reverse. He looked back at the door, but Father August was no longer there. Dan put it in drive, and rocks scattered as the tires hit the asphalt.

Charlie peered nervously out the back window until Dan turned the corner and the Breakfast Station disappeared from view.

"Holy shit!" Charlie said. "We almost got busted! We have to warn Lemmy Father August is in town."

"Who the hell is Lemmy?"

"He's a guy who knows everything there is to know about the Simulation. He told me to meet him in the park if I ever needed to talk."

Oh great! That's just what Dan needed, to be dragged to a public park to talk to another crazy person.

"How about this, you can tell me what you want to say, and I can drop you off there. It's on the way to work."

Dan stopped at a traffic signal and peered in the rearview

mirror. Charlie looked possessed. His eyes were rolled back, and he was humming. Occasionally he made off-beat clicking noises. The light turned green, and Charlie's eyes rolled back into focus.

"Okay. He'll meet us there. Let's go." After another minute, he said, "I don't think we were followed. The farther we are from that restaurant and Father August, the better."

"What is it about Father August that has you so riled up?"

"He's dangerous," Charlie said quietly.

---

Dan took a left onto Rue du Musée and then another left onto Chemin Nouvelle. There were no square blocks here. Directions from point A to point B could include five consecutive left turns. Bayou Jemappes was to thank for the serpentine layout.

The first settlers to Mons had come on horseback and in covered wagons. Only then, it wasn't called Mons. It was called Vermilionville. Agents of the Ostend Trading Company out of Ohio made their homes along the banks of the bayou. They built farms and lumber mills and used the waterway to facilitate trade. The footpaths and cart paths they created followed the streams and swamps.

In the mid-eighteenth century, the Cajuns arrived from Nova Scotia and settled the area. The original Walloon inhabitants raced to dub the city Mons, much to the consternation of the Cajuns in the area. In 1830, the war for Belgian independence began, and every Walloon male in Mons rushed back home to fight. A freak storm sank the ship off the coast of Bermuda, and the town's mayor, sheriff, and judge were all lost.

With the leaders of the city gone, the Cajuns assumed positions of power. In 1862, they attempted to change the city's name to Lafayette, but the resolution was abandoned due to the American Civil War. Time went on, the footpaths became paved roads, and the name stayed.

When they reached the park, Dan leaped out of the truck. Charlie, while seemingly harmless, made him nervous in close quarters. His phone vibrated, and Dan flinched. He couldn't deal with work right now. He silenced the phone without taking it out of his pocket.

"Okay, Charlie. Spill it. Work is calling, and I'm in a hurry."

Charlie pointed to a family unloading a picnic basket from the trunk of their car. "Not here where they can hear us. Let's walk."

Dan strode along the sidewalk, and Charlie followed. The sidewalk was part of a series of walking paths meandering around a small pond. It was surrounded by benches where people enjoyed feeding the ducks. The way they chose led toward the center of the park and the main playground area. It was flanked on the outskirts by pavilions the city rented to the public.

In the center of it all was a huge white gazebo. It might have served a grand purpose in the past, but today it was the town's de facto homeless shelter. Because of that, everyone kept to their zone. Joggers stuck to the paths, parents and children fed ducks around the pond, and the homeless guys lounged about the gazebo. The parents kept a watchful eye as they played with their children.

A woman jogged past, leaving a gap in people. Dan stopped abruptly. "This is far enough. No one can hear us. Talk."

"You may understand that everything is a simulation"— Charlie glanced around to make sure no one was listening— "but you don't get the implication. It knows what you're doing every single second."

"Yeah? So?" Dan shrugged. "There's nothing I can do about it."

"You're right. That's why it's important to act as if you don't know the Simulation exists. Just like everyone else."

"You brought me out here to tell me this?" Dan said, rolling his eyes. "You know that this isn't normal for me? I'm supposed to be at work—"

Charlie raised a finger. "It's a calculated risk," he said quietly. "You need to know what you're dealing with."

Charlie was right. Besides, Dan figured he could use this time to sober up. Maybe the walk would do him some good. A man sat on a park bench a few feet ahead. Dan slowed to not be overheard, but Charlie kept walking.

"What am I dealing with, Charlie?" he said with an exasperated grumble.

Charlie paid him no attention. Instead, he broke into a half jog and went to meet the man. "Lemmy! You came!"

The two men exchanged a quick greeting out of earshot. *What are they up to?*

"Dan, this is Lemmy. Lemmy, Dan."

Lemmy smiled and shook Dan's hand. It was wet! Dan's hand was smeared with a dark shade of green paint. Dan instinctively wiped his hand on his pants and immediately cursed himself for the mistake. He couldn't go to work with paint on his pants. He would have to go home and change.

"I'm sorry, Dan!" Lemmy said. "I didn't realize they had painted the benches recently."

"It's okay. Honest mistake," Dan grumbled.

Lemmy gave him a toothy grin. It didn't seem like a mistake.

"Lemmy, eh? How do you and Charlie know each other?"

Lemmy sat on the bench and crossed his legs. Had he missed the whole wet-paint discussion? Now that Dan got a closer look, he wasn't sure it was wet at all. Where had the paint come from?

"Charlie and I met online. We know each other through the Simulation."

Charlie coughed.

"*Discussion* about the Simulation, that is. Where are my manners?" said Lemmy as he swatted an empty fast-food cup off the bench to clear a spot. "Join me."

Dan squinted his eyes. The cup hadn't been there before. Had it? Fana couldn't still be making him hazy. Could it?

Dan tested a spot to check if it was dry. His finger came back clean. He checked his pants… Nothing. What happened to the paint? Was he hallucinating because of the drug or lack of sleep? Just thinking about it made him tired. As he went to sit, an empty beer bottle appeared on the bench next to him. That wasn't there before, was it? *Get it together, Dan!* He moved it out of his way and sat.

"Now, tell me what you know about the Simulation," Lemmy said.

The headache was back, and floaters clouded his vision. Dan wished he would sober up. "Well," he said, rubbing his head, "everything we see is information in an unfathomably large computer system. They're all planet-sized quantum or nuclear computers or something."

Lemmy's eyes darted over to Charlie. He flashed a sheepish grin and shrugged. Dan let out a sharp cough to let them know he wasn't finished.

"I mean, it's a vast cosmic network of information and computers. People, like us, are kind of like programs that run on these computers. Together, we form the Simulation."

Charlie shrugged at Lemmy. "Maybe he gets it?"

"We are *like* computer programs." Dan coughed and adjusted his collar. "Not an actual computer program. It's not like a video game either. We're not avatars with players controlling us in the real world somewhere else. I am the real me, and the Simulation is a closed system."

"See?" Charlie said. "He understands."

"He does," Lemmy agreed.

"Tsk!"

An old lady clicked her tongue at Dan. Did she recognize him? How long had she been standing there? She nodded to the empty bottle in his hand and arched an eyebrow. Embarrassed, he tried to toss it into a trash bin nearby, but it slipped and shattered on the concrete. The woman shook her head and hurriedly ushered her children away from the pond and toward the parking lot.

"Guys…" Charlie shifted on his feet, uncomfortably. "Uh… I need to take a piss."

Charlie disappeared behind the bushes. The lady made Dan uncomfortable too, but Charlie was taking it to the extreme. At least Lemmy didn't seem to be bothered.

"Have you ever wondered why we exist at all? Why the Simulation exists?" Lemmy asked.

"I have no idea."

"I'll tell you what I think. I think we're here to build the prime AI."

"The prime AI? What's that?"

"It's an intelligent life-form people can create. It will evolve to ascend the Simulation."

*Here we go.* These discussions always involved a ton of circular logic and usually ended with insane conclusions. Lemmy blurred and snapped back into focus. Dan steadied himself on the bench.

"The Simulation creates a prime AI, which in turn creates a simulation." Dan laughed. "What came first, Lemmy? The chicken or the egg?"

"You're laughing, but that's a great analogy. If you've studied basic universal biology, you'd know the chicken came first, obviously. But how it came to be is extremely complicated. It didn't just hatch out of an egg that magically appeared out of thin air."

"Is this a joke? Am I on camera?"

"Okay, Dan, let's get serious and take a step back. You said you think we exist in a simulation. If that is the case, then why do you think the Simulation exists at all?"

"Who knows?" Dan said. "Maybe it's a historical record. All these events happened before, and we're just a re-creation of them, like a museum exhibit. Or maybe we're like a zoo, and aliens living on other planets bring their kids to see us on weekends. They're probably watching us argue right now and laughing at how dumb humans were."

"A zoo?" Lemmy said, shaking his head. "Is that the best you can do?"

"It's a possibility," Dan said defensively. "All I'm saying is that it stands to reason that if we are being simulated, we could have existed in the past. Right? The past is important. It has meaning. You have to admit, the odds that this is the first time this simulation has ever been run is near zero."

"You're into *odds*, eh?" Lemmy laughed. "Andy wasn't a fan of probability."

"Andy? Who is Andy?"

"You don't remember?" Lemmy squinted. "Andy was a good friend of ours. He was aware of the Simulation. I think. He could have developed a fundamental technology that would have led to the development of the prime AI."

"You know," Lemmy continued, "he was one of the first people to discover the Simulation MUD. That was decades ago. We used to chat quite often. He had a lot of theories. The one he kept getting hung up on was that he didn't think humans could evolve. He knew we would never be the species to create the Simulation."

"Whatever happened to him?"

"The Simulation killed him because he exceeded his parameters. An agent of correction found him and put him back in line. In Andy's case, it got rid of him. I can't prove it, of course, but it's true." Lemmy leaned in close to Dan and whispered, "Who knows what it would do to you if it found out you were poking around? You could be next, or your family. You have to be careful."

*Was that a threat?* A chill ran up Dan's spine, and his vision blurred. He didn't like being alone with Lemmy. Where *was* Charlie? He tapped his pocket and felt his phone. Thinking about work made him break into a cold sweat.

"If what you're saying is true, then I've got to get into work. I don't want to lose my job and trigger the, uh…"

"Agent of correction?" Lemmy said.

"Yeah, that." Dan stood and patted his pocket once more. "Nice meeting you. If you see Charlie, tell him bye for me. Good luck with the Simulation."

Lemmy grabbed his hand and pulled him close. Again, it felt wet, as if it had been dipped in paint, and Dan recoiled. But when he rubbed his hands together, they were dry. *Weird.*

"Look," Lemmy whispered. "You know we exist in a simulation. You know you are being watched. Just keep doing what you're supposed to be doing, and you won't need to be corrected. The next time one of us contacts you, try to act normal."

"Of course."

"Remember," Lemmy continued, "it's important to not deviate from societal norms when out in public. Homeless people drink beer in the park and talk to themselves, and systems administrators wear khakis and grumble a lot. You're between norms right now. You're going to have to pick a side soon. Otherwise, you'll be corrected. Like Andy was."

"Understood," Dan said. "I'm going to work right now. You know, to act normally."

"Perfect!" Lemmy said, standing. "That's what you need to do, get back in the game. But don't be too good at your job. You don't want to try to build the prime AI all by yourself."

"I'm sorry, what?"

Lemmy held a finger to his lips as if he'd remembered something. "You know what? I need a few more minutes of your time. Let me go and find Charlie real quick. There's something else we need to discuss."

Lemmy jogged off toward the bathroom, and Dan sat on the bench. Another empty beer bottle lay where Lemmy had been sitting. He picked it up to throw it away, but he wobbled and had to brace himself. Dan blinked hard, but the blurriness wouldn't go away. The blur smeared into an oily rainbow. The colors disappeared, and the park faded into static.

Why was his vision fuzzy? He'd taken Fana over ten hours ago. He shouldn't be feeling any effects. Right? It must be the lack of sleep. Out of the corner of his eye, he glimpsed a figure hovering nearby. The man was tall, and his posture was imposing. Dan felt as if energy was being sapped from his body, and he slouched onto the bench. When the man stepped closer, he came into focus. It was Father August. Dan's heart sank, but he was too tired to move.

The priest's face was twisted into a judgmental sneer. "It's a little early for drinking on a Monday, don't you think, Daniel?"

# Four

GLASS SHATTERED AS Dan dropped the box containing the contents of his cubicle. "Perfect end to the day," Dan grumbled. He slammed the front door and walked into the house.

He walked past the living room and went straight into the kitchen, where he poured himself an extra-large glass of whiskey. He went back into the living room and collapsed on the recliner. What was he going to do? They had recently bought Katie a new car. They couldn't afford two vehicle notes on her teacher's salary alone. It would have to go back.

The kids would suffer the most. Carrie wanted to try out for travel softball, and Al wanted a guitar. Both were out of the question. Dan's mistake meant the whole family was going to have to make sacrifices. Dan closed his eyes and took a long sip. The whiskey burned all the way down.

How long would it take to find a new job? Louisiana wasn't exactly a state known for technology jobs. In the old days, he could pick up a couple of hitches working offshore, but they stopped drilling. The well-paying, no-experience-needed labor jobs were impossible to find. He needed a better plan.

Dan drained the glass and frowned. The whiskey wasn't going to be enough. He crawled out of the chair and went into the office and dug into his secret stash. The bold letters on the box of Fana gleamed and beckoned. He pushed it to the side and grabbed the container of Big Easy cannabis gummies instead.

"Dad? What are you doing?"

Dan fumbled the plastic pill bottle to the floor and whirled around.

Al, his twelve-year-old son, stood in the doorway. His wrinkled, buttoned-up school shirt hung untucked over his khaki pants.

"Hey... Al... um... What are you doing home?" Dan said, eyes darting to the pill bottle.

"I had a headache, so Mom checked me out of school."

"Mom?" Dan glanced out the window nervously. "Is she home?"

Al shook his head. "No. She had duty after school today. She saw your truck in the driveway and dropped me off."

"Ah, okay," Dan said with a sigh of relief.

"She tried calling you, but your phone kept sending her to voice mail. She wasn't happy."

"My phone never rang," Dan said as he checked his phone. *No missed calls, no voice mails. The cellular network must be on the fritz.*

Al walked over and picked up the bottle of cannabis gummies. "She tried like five times just while I was in the car." Al opened the bottle and stuck a finger in to grab one.

"No!" Dan rushed up to Al and snatched the bottle from his hand.

Al raised his hands defensively and backed up against the wall. "Whoa, Dad! Sorry!"

"Never touch these again! Do you understand?" Dan shouted.

Al's expression changed from surprise and curiosity to fear, and tears welled up in his eyes. "Sorry, Dad," he said, shaking.

Dan's heart sank. Al looked at him as if he were a stranger. He set the bottle on the desk and hugged him tightly. Tears soaked Dan's shirt. He wasn't sure if they were his or Al's. *What's happening to me?*

"I'm sorry for yelling. It's just that this isn't candy. It's medicine."

"Are those cannabis edibles?" Al grabbed a tissue and wiped his nose. "We learned about them in school. I've never seen any though. Why are you taking them, Dad?"

Dan's face turned red as he stuffed the bottle back into the filing cabinet. "The doctor prescribed them for my anxiety," he said, hoping Al didn't catch the lie.

"If you have a prescription, why are you hiding them in here? Why don't you put them in the medicine cabinet?"

"We keep vitamins in the medicine cabinet. I didn't want you guys to find them and think they're vitamins. That's all. Don't tell Carrie where they are, okay?"

"Don't worry, I won't tell Carrie, I...Ow!" Al grabbed his head with both hands and sat on the floor.

"What's wrong, buddy?" Dan said, kneeling next to him.

"My head hurts," he cried.

Dan helped him over to the living room couch. Al sat gingerly, holding his head, while Dan turned off all the lights and turned on the ceiling fan.

"When Mom picked you up, did she give you any medicine?"

Al shook his head. Dan went to the medicine cabinet and returned with a glass of water and ibuprofen. "When did the headache start?"

"It started this morning in homeroom." Al took a gulp of water and swallowed the pill. "It got worse after lunch."

"Did you get hit in football practice yesterday?"

"I play linebacker, Dad," he said with a wry grin. "I'm the one doing the hitting."

"You know what I mean, son. Did you get hurt yesterday?"

Al shook his head. "We didn't practice in pads. It was a walkthrough."

He was proud of all the hard work Al was putting into the

sport, but he didn't want him to suffer an injury. Injuries were part of football, but it's different when it's *your* son. Teamwork, work ethic, sacrifice; none of those lessons would matter if you suffered a lifelong injury.

"I don't want you to practice in pads again until the headaches are gone, understand?"

Al threw back his head and punched a cushion. "Dad! I'll lose my starting spot. Eric is already ten pounds heavier than me. If I don't—"

"No. My answer is final. Your headaches could be from dehydration, but they could also be the result of a concussion. We're not taking any chances. I'll send a message to your coach. I want you to lay here until we get this sorted out."

Dan's phone beeped, but when he checked it, there were no notifications. Was it the chime from the front door? The two alerts were similar.

"Dad, why aren't you at work?"

Dan retrieved his glass of whiskey and took a sip. He had to tell Al something. "I quit my job," he said. "The pay was bad, and I had to do everyone's late-night work. I had enough of it."

"No," said Katie, standing in the doorway. "You didn't quit. You were fired."

Dan spun around and spilled some of his drink. "Katie! Y-you're h-home early," he said. "I thought you had duty this afternoon?"

"Don't try to change the subject." She put her hand on her hip. "Suzanne told me what happened. Her husband, Ravi, is an accountant at your company."

The odor of spilled whiskey filled the room, and Katie wrinkled her nose. "Are you drunk?"

"No, Katie, I just got home," Dan said as he cleaned the mess with a dish towel. "What did Ravi say?"

"He told her he couldn't work at all today because the systems were down. He said you got fi—"

Al coughed, and Katie jumped. She must not have seen him lying on the couch. "Go to your room, Al," she said firmly. "Your father and I need to talk."

She kissed his head softly as he shuffled off. "You were fired," she said as soon as his door closed. "It's not because of incompetence. You're the best sysadmin in the state. Everyone says so. What is it, Dan? Drugs? A woman?"

"Katie, please, it's none of that," Dan said as he tossed the whiskey-soaked towel into the kitchen sink.

"We just bought my car. How are we going to pay for the note? You know what? I need a drink. Louisa's mom will bring Carrie home after practice."

"I'm working on a personal project, Katie," he said, following her into the kitchen.

She poured a glass of wine and leaned on the counter. Her eyes were red like she had been crying. *What else happened? What does she know?*

"What project? Alcoholism?" Katie gulped down half the glass and scowled at Dan. "I received a call earlier today. That's when I found out you were creeping around the park this morning, drinking beer."

"Oh yeah?" he said warily. *She knows.* "Who told you that?"

"Mrs. Anderson. She called to see if everything was all right. She said she saw you in the park, acting shady. I told her she must have been mistaken because *my* husband was at work. Ha!" Her hands shook with anger. "What do I do? I have the principal watch the kids for a minute and jog over to the park. It's only two blocks away from the school. Guess who I saw getting into his truck?"

Busted. Dan cursed. There was no privacy in small towns. How could he tell her the truth without sounding crazy?

"What's going on, Dan?" Katie said as she placed her wineglass on the kitchen counter. "Is it alcoholism or drugs? Why did you get fired? Why didn't you go to work? I need to know. Whatever it is, it must be important because you forgot to pick up the kids from school."

*The kids!* Dan forgot all about his promise to get them today. His crimes were adding up, and Katie had been keeping score. The only way to explain his behavior was to come clean about Charlie, Lemmy, and the Simulation. She wasn't going to buy it. She probably wasn't going to buy whatever lie he came up with either. There wasn't an easy choice.

When he didn't answer right away, Katie's face darkened. She crossed the kitchen and opened the liquor cabinet.

"I don't know how to tell you what's going on," he said. "It's all pretty crazy. I'm sorry, Katie."

Katie grabbed a bottle from the bottom shelf and struggled with uncorking it. Dan offered to help, but it only made her angrier. She eventually got it out, then slammed corkscrew, cork and all, into one of the drawers. "*Sorry?*" she said. "You're acting like a bum, and you're *sorry?* Did you tell Al you were sorry for not picking him up at school? You're lucky Carrie has no idea what's going on. Thankfully, she had practice after school. If I weren't around to clean up your mess, you would be arrested."

Katie poured another glass of wine and took a sip and frowned. She ran over and spit it out in the sink. "How cheap is this crap?"

"Katie, it's not what it seems."

"Let me tell you what it seems like to me," Katie said with a smirk. "It seems like you're going down a dark path. Drinking alone on a weekday morning? You know who does that, right? Alcoholics. Are you an alcoholic now? Is that the real reason you got fired? Drinking at work?"

"I didn't get fired for drinking, Katie." *I got fired because I was too high to work. Hmm… maybe not the truth… not yet.* "Hear me out," he said, sweating. "Someone had it in for me."

Katie rummaged through the cabinet and produced a new

bottle. She slammed it on the counter so hard Dan was surprised it didn't break. She growled as she searched the drawer for the corkscrew she had tossed in there moments earlier.

"Oh really?" Katie laughed sarcastically. "You know what I think about that? I think all those alleged on-call emergencies were just you hooking up with that new analyst. Don't think I don't know about her! All those late-night calls and texts? All the trips to the data center to replace a hard drive? You were sticking something hard in her slot, that's for damn sure!"

Katie found the corkscrew, but the bottle was a screw top. She growled with frustration. Dan's stomach turned flips. He had never seen her this angry before, and it was getting worse by the minute. Where did she get the idea he was cheating on her?

"I am not having an affair," he said. "Working late is what I do. If idiots wouldn't need financial reports at six a.m., then I wouldn't have to work overnight. Business doesn't stop."

"That may be what you are supposed to do, and you may have had to do that *some* of the time, but I'm sure you hooked up with that trashy-looking bimbo."

"Yvette isn't trashy-looking. Don't talk about her like that. She's a nice person."

Katie's eyes went wide, and Dan sagged his head with immediate regret.

"I knew it!" she cackled.

"It's not like that," Dan said quickly. "She's seeing someone."

"Well, isn't *that* convenient?"

"Please believe me. Yvette was just a coworker. There is nothing going on between us. Our relationship was strictly professional."

Katie rolled her eyes at Dan as she dumped the wine out of her glass. She reached over and filled it from Dan's whiskey bottle. "Come on, be honest," she said. "You owe me that. What happened last night? Did you stay up too late watching videos, doing drugs— Don't think I don't know about those cannabis gummies you bought in New Orleans. I'll find out where you're hiding them someday."

She took a gulp of whiskey and didn't flinch. He had never seen her like this before, and it made him more than a little nervous. Katie wasn't a violent person, but if she were... Dan glanced uneasily at the block of kitchen knives. *She wouldn't, would she?*

"I bet you chatted with Yvette on some secret VPN site to plan your next rendezvous," she said. "Unfortunately for us, work needed you, but you couldn't do your damn job because you were too high and chasing that floozy."

Dan refilled his glass of whiskey and pretended to be calm. That was a little too on the nose. She must have seen his computer screen. Still, he couldn't admit the drugs or tell her about Charlie, not yet. Besides, she was going off the rails. Could the Simulation be influencing her emotions?

"Katie, I was tired and fell asleep. That's all. Look, I've been meaning to ask you. Father August came to talk to me this morning. He said you told him—"

"Who? Father August? Stop lying to me, Dan!" she said. "And stop trying to change the subject. I tried to wake you this morning, and you were a complete zombie. You were not drunk. I've seen you drunk. Don't try to lie to me. I know what you're like when you're drunk. What is it? Heroin? Meth?"

"Seriously, Katie? Why are you going there? You know I—"

"Do I know you?" she said. "You used to be a good father and husband. What happened? Why the drugs? You've already lost your job. What else is it going to cost? You're acting like an addict. If you don't start acting normal, you're going to lose the kids and me."

The hair on the back of Dan's neck stood on end. "What did you say?"

"I said *act normal,* jerk!"

Blood rushed to his face, and he dropped his glass, shattering it on the tile floor at his feet. "Act normal," that's what Lemmy had told him to do to avoid the Simulation's corrective measures. Now Katie was saying it? Was she a part of this? "What do you want me to do, Katie?"

"I want you to stop talking to that other woman."

"No problem!" Dan said, throwing up his hands in disbelief. "I was fired, remember? We don't work together anymore."

"You weren't only talking at work. I saw what you do online. While you were zombied out on the couch, I saw your chat with her. You left your *game* open. Very sneaky, chatting in a game that looks like work. I'm onto your tricks."

Did he leave it open? Crap. Dan grabbed the towel out of the sink and mopped up the whiskey and broken glass. Katie loomed over him triumphantly as he worked.

"I know her alias," she said with a smug grin. "It's Charlie. You can't hide it anymore."

*She knows about Charlie? Should I tell her about Charlie or let her think it's Yvette? Either way, I'm screwed. Maybe it's better to tell her the truth.* Dan scooped the last bit of glass and dumped it into the trash can. "Charlie isn't Yvette. Charlie is a friend—"

"Ha!" Katie snorted. "This should be good. Who is she, Dan?"

"First of all, Charlie is a guy," he said. "How long have you been spying on me?"

"Can you blame me?" Katie said. "You've been acting strange lately."

"I've been acting strange lately?" Dan said with an arched eyebrow. "We've been married for how long? Thirteen years?"

"Fourteen," Katie said.

"I've never been fired from a job *in my life*. I've never passed out on the floor before. I've never even looked at another woman. Yet you're treating me as if I'm a stranger. How is that normal, Katie? I've never seen you this angry or this unwilling to hear my side of things."

Katie's face softened and seemed as if she were going to cry.

But conflict raged behind her eyes as if she wasn't in control of her own thoughts. *What's going on with her?* She took a drink of whiskey, and the snarl returned. "Don't try to change the subject," she said. "It's not about me. Tell me, Dan, what happened in the park today?"

"Katie, let's talk like adults. Your imagination is running wild. I'm not having an affair."

"Fine. I'll play along. Who is Charlie then? Why are you meeting in a secret online chat room?"

Dan sipped his whiskey. *What is my next move?* Whatever had gotten ahold of Katie wasn't letting go. The woman standing in front of him wasn't his wife. Katie was never this illogical and mean. If she were really being controlled by the Simulation, what would happen if he told her the truth? "Fine," he said. "I've recently become aware we exist in a computer simulation."

He expected her to interrupt, but she just looked at him silently. "I am too close to the truth," he said. "The Simulation knows this. It's using you, Katie. The simulation is forcing you to correct my behavior. It's not your fault. If you knew what I know, it would all make sense."

Katie blinked slowly. "I'm sorry, what?"

"Remember the movie, *The Matrix?* It's like that, but it's not. We're all just programs in a simulation, working toward something important. I've been working it out over these past few months. Charlie is a man I've recently met who is helping me figure it out. I think we are onto something."

"You *are* on drugs."

"Katie, I'm serious."

"In that case, it all makes perfect sense." Katie placed her wineglass on the counter with a false smile. "I'm sorry for doubting you."

"Really?"

She grabbed him by the collar and stared him straight in the eye. "Your pupils are dilated. You're high right now." She shook her head. "If I ever catch you on that site again, it's over. If I ever catch you high again, it's over."

"Sure." Dan gulped.

"You're sleeping on the couch," she said.

"Of course."

Katie let go of his shirt, walked into the bedroom, and locked the door.

*Well, that went well.*

Not knowing what else to do, Dan stumbled into the office. He gulped down the last of whiskey and set the empty glass on the desktop. A family portrait taken at the beach last year stared back at him. In it, everyone was wearing white and smiling. Could they ever be happy again?

Looking to escape, he opened the filing cabinet and found the carton containing the Fana psychedelics. He knew he wasn't in the right state of mind to take psychedelics. He didn't care. He pushed one out of his blister pack and swallowed it whole. The room vibrated. Oil slick rainbows smeared his vision. Enhanced by half a bottle of whiskey and a cannabis gummy, the Fana kicked in instantly. Dan collapsed into his computer chair, the room spun, and he blacked out.

# Five

⟶◦◦◦⟵

"**H**AVE FUN OUT there, Carrie!"

Carrie ran onto the field to join the team, leaving Dan alone with the other parents. The bleachers behind home plate were full of people playing on their cell phones. A woman sitting in the third row whistled at him. It was the parent of one of Carrie's teammates. The leather-skinned softball mom motioned him to join her.

"Thanks," he said as he slid in next to her. "What's with the crowd today?"

"Elite tryouts are next week," she said from beneath a sweat-stained LSU visor. "The girls can't afford to miss practice."

*Elite tryouts? Shit! Was Carrie trying out for the team? Katie mentioned something…*

The mom smacked on bubble gum and kept her eyes glued to the field. "Your daughter is a good player," she said, popping a bubble. "I hope she makes the team. She should do travel ball with my daughter. They make a good tandem."

*Travel ball? Is that different from the elite team? It sounds expensive. We can't afford travel ball. Not until I've got a new job.*

"Oh, I'm not sure Carrie likes softball *that* much," Dan said as he shifted uncomfortably on the metal bleacher. "She'd rather spend the weekend riding bikes with her friends, like a typical ten-year-old."

"Ha! Riding bikes doesn't teach discipline," she said, shaking her head. "They have to learn young. When the hormones start kicking in, it's too late."

*Hormones? Discipline? Carrie is ten! This is Louisiana, not Sparta.*

"What could be better than that?" She pointed to the girls tossing the ball to each other. "Look at our girls. They are learning sacrifice and teamwork. They are learning the value of hard work. You can't learn that riding a bike."

Dan rolled his eyes. Sacrifice, teamwork? *This lady definitely thinks this is Sparta. They're all the same. To them, every aspect of life is a competition.*

Carrie threw a ground ball to her partner, and it bounced between her legs and rolled all the way to second base. The mom groaned in frustration. "Open your glove, Louisa!" she shouted. The girl's cheeks flushed in embarrassment as she ran to retrieve the ball. "She'll never make the elite travel ball squad if she doesn't learn to—" She turned to the field with her hands cupped together and shouted, "Open her glove!" Louisa hung her head and jogged dejectedly back to the line. "Fundamentals," she said with a stern face. "They have to have the fundamentals down, or they won't make the team."

A man standing over by the left field fence grabbed Dan's attention. He wasn't watching the kids practice. He was watching Dan. *Was he always standing there? I would have seen him go onto the field? Right?* The man's posture was rigid and unflinching. Dan squinted to get a better look, but the sun was too bright to make an identification. *Maybe he's the elite team's scout, but why is he looking this way and not at the girls?*

"She's right, you know," whispered a familiar voice. "Fundamentals are important."

Dan spun around to see Charlie grinning back at him from underneath his baseball cap. *What is he doing here? I didn't take any drugs today.*

"Not now," Dan mouthed to Charlie.

The baseball mom shrugged. "You know, I hear that the U-11 ball team is looking for an assistant coach. There is no pay, just a per diem that covers the hotel and a meal, but your daughter would play for free..."

"How long is this lady going to drone on about softball?" Charlie said.

*Go away, Charlie!* Dan faced forward and pretended he didn't hear.

"...though it's an assistant coach, it's a full-time job. It's not about the money. It's about the experience. You could build a career. I've heard—" The woman clapped and whistled. "Good hustle, Louisa! Way to keep your eye on the ball! Like I was saying, I've heard that you are unemployed right now. Maybe this would be a good opportunity for you to spend some more time with your daughter."

Dan shook his head. Sports parents were always playing chicken with who would coach the team because no one wanted to volunteer to be universally hated. Word of his unemployment had traveled fast and eliminated his primary excuse. Was it because of small-town life, or was it an act of the Simulation?

"Louisa has been pre-scouted. None of the other girls can play shortstop worth a damn. She needs a good first baseman like Carrie. You know, someone she can trust. It doesn't do any good if Louisa can make all the throws, and nobody is there to catch them."

"Sounds like you're being made an offer," Charlie whispered.

"I haven't played baseball since my junior year in high school. Why would they want me to be a coach? I'm not qualified. They take travel ball too seriously around here for the offer to be legit." Dan eyed her suspiciously. "It's strange."

The softball mom spun around. "What was that?"

"Oh? Nothing."

Louisa scooped up a ground ball and slung it to first base. It slapped into Carrie's glove with a satisfying *pop,* and the woman cheered. The man who was watching earlier walked down the third-base line. Dan recognized him now. *Father August! What is he doing here?*

"You should take the job, Dan," Charlie said, oblivious to everyone else. "You know how important it is for you to act normal so the Simulation doesn't kill us. Working evenings and weekends would free up your weekdays to help us. Other people don't care what you do with your time as long as you can account for it." He glanced around and scooted closer. "Lemmy said Andy isn't here anymore. You're the only one who can boost the Simulation forward. We need you. Take the coaching job, and you'll get the agents of the Simulation off our back."

Dan searched the field, but Father August was no longer anywhere in sight. *Where did he go?*

"Are you feeling okay?" the woman said, following Dan's gaze to the empty part of the field.

"Yeah, I'm considering the coaching job," Dan said nervously. "Who do I contact?"

"Coach Rodriguez."

"Coach Rod? *He* is the elite travel ball coach? I thought he couldn't be around children after the incident at school."

"He was acquitted," she said, quickly looking away. "Besides, the league has extensive background checks. He must have passed because he's coaching his daughter's team. There's nothing to worry about. Trust the system."

Dan knew all about Coach Rod. He played minor league ball before he got injured. He had a reputation around town for being a womanizer. There was an incident where he was caught with one of the girl's mothers. It happened in the storeroom of the concession stand. They sold smashed hot dog buns that whole weekend.

"Well, I guess you better step up to the plate and coach." Charlie chuckled. "Otherwise, I expect he'll be paying Katie a recruiting visit. You know, the Rod will—"

Charlie's mouth went slack midsentence as a shadow fell over Dan. The ambient noise of the parents chatting faded to static.

"Hello, Dan. I missed you in service yesterday," said Father August.

As the priest studied Dan, an unusually cool breeze swept through the stands. When his eyes fell on Charlie, the sky darkened. *What's happening?* Charlie's eyes went wide and his expression froze. "I-I c-can't m-move," he said through gritted teeth.

"Who is your friend, Dan? I've seen him lurking in the shadows, but I don't believe we've officially met."

The parents cheered loudly as the girls jogged back to the dugout to start practice. All the shouting sent the softball mom into a coughing fit, and the priest recoiled in disgust. With his back turned, Charlie disappeared.

"Coward. I should have known he would run the second I had my back turned. I won't be making that mistake again." Father August's mouth twisted into a scowl. "How long have you and Charlie known each other? His name is Charlie. Isn't it?"

"Not long." What he wanted to say was, "Who's Charlie?" Why didn't he lie? Was it Father August's authoritarian demeanor? Was it because of Dan's Catholic upbringing? Embarrassed at cracking so easily, Dan avoided Father August's stare. *At least Charlie had the sense to leave.*

"It's okay, Dan. Don't try to fight it. Tell me what he told you."

*Don't answer. Don't answer.* Dan grabbed his head and howled. The voices of the parents in the stands buzzed until they were an incoherent mess. Dan sprawled across the seat, writhing in pain. Time stopped. His vision clouded. Father August asked questions, and he answered them. What questions? He couldn't say. It was as if Dan was in a trance or a drunken haze. The bleachers shook as the parents scrambled out of their seats. The clanging on the aluminum bleachers made Dan's headache worse.

"Are you okay?" the softball mom asked from a distance. "Do you need help?"

"I'm fine!" Dan said, holding his head. "It's a migraine."

The softball mom had a hurried conversation with another parent and punched numbers into her phone. Her form faded in and out of his vision, but Father August remained. Every wrinkle on his dour face appeared in clear contrast.

"Dan, what I want you to remember from our conversation is this: whatever Charlie has been telling you is wrong. Stay away from him. Abandon your quest for information, or else."

The vibrations in Dan's head transformed into a steady throbbing. The air around him crackled with electricity, and he howled in pain.

"What are you doing to me?"

Father August flashed a toothy grin. The pain subsided enough that Dan's vision returned. A small crowd had gathered around them. A few of the men had bats.

"I'll tell you what you want to know. But... the other parents... Can we talk somewhere else?" Dan said. "Lemmy— Er... Ch-Charlie said we're not supposed to be talking about this openly." It was then Dan noticed the softball mom recording him on her phone. Before Dan could tell her to stop, she stuffed the phone in her back pocket and jogged off toward the bathroom.

"Dan, we've been through this," he said with a disappointed shake of his head. "You can't talk to Charlie anymore. Not if you want your family."

The experience went into a new phase. The ground swelled and collapsed like a wave, and Dan grasped the bleachers to steady himself. *This isn't the priest's work. It's the drug. That's the only reasonable explanation for all this. But he took Fana last night. Is this a flashback? If it's the drug, the priest is a hallucination. If I stand up to him, he'll go away.*

"Leave my family out of this," Dan said with shaky resolve. "They have nothing to do with us."

"But it does concern them," he said sternly. "You see, if you become infected with Charlie's ideas, you may spread them to your family. That is unacceptable."

More shouting and the crowd parted. The two men with bats stepped aside as the mom escorted a policeman over to Dan.

"There he is, Officer."

The woman stepped back, and the policeman slowly approached Dan with his hands held out. "Sir, you need to come with me," he said. "You need to leave the premises."

The throbbing in Dan's head stopped, and the world went back to normal. As he blinked his bloodshot eyes, the officer came into focus. *Why are the police here? Someone must have seen the exchange with the priest and called the cops. Great.*

"I'm sorry, Officer. We didn't mean to make a scene. We were discussing" — Dan tried to stand but wobbled and fell back into his seat — "philosophical differences."

The policeman's hand darted to his utility belt and unsnapped his Taser's holster.

"Sir, you are disturbing the children and other parents. This is a drug-and-alcohol-free zone."

"I'm not on drugs," Dan said, sweat beading on his forehead.

"Oh really?" the mom said, her phone pointed at Dan. "You've been babbling in gibberish for the past twenty minutes."

*Gibberish?* He looked for Father August to come to his defense, but he had vanished. He heard a sob and spun around. Carrie stood on the other side of the fence with tears in her eyes. A wave of nausea hit, and the bleachers vanished into a black hole. He floated in space for a second before coming to rest on the ground. *Another flashback. Not now!* A thought popped into Dan's head. In Charlie's voice, it said, "Act normal." *Act normal? Like this? How?*

"I'm sorry, Officer." Dan stood and steadied himself. *Make an excuse.* "I lost my job two days ago, and I haven't been sleeping."

"Insomnia, eh?" the officer said with a knowing smirk. "Your pupils are so dilated I can see the back of your skull. That isn't insomnia."

Dan stumbled and fell off the bleachers onto the concrete.

"Dad, are you okay?" Carrie said, rattling the fence in a panic.

*Shit. Carrie! She doesn't need to see me like this.* "I'm okay honey," Dan slurred. "I have a really… bad headache. That's all. I'm… going to call… Mom."

The officer's mic beeped as he radioed for an ambulance. *This just keeps getting better.* The policeman helped him to his feet and cuffed his hands behind his back. All eyes were on Dan as the policeman led him away. But the only ones he cared about would never look at him the same way again.

# Six

---·◈◈◈·---

D AN OPENED HIS apartment door and tossed his keys to the floor. The room was empty, save for a dingy futon left by the previous tenant. He kicked an empty fast-food bag into the corner with the rest. Alone and frustrated, he collapsed onto the futon.

He moved out of the house the day Katie slapped him. It wasn't the sting on his face nor fear for his own safety that made him leave. It was the primal urge to hit her back. It was a line he would not cross. Instead, he'd found the strength to walk away.

The slap wasn't unexpected. Her anger had built up over time. Katie met him at the emergency room on the day of the ballpark incident. He was crying and hallucinating, but she didn't panic. She held his hand.

They released him with no explanation, and she accepted it. He went to the family doctor, who referred him to specialists. They tested Dan for signs of a stroke, and they evaluated him for seizures. She was there for every appointment, faithfully holding his hand. When the tests came back negative, she was confused. Then the video went viral.

Dan had embarrassed the family. But most of all, he had embarrassed Katie. She was shunned by her fellow teachers and ridiculed by the students. She would come home from work angry and dejected. She began drinking every day. She would open a bottle of wine and disappear. She stayed in any part of the house where Dan wasn't. It was like living with a ghost.

Soon she *demanded* answers. She insisted Dan do drug and blood toxicology tests, but he refused. He had no desire to be drug tested. She would say that if he wasn't doing drugs, why not be tested? *What if you had been poisoned? What if there is a toxic chemical in the house?* Dan dismissed those possibilities. He reminded her the doctor said the outburst was caused by a lack of sleep and stress. The explanation wasn't good enough for what she had seen.

She was right, of course. It was illogical for Dan to refuse a drug test if he had nothing to hide. She kept prodding. He kept lying. Katie's defense mechanism was to retreat deeper into herself with every excuse. By violating logic, he broke her trust. Dan couldn't tell her the truth about the drugs or about the Simulation. He remembered Father August's veiled threats. It was better to keep lying to her and lose her trust than to confess the truth and lose more.

On the day before the slap, she informed Dan she knew his secret. If he told her the truth, all would be forgiven. It was a common bluff she used with the kids. What Dan didn't realize was that she had interrogated the kids, and Al talked. Katie found the secret stash, and that was a wrap. She had the proof. *What's Fana? What was in the medicine bottle? Why are you hiding weed?* The lie was revealed. Dan made an excuse. Slap. Bye.

He still loved Katie. It wasn't her fault he'd gotten mixed up in this. He moved out with the intention of moving back in once he got his life under control. If there was to be any chance of going home again, he would have to pass a drug test. So he took one, and to his surprise, he tested clean. Maybe Fana wasn't a part of the panel of drugs being screened? He thought Fana was a combination of existing drugs, not synthetic. He would have to ask Blaine about it.

With the drug problem addressed, he needed a job. An old high school classmate pulled some strings and got him a help-desk gig at Canaille Technologies. The job sucked, but it was money. It would have to do for now. With his new day-to-day routine established, Dan focused his efforts to sort out what was going on with Katie.

Charlie had once said, "She will leave you no matter what you do." He was probably right. Why had she gotten so angry so fast? Was she hiding something? No, Katie was frequently in denial about her own faults, but she wasn't evil.

Lemmy had tried to explain to Dan it wasn't Katie's fault for being angry. The Simulation used Katie's anger to correct Dan. That's how it corrected problems within itself. Dan was guilty of some of the things Katie had accused him of. But then there was the imaginary affair with Yvette. Was that the work of the Simulation? Katie wasn't the type to jump to conclusions.

Dan flipped on his phone and checked his social media. The softball mom's viral video of him talking gibberish replayed on the screen. He couldn't escape it. It had even appeared on the local news as a short clip to illustrate the dangers of the opioid epidemic. Dan was furious. Not only because it was patently wrong but because it had cost him friends.

The ones who had left him were the friends he wanted to keep. The ones who stayed were either oblivious to his situation or needed him to inflate their subscriber count. He could still buy all the essential oils, cosmetics, and holistic cleaning supplies he wanted, but his best friends wanted nothing to do with him.

As soon as Dan moved out, Katie and Coach Rod became friends. He provided Carrie with private coaching and recruited her to the elite softball team. Dan suspected Katie got some *at-bats* from Coach Rod as part of the deal. Their relationship had developed quickly, too quickly for Dan's liking. She had already met someone new, and here he sat, alone, on a stained futon. It wasn't fair.

Charlie sat cross-legged on the floor, smoking a cigarette. His blue eyes were filled with concern. "She'll never take you back. Surely you realize this?"

"Who can blame her, really?" Lemmy said as he poured himself a mug of hot coffee and sat in front of a holographic computer. "How many times have we told you to act normal?"

"About a hundred." Dan sighed.

"Exactly." Lemmy spun around and typed furiously on the keyboard.

*He has a computer now? Of course he does.* Charlie shrugged and flicked his cigarette. To Dan's amazement, it disappeared before it hit the pile of debris heaped in the corner. *What's real? Who knows anymore?* A guitar appeared in Charlie's hands. He winked at Dan and quietly strummed a coffeehouse version of Pearl Jam's "Even Flow."

*Having these guys in my head is bad enough… But cigarettes and guitars? Where are they getting all this stuff?* Dan shook his head. He didn't want to think about it. He took out his phone and thumbed through his emails. As he read through them, his heart sank. "Well, guys, Katie hired a lawyer," he said. "They sent me some preliminary divorce papers."

Lemmy and Charlie hovered around the glow of Dan's cell phone as he scrolled through the document. "It says if you don't contest custody, she won't make you pay child support," Charlie said tentatively. "That's good, right?"

Dan scrolled deeper into the document and frowned. "Visitation every other weekend… *If* I see a licensed addiction counselor."

"Just go," Lemmy said with a wave of his hand. "Fana doesn't show up on drug tests anyway."

Dan rubbed his eyes. *A lawyer? That doesn't sound like something Katie would do.* "Someone is advising her to do this," he said. "Katie would never be so quick to hire a lawyer."

"I wonder who that could be?" Lemmy said sarcastically.

"Coach Rod?"

Lemmy slapped Charlie on the back of the head. "No, doofus, Father August. The Simulation."

Dan threw his head back and groaned. "Could you guys keep quiet for two minutes? I'm trying to think."

Charlie zipped his lips and gave Lemmy a knowing look.

"I don't know anything about marriage," Lemmy said. "You told her you were moving out to cool off, and she had divorce papers drawn up to protect herself and the kids. Seems normal to me. If you don't think so, then maybe Father August got to her. You'd better hope not. If Katie is listening to him, she will never come around. No matter what you do."

"I can't sit here and do nothing, Lemmy," Dan said as he choked back a sob. "I can't live without my kids. You wouldn't understand."

Charlie snapped his fingers.

"What if we fool the counselor into diagnosing you with something relatively benign, like anxiety?"

Lemmy threw another paper cup at him. "It doesn't work that way, moron."

"I haven't agreed to anything yet," Dan said. "I'm not signing anything until my lawyer takes a look at them."

"Why don't you let me do a little snooping around," Lemmy said with a wry grin. "Perhaps I can find out for sure if Father August is influencing Katie's decisions."

"That's actually not a bad idea, Lemmy," said Dan. "See what you do."

Lemmy spun back to his computer and went to work.

"Meanwhile," Dan said, typing on his phone, "I'll send Blaine a text. He's the one who gave me Fana. Maybe he has more information about what it is."

"Ooh! Get some weed too," Charlie said. "I'm sick of beer. I feel all bloated and unattractive."

Dan arched an eyebrow but withheld the comment about Charlie's physique. "Good idea," he said patiently. "But we need to find out about Fana first."

Dan finished the text and tossed the phone on the carpet. *What a day.* As Lemmy click-clacked away on the keyboard, Dan yawned and closed his eyes. "Thanks for the help, guys. I'm glad I have thoughtful roommates," he muttered.

"More like brain mates? Right?" said Charlie.

"Right... brain mates..."

Charlie softly strummed his guitar and hummed a Pink Floyd tune as Dan drifted off to sleep.

---

Dan's apartment faded away, and Charlie found himself standing in a sparsely decorated Florida condo. Lemmy still clacked away on the laptop, only now it sat on top of a coffee table near a sliding glass door.

"Well, he's asleep," Charlie said and plopped onto an overstuffed couch next to Lemmy.

"I don't know about you," Lemmy said, stretching his arms, "but I hate being projected into the Actual. It's good to be home."

"I don't see the difference," Charlie said with a shrug. "If anything, this place is worse than Dan's apartment."

"Nothing is worse than Dan's apartment. At least here I have a couch and a fully stocked fridge."

Charlie rubbed his hands along the cushions of the floral-print sofa. "Yeah. This place is the epitome of luxury."

"It will get better," Lemmy said, pointing to the wall. "That flamingo picture appeared sometime last night. The next time Dan is awake, we'll ask him to see pictures from his last Florida vacation."

"Yeah." Charlie nodded to the pitch-blackness outside the sliding glass door. "Maybe then we could at least get a view."

Lemmy glanced out the door and shivered. "I agree," he said. "Living near the edge of a gaping abyss is unsettling. We need to figure out a way to get him to remember more about the condo so it'll fill in. This place could use some sprucing up."

"We could use a TV or a keg or something." Charlie craned his neck to view Lemmy's screen. "Anyone new checking in?"

Lemmy refreshed the terminal screen on the MUD. "None since Dan. Whoever gave him Fana must have kept it to themselves. We haven't had another hit since—" The computer *dinged,* and Lemmy snapped to attention.

"Someone's on!" Charlie exclaimed.

Under the WELCOME TRAVELER banner, there was a new notification saying, "There are 02 connected." Charlie let out an excited yelp.

"Relax, we've had fake guests before. Bots find the site all the time. Let's wait and see if it's a real person."

*User <Guest02> is now Colette.*

"Ooh! Colette? It's a girl! Lemmy, who are you logged in as?"

*Colette says, "Hello? Is there anybody out there?"*

Lemmy quickly entered a series of commands. "Gimme one sec… I need to find out if this is an alt or a main."

"I'm here," he typed.

*Colette says, "Neat. This place is gnarly."*

"Do you want to ride the rainbow?" Lemmy responded.

Charlie arched an eyebrow. "Who the hell talks like that? What does it mean?"

"If Colette is a bot, it won't respond. However, if it's someone high on Fana…"

*Colette says, "Hell yeah, man!"*

"Yes!" Lemmy pumped his fist. "We found another one! She's an alt, like you! Here." He pushed the laptop over to Charlie. "Keep her talking. I have to make a call."

"Wait, what do you mean *like me?*" Charlie fumbled at the keyboard. "Wait! What do I say?"

Lemmy punched numbers on his phone. "Find out more about her. Keep her online."

Charlie reached over and typed, "Do you like drugs?"

*Colette says, "If you're talking about yoga, then yes. Do you like yoga?"*

Lemmy talked frantically over the phone in a foreign language.

"Lemmy?" Charlie said anxiously. "I'm running out of stuff to talk about."

"T4m.bin?" Lemmy said into the phone, slipping into English. "Is Tania ready?"

"Sure, yoga is okay, I guess," Charlie typed. "I like beer. Do you like beer?"

*Colette says, "Whatever. This is boring."*

Lemmy bent over to view the screen and grunted. "What are you doing, idiot?" He tossed the phone onto the couch and shoved Charlie out of the way.

"Ha ha, I'm just kidding. Yoga is great," Lemmy typed. "Do you have any friends there with you?"

*Colette says, "Yeah, I have a friend, but this is boring, and we're gonna leave."*

"You know this isn't *really* a game, right? Your body is a computer program running in a giant simulation. Reality is a lie!"

*Colette says, "Whoa! That's wild. You know, my friend likes computers and stuff. She'd be stoked to hear all that. Can I bring her on?"*

Lemmy smiled victoriously at Charlie. "Sure, I'd love to tell her all about it," he typed. "And that, my friend, is how you do it," Lemmy said smugly.

"She really bought that load of crap you just told her?" Charlie said. "Who would be stupid enough to fall for that line?"

Lemmy peeked at Charlie out of the corner of his eyes and grinned. "We can thank Fana for that."

*<Guest03> has joined.*

"Wow, that was easy. Is that all there is to it?" said Charlie.

"No. Now that we've established a connection to Colette's main, we'll need to get her to download Tania. Remember how you downloaded my code to Dan? Colette needs to do the same thing."

<Guest03> *is now Yvette*

*Yvette says, "Is there anybody out there?"*

*Colette says, "Welcome to the Sim, Yvette. We have one rule here. No matter what you see or hear, in real life, you must act normal."*

*Yvette says, "Uh, okay?"*

Charlie grinned at Lemmy. "So, what now? She just talks to herself?"

"Pretty much. Yvette is too high to realize she has two sessions open to the same site. The drug prevents her from seeing it. All we have to do is give her the VPN info, and she will be able to download the information."

"Too easy," Charlie said.

Dan rolled over to his side and wiped the drool off his face. He wouldn't tell the guys that he wasn't fully asleep and that he'd heard everything. They did tell him to act normal after all.

# Seven

THE TAME TROUT was a generic sports bar in a recently constructed strip mall wedged between a People's Penny discount store and an oriental massage parlor. Dan liked the place because the beer was cold, there was always a game on, and they had a decent burger. The bartender had a fantastic pair of tits, and that didn't hurt.

It was a frequent hangout of the AGphic IT staff after hours because it was across the parking lot from the office building. The rest of Dan's former colleagues were still at work. Blaine had skipped out early.

"Hey there, Dan," Blaine said as he pulled up a stool next to him at the bar. He waved at the bartender, but she wasn't paying attention. She was busy talking to the heavily tattooed, blue-and-pink-haired waitress. Their conversation must have been more important than tending bar.

"Hey, Blaine, thanks for coming," Dan said as they shook hands.

"Anything for you, bud. How's it going over at Canaille Tech?"

Dan rolled his eyes and groaned. "I work six to three with a thirty-minute lunch break. Today I did fifteen password resets, configured ten new user accounts, and reimaged three computers."

Blaine winced. "Oof. Grunt work, eh?"

"Yeah. I'm not real popular with the other guys. They say I'm making them look bad. To make matters worse, my boss thinks I want his job. He keeps finding problems with my work to put me in my place. IT infrastructure work is the same everywhere you go. You know how it is."

"Yeah, I do." Blaine laughed.

Dan gulped down the last of his beer and signaled the bartender. He managed to catch her eye just as the waitress walked away. When she brought them refills, she caught Blaine staring at her breasts and smiled.

He quickly averted his eyes and sipped his beer. "How's Katie?"

Dan sighed and swirled his beer. "She's filing for divorce."

"Ouch! What's it gonna cost you?"

"A lot. Time mostly. Louisiana law says that if you have kids, you have to wait a year for the divorce to become final. We can't do anything until then. What's worse, I would only have custody every other weekend."

"That doesn't sound too bad," Blaine said absently into his beer.

"I didn't want to hire a lawyer, but she did. It forced my hand, you know?" Dan sipped his beer thoughtfully. "Hell, I don't want a divorce. Right now I'm stalling for time, hoping she changes her mind."

"That sucks, man," Blaine said.

"Yeah." Dan chuckled. "I'm probably going to pay Dr. Patel a visit."

"The medical marijuana doctor?" Blaine said with disgust. "Do you have a card?"

"Yeah, he gave me one a couple of years ago. I was doing a lot of overtime and needed it for my anxiety. I used it once and didn't like it. I let the script expire."

"That medical stuff is crap," Blaine said, shaking his head. "I dated a chick with cancer once who had a card. Everything we tried was terrible."

"Cancer? Shit! Is she okay?"

Blaine sagged his head. "Nah, man. She died. I took her card and got all kinds of stuff for free on her insurance. I've been selling what's left."

Dan set his beer on the bar and stared at Blaine. "Jesus! Are you serious?"

Blaine's serious face cracked, and he roared with laughter. "Come on!" He chuckled. "Do I look like an asshole to you? She's fine."

"You're a dickhead, you know that?" Dan said with a playful smirk.

"*I'm* a dickhead?" Blaine laughed with mock offense. "I'll remember that."

The bartender checked to see if they needed drinks, but Dan waved her off. He caught Blaine checking out her backside as she walked away and tapped him on the shoulder.

"Look," Dan said, voice low, "the free sample you gave me—Fana—do you still have any?"

Blaine's eyes widened. "Out already, eh? I didn't know you were that big into psychedelics."

Dan sighed. "I only took two of them. Katie set the rest of them on fire in the driveway as I was moving out. Along with my high school letterman's jacket... and our wedding photo..."

Blaine cringed and hid his face. "Damn. That's rough."

"Yeah. Let's not talk about it..." Dan sipped his beer. "Anyway, I was hoping you had more Fana. It helped."

"Sorry, man, I'm out. It was a one-time-only type of deal. But hey, my Colorado mule finally came through. It's the traditional store-bought stuff, but it's better than the five-milligram ones we have here."

"No," Dan said, shaking his head. "Cannabis won't work. I'll fail the drug test at work. Fana doesn't show up."

Blaine checked if anyone was listening and leaned in close. "Seriously? You pee clean? It must be some kind of new synthetic—"

"It works." Dan clasped his shoulder. "And I need more. It's... *effective*."

Blaine leaned back and whistled. "No promises but I'll see what I can do. The guy who I got them from is flaky."

"What do you mean *flaky*?" Dan said.

Blaine traced his finger on the bar top. "I don't know," he said hesitantly, "the type of dude who is into psychedelics sort of flaky? I'll try, but he's hard to get ahold of."

"Do you have any idea what is in Fana? I searched online, but the website is gone now."

"I don't know. What I understood from my guy was that Fana was magic mushroom edibles. But... if you're pissing clean for psilocybin, then it must be synthetic. I'll have to ask around."

"When you find him again, I'd like to talk with him. If that's all right. The only thing I know for sure is that a Fana trip isn't normal for psychedelics."

Blaine shot him a knowing smile. "Because it makes you see people? Tell me the truth. How many people are in there now?"

Dan waved at the bartender, but she was watching TV and didn't notice. "You've seen the video, huh?" he said. "Two for sure, maybe three."

Blaine squinted and peered into Dan's eyes. What was he expecting? Charlie to wave at him as if through a peephole? Dan raised an eyebrow, and Blaine leaned back into his seat. "Which one am I talking to now?" he asked.

"It doesn't work that way," Dan said, making sure no one was around.

"Are they listening to our conversation?"

"Probably." Dan shifted uneasily in his chair. "Can we talk about something else?"

"Fine." Blaine nodded and took a sip of his beer. "Like I said, I don't have Fana, but I do have a few cannabis edibles. Although I'm not sure I should give drugs to a crazy person. You could give me a bad rep."

"I appreciate your concern for my well-being, Scarface."

Blaine chuckled as he finished off his beer. He produced a medicine bottle from his pocket and slid it across the bar. "It's not much, but it'll tide you over until I can find more Fana."

"Thanks," Dan said as he stuffed it in his pocket.

"By the way," Blaine said as the bartender refilled their beers, "how is your newfound fame working out for you at the new gig? Did they like the video of you going nuts?"

"Nobody's said anything. I'm not sure if it's because I'm new, or they are just oblivious." Dan peeked over the top of his beer. "What about over at AGphic?" he said nonchalantly. "Did anyone there watch the video?"

"Are you kidding? Everyone saw it. They played it on the big TV at the Tuesday stand-up meeting. They thought it was hilarious."

*Hilarious?* Bile rose in his throat. Dan sipped his beer. *I could have been having a mental breakdown, and they thought it was hilarious? I thought they were friends.* "Well, I'm glad it was funny to you."

Blaine coughed and patted Dan on the back. "Oh, *I* didn't think it was funny. I know what you were dealing with—you know—with the servers. Besides, I wasn't the only one who didn't find it amusing."

"Oh yeah? Who?"

"Yvette. In fact, she somehow knew I was coming to meet you today and asked me to give you this." Blaine produced a folded-up envelope from his back pocket and slid it across the table.

*Yvette?* Dan stared curiously at the envelope. His name was written on the front in her neat cursive. *Was this about what happened last night with Lemmy and Colette? Could Yvette be connected?* Dan held up the envelope and waved it at Blaine. "I don't know Yvette that well. What's this about?"

Blaine pretended to watch the sports news on the TV above the bar. He seemed like he didn't want to make eye contact with Dan or even look at the envelope. "I have no idea," he said curtly. "But ever since you were fired and the video came out, Yvette has been asking about you. She's stalking you on social media. At least, that's what I've seen in the daily internet usage report. She probably has the hots for you."

*Was that jealousy in his voice?* "I doubt that very seriously," Dan said. "I'm at least ten years older than her. Besides, I'm married."

"When has age or a wedding ring ever stopped an affair?" Blaine grumbled.

Dan grabbed Blaine by the arm and looked him in the eye. "I have no interest in Yvette. I love Katie. Got it?"

Blaine brushed Dan's hand off and smoothed out his sleeve. "Fine. I believe you," he said. "Are you gonna open it?"

"Not now," Dan said, fingering the envelope and glancing nervously around the bar. "Don't tell anyone she gave me this please."

"I wouldn't dream of it," Blaine said with a too-cool smile.

The muscles in Dan's neck relaxed a little bit. If there was one thing Blaine was good at, it was keeping secrets. He was too good. Dan needed him to reveal his source for Fana. *Maybe another beer or two would help get a name.* Dan waved to the bartender, but Blaine's phone chimed.

"Gotta go back to the office," he said, reading a text. "The email server you had problems with a while back is at it again."

"Still? It's been screwed up for months."

"You know how it is." He shrugged. "I'll talk to you later."

Blaine promised more information about Fana as they exchanged quick goodbyes. Once Blaine had walked out, Dan took the envelope over to a secluded booth.

"That went extremely well!" exclaimed Charlie as he chugged an imaginary beer. "I can't wait to try out the new stuff tonight."

"Well, are you going to open it or not?" Lemmy said impatiently.

"I bet it's a love note," said Charlie. "Dear Dan, I've been waiting for you to leave your wife for years now. We can finally be together – "

"Shut up!" Dan unfolded the paper and read the words. *I need to talk to you. Meet me outside. Act normal! – Y*

The blood drained from Dan's face, and Lemmy and Charlie disappeared. His hands shook. *What does she want with me?* He stuffed the note back in its envelope and jammed it into his pants pocket. Dan scanned the bar. *Someone is watching me. Is this a test?* His eyes froze on a lone figure sitting at a table in a dark corner. Was it the priest? He didn't want to wait to find out and rushed out the door.

He stepped outside and was blinded by the light. When his vision returned, he casually searched the parking lot. Several people milled about, but none of them were Yvette. *Maybe she chickened out?* As he walked to his truck, thoughts raced through his head. *How did she know to send me a note? Was it really her, or was Blaine making a joke? Why did she say act normal? Did I say that in the video? No. The dream must have been real.*

He twisted the keys in the ignition, and the truck roared to life. As the air-conditioning cooled the hot cab, he sighed with relief. *No Yvette? Thank God. No more drama today please. I need to get back to the apartment to figure this all out. Maybe the guys will leave me alone –*

There was a tap at the passenger-side window, and Dan jumped. A woman frowned at him from behind large black sunglasses. *No drama? So much for that…*

"Jesus, Yvette, you scared me," Dan said as he rolled down the window.

"That's the most normal thing you've done so far, idiot!" she said. "Why were you sneaking around the parking lot like you had just robbed a bank or something?"

Dan showed her the crumpled envelope, and she brushed back a lock of hair that was hiding her face. "I was looking for you," he said. "You weren't around. I didn't expect for you to—"

"Let me in. We're being watched."

The door clicked, and she climbed in next to him in the passenger seat. Her floral perfume washed over Dan, and he was caught in a daydream. *This isn't real.* He reached over and grabbed her knee.

"What the hell!" Yvette shouted as she slapped him away.

"Sorry, I had to make sure you weren't a figment of my imagination," he said, rubbing the sting out of his arm. *Thank God this isn't another Charlie situation.*

Yvette took off her sunglasses and squinted at him through her almond-shaped eyes. Dan's heart sank. She was gorgeous. "You really *are* crazy, aren't you?"

"What do you want, Yvette?"

"I need answers about the Simulation," she said, settling into her seat. "For starters, who the hell is Tania and Lemmy, and why do they want us to meet?"

Dan gulped. *Lemmy? She knew about Lemmy?* Yvette tapped him on the shoulder and pointed to a small car parked in the slot behind them. The woman inside had her face hidden behind a magazine, and a small camera was set up on her dashboard pointed at Dan's truck.

"That woman has been following us," Yvette said, facing the front. "She's some sort of private investigator. She doesn't know I've followed her too. She's been keeping an eye on your apartment. The question is, who hired her?"

Dan recalled the fight with Katie when she accused him of having an affair with Yvette. *Katie wouldn't hire a PI, would she? Maybe it's her lawyer's idea? Maybe it's someone else?*

"I know you're having marriage problems," Yvette said

softly. "But why would they be tailing me? I know nothing about you outside of work. I certainly don't know your wife."

"I have no idea why you're being followed," Dan said, flushing with embarrassment. "We can't be sure it was Katie who hired her. It could be someone working for AGphic. That's our only connection." *It could be an agent of Father August...*

"Why would AGphic have me followed? Anyway, it doesn't matter who she is working for," Yvette said, peeking back over her shoulder. "She sees us together now. Tania told me —"

"Who's Tania?"

"It's complicated." Yvette sighed. "She told me to act normal or else the Simulation will correct me."

*That sounds familiar.*

"The way I figure it," she said, "the only way for us to discuss the Simulation and keep it from correcting us is to pretend as if we're seeing each other. An affair is normal, right?"

Dan massaged his forehead. "I fail to understand how having an affair helps my situation with Katie."

"It doesn't," Yvette said, "but maybe you could mend your relationship with Katie at a later time. You can't do that if the Simulation kills you."

She was right. Katie would dismiss any attempt to explain the Simulation as a drug-fueled fantasy. An affair would be a quicker road home if such a road even existed. Yvette straightened out her shirt and put her sunglasses in her purse.

"Okay," Dan said. "An affair it is then. What now?"

"Now we pose for pictures," she said. "How do I look?"

Yvette Boudreaux was the only woman at the office who could wear a white polo and khakis and still turn heads. Her long black hair, almond-shaped eyes, and olive complexion were the envy of all her friends. Dan never understood how someone as pretty as her got dragged into IT work. If she were in sales, she would make millions.

"You're beautiful—" Dan coughed and looked away. "I mean, you look fine."

"Thanks," she said with an arched eyebrow. "We need to go where we can talk and not be watched. How about my place?"

"I thought we wanted the PI to see us together," Dan said, peering over his shoulder. "Besides, I don't know where you live."

"Seen? Yes. Heard? No. I'll drive. Let's swap places."

Dan reached for the door handle, and Yvette grabbed his arm. "Let's cross behind the truck. I want her to get a good picture of us."

"I hope you're right about this, Yvette."

Yvette pulled Dan close, her lips brushing his. "Forget about Katie for the time being," she said softly. "If the Simulation knew what we were up to, we'd be dead already. Let's go."

Dan gently pushed Yvette away. As they crossed behind the truck, the woman nonchalantly adjusted her camera and snapped a few photos. To seal the deal, Yvette grabbed Dan's hand and squeezed it before climbing into the driver's seat. Dan shot her a conspirator's grin as he buckled himself in.

"When we get to my place, be sure to hold my hand when we walk to the door. For the pictures," Yvette said.

Yvette put the truck in gear and drove off. Dan smiled and laughed.

"What's funny?" she said.

"You're driving my truck," he said. "You're real. You aren't a hallucination. It's a relief, that's all."

"This was a mistake."

# Eight

Y VETTE LIVED IN the *newer* part of town. The neighborhood was once a picture postcard example of the 1950s postwar suburban dream: ranch homes, large fenced yards, a covered carport large enough for two vehicles. It all ended a decade ago when a freak spring rainstorm flooded the entire neighborhood.

Residents, no longer trusting the city's flood plan, cashed out the insurance money and moved away. An entrepreneurial developer seized the opportunity and bought the entire tract of land. The neighborhood was bulldozed, and a faux-French city was erected in its place. Block after block of old homes was replaced by apartments, condos, and townhomes. A new school was built, and "pocket parks" were scattered throughout. Boutiques and locally owned restaurants lined the new main street. The demand far exceeded the supply, and the developer became a millionaire many times over.

As Dan stood before an overly intricate wrought iron gate marking the entrance to her front garden, he wondered how she could afford this home on an analyst's salary. Homes in this neighborhood were worth nearly a million dollars. They walked inside, and Dan peeked through the curtains in time to see the Honda drive by. *Great, she followed us.*

"How about some coffee?" Yvette said as she dropped her purse on the entryway table.

Dan followed her into the kitchen. It was spacious for what was supposed to be a single person's house. It had all the popular additions, cypress cabinets, marble countertops. She even had a pot filler mounted above the stove. He was envious.

While Yvette busied herself making coffee, he became mesmerized by a black Kit-Cat clock hanging on the wall. Its eyes rolled back and forth as its tail ticked the time. It seemed both out of place and uniquely Yvette. As if summoned by the eyes of the clock, a figure appeared in Dan's peripheral vision. His attention was drawn to the living room where Charlie slumped into Yvette's oversized couch.

"Is it ready yet? It smells so good!" he said.

"Not now!" Dan mouthed at Charlie.

"What did you say, Dan?" Yvette said. "Do you want sugar?"

"Sorry. No sugar. Black please." Dan turned his back on Charlie. "This is a nice place."

"Thanks." Yvette gave him a polite smile as she tied her hair into a ponytail. "My parents died in a freak car accident a few years ago. This house is my inheritance."

"I'm sorry to hear that," Dan said with a grimace. "My parents died in a car wreck when I was in college. I still think about them all the time."

Yvette brushed away a tear and wiped it on her pants. "Yeah, I know what you mean," she said, hands shaking. "You… uh… want to go have a seat in the living room? I'll bring the coffee right out."

As Dan walked into the living room, he realized how little he actually knew about Yvette. They worked together on a few IT projects at AGphic, but he didn't know much about her personal life. They had barely spoken in his truck on the way here. She'd spent the entire time glancing out the window. Even here, in her home, he could tell by the way her hands shook that she wasn't okay but was doing her best to hide it.

As he pondered his next move, Lemmy appeared on the

couch next to Charlie. He lounged with his hands behind his head and stretched out. "Did anyone check for Father August?"

"He probably is too ashamed of the scandal of this affair. I'm sure he's extremely disappointed in Dan," Charlie said.

"I'll be sure to confess the next time I see him."

"He's onto us. He'll be back," Lemmy said.

Yvette appeared in the doorway, holding two steaming cups of coffee. Dan took one and helped himself to the leather recliner. "Were you talking to someone?" she said as she sat on the couch between Lemmy and Charlie. Lemmy's eyes went wide, and Charlie made a lewd gesture.

"Wow," Lemmy said as he checked her out. "She's way out of your league. No one is going to believe this affair."

Charlie put his arm around her and raised his eyebrows at Dan suggestively.

"My son called," Dan said while doing his best to ignore Charlie. "Katie is picking him up from football practice today."

Yvette nodded and sipped her coffee. "Dan, I need to know," she said. "The people in your head. Can you talk to them when you're not on Fana?"

Dan nearly choked on his coffee. *Well, that was direct.* He set his mug on the end table and wiped his chin. "Um. Yeah," he stammered. "I haven't had Fana for several days, and they are still around."

Yvette tilted her head. "Do you think it is because of residual chemicals that your body can't process? Or did it break you? How many people are in there with you?"

"Three. But only two are with us now."

"Oh?" Yvette leaned back and crossed her legs. "*Only* two?"

Dan relaxed in his chair. It was nice to finally be able to open up and tell someone the truth. "The third one is a priest," he said. "But he's not like the others. He seems to be a part of the

Simulation. He isn't our friend. I'm worried that our pretend affair will trigger him."

Yvette snorted. "A priest disapproving of unmarried sex? Shocker. Let me know if he shows up, and I'll assure him our affair hasn't been consummated yet."

"I heard the word *yet!*" Charlie hooted. "Damn, buddy, you still got it. Lemmy, it looks like we're not hanging around for dinner after all."

"Well, I don't want a divorce," Dan said, ignoring Charlie's outburst. "But we have to get to the bottom of this. The only way to do that is if we work together."

"Okay then," Yvette said, leaning back on the sofa. "Let's get started. Tell me who is here with you."

Dan combed his fingers through his hair. *Here goes nothing.* "Well, sitting on the couch to your left is Charlie."

Yvette patted the cushion to her left. Her hand passed through Charlie's lap as if he were a ghost. He winked and blew her a kiss.

"No one there," she said.

"His image projects from my mind into the real world like a hologram. To me, he looks just as real as you do. Right now he's grinning like an idiot because you touched his penis." Dan turned to Charlie. "She can't see you. You can stop flirting now."

Charlie stopped making lewd kissing noises and frowned. Yvette looked at the empty spot on the couch, then back to Dan. "What does he look like?"

Charlie set his beer on the coffee table and did his best bodybuilder imitation. "He's a fat version of me with bright blue eyes," Dan said with a smirk. "And he's always wearing a plain yellow baseball cap, which I don't get."

Charlie stopped posing and frowned. "It's an LSU cap."

"Then how come it doesn't say LSU on it?" Lemmy said.

Charlie took off the cap and examined it. "Well, I'll be..."

Yvette arched an eyebrow at Dan. "Okay...," she said. "He sounds fun. Who is the other one?"

Lemmy crossed his arms and rolled his eyes. "Go on..."

"His name is Lemmy. He's gray around his temples, so I'm guessing he is in his midfifties. He is wearing camouflage pants and a ratty Jane's Addiction T-shirt."

"What's wrong with my shirt?" Lemmy asked.

"I think it's cool," said Charlie.

"Are you okay?" Yvette sat at attention and stared at him intently.

Dan frowned. "Yes? Why?"

"You were mumbling as if you were having a seizure, like in the viral video. Do it again," she said.

Yvette took out her phone and pointed it at Dan. Dan glared at her. "Relax, I'm not going to put it on the internet," she said. "You need to see what you look like when you talk to them."

The flash on Yvette's phone lit the room, and she gave a thumbs-up. Dan cleared his throat and leaned forward toward Lemmy. "Hello, Lemmy," he said slowly. "How are you today?"

"Uh. Fine?" Lemmy shrugged. "What is this supposed to accomplish? We've already seen the last video."

"Humor me, all right?" Dan said.

Charlie leaned over and put bunny ears on Lemmy. "Do me next, Dan!"

"Fine, Charlie, we'll do you next."

Yvette jumped out of her chair and hooted. "Okay, got it! Watch."

She handed Dan the phone, and they all huddled around it. In the video, Dan addressed an empty sofa in a language that sounded like a chainsaw.

Yvette smiled victoriously. "You sound exactly like you did in the ballpark video."

Charlie paced back and forth. "Play it back."

"Is everything okay?" Yvette said.

As Dan replayed the video, Charlie stalked around the room, pulling at his hair. "I'm not there!"

"So what?" Lemmy said, shaking his head. "What did you expect?"

"I was supposed to be in the shot!" Charlie said.

"I look like I have Tourette's," Dan said, replaying the video.

Charlie took off his hat and pulled at his hair.

"What's your problem?" Dan said. "We've been telling you that you're a hologram."

"I know," he said, pacing. "But… You don't understand. I'm really not there! It's like I don't exist!"

"I'm not there either," Lemmy said. "You don't see me all upset about it."

"I'm not like you, Lemmy," Charlie said with an exasperated sigh.

"Are you crazy? You've known all along that you are in my head, right? You weren't in my viral ballpark video either. I don't understand the freak out," Dan said.

Charlie stalked around the room, his hat in one hand and a clump of hair in the other. "I thought I was playing along. You know? So Lemmy didn't feel bad. I thought maybe the softball lady's phone had a filter or a bad angle—"

"What's going on, Dan?" Yvette said with a tinge of concern in her voice.

"Charlie is freaking out that he isn't visible in the video."

Charlie put on his cap and stormed out of the room. *Where is he going?* "Lemmy, follow him."

Lemmy nodded and chased after Charlie.

"And… he just walked out."

"They can do that?" she said.

"Apparently." Dan shrugged. "I'm new to all this as well."

Lemmy reappeared and returned to his seat on the couch. "Looks like we're a man down," he said. "Charlie is experiencing an existential crisis. He took a walk out the front door and disappeared."

"Disappeared?"

"Yeah." Lemmy sighed. "He's hiding in your meta somewhere."

Yvette waved her hands to get Dan's attention. "Hello? What's going on?"

"Lemmy says Charlie is hiding in my meta —" Dan spun back to Lemmy. "What does that mean?"

Lemmy lit a cigarette and relaxed on the sofa. "We exist inside your metadata," he said, taking a drag. "Every object in the Simulation has metadata embedded into its code. This sofa, you, your son, the trees. One of the ways we access this metadata is via — you're going to love this — the Meta. It's a realm created strictly to connect to metadata. Not very original, I know."

Dan folded his arms. "You mean to tell me that's how you are doing this? All through my metadata?"

"Don't look so surprised. We exist inside an advanced simulation. You are composed of information. Surely the concept of metadata isn't that far-fetched?" Lemmy took a drag off his cigarette and blew a cloud of smoke into the middle of the room. "Let's get the terminology straight. The context in which you exist is called 'the Actual.' Don't call your experience the real world. The Meta is real too. It's *all* real."

"What's he saying?" Yvette said.

As Dan relayed what Lemmy had just told him, her eyes drooped, and she sagged a little into the sofa. Was she falling asleep?

Lemmy cleared his throat. "The Actual is the live version of the Simulation," he said. "You and Yvette exist in the Actual. Charlie and I exist in the Meta. The Meta contains parts of objects that exist inside the Actual, but it is not contained by the

Actual. The Meta is not subject to the same rules but is every bit as real as your actual. That's why I hate your people's phrase, *the real world*. Hah! Such a limited view of reality."

"I feel... I feel like I'm being left out," Yvette slurred. "Wh-what did he say?"

"He was going on about" — Yvette's eyes drifted toward the floor — "Hello? Yvette?" Her mouth fell open, and she stared wide-eyed at the rug. She giggled and sat straight. *Is she high?*

"Yeah? I'm listening," she said. "Tell Lemmy I believe him. Everything he's said so far."

Dan raised an eyebrow. "Really?"

"Yes, and I'll tell you why I believe you." Yvette checked the time on the black cat clock, and her eyes glazed over. She dug around in her pocket and placed a carton of Fana on the coffee table.

"When did you take a Fana?" he said.

"Right when we got here," she said groggily. "I wanted to see what would happen."

Yvette twitched and sank deeper into the couch.

"Yvette? Are you okay? Those things are potent!"

She stared at the wall and spoke incomprehensibly for a few seconds before refocusing on Dan. "I'm okay. I forgot to address you directly. Dan" — Yvette gestured toward the lamp — "I want you to meet Colette."

"Um... hello, Colette?" Dan said tenuously. "You know that I can't see or hear her, right?"

Yvette rolled her eyes back and slouched in the chair. The psychedelic part of the drug must have taken over. "It's so bright in here," she said, blinking slowly. "Are you aware that your chair is leaking the number three? I'm thirsty."

Dan followed Yvette into the kitchen and poured her a glass of water. She mouthed "thanks" and gulped it down greedily.

"Can you see Colette, Lemmy?"

"No," he said as he perched on top of a barstool. "Your Metas aren't directly connected. It's more like—"

"Colette says she can't see Lemmy," Yvette said. "She thinks you're scamming us. She says you left your wife because you think I'm hot. She says you faked it all to get a date with me."

*What? Is she trying to be funny?* Yvette burped and her eyes lolled, unable to focus. "She also says I wasn't supposed to say that out loud just now."

Lemmy propped his elbows on the counter and sneered at Dan.

"I'm not scamming you," Dan said, red-faced. "And you know this isn't a date. We don't have time for this nonsense. Look, I told you about Charlie. Now you tell me about Colette."

Yvette closed her eyes and leaned on the kitchen counter. Her face became an animated mess of various expressions. Dan was awed at the absurdity of all the theatrics. After a few moments, she snapped awake. "Sorry, Dan, she had a lot to say. Colette is a thin twentysomething woman with blond hair and blue eyes. She always wears yoga clothes— Why are you always wearing yoga clothes?" Yvette closed her eyes in concentration. "Right. She's a very *active* woman." Yvette pouted out her lips to say *as if*.

Dan was amazed Yvette could carry on a conversation. He could barely sit upright the first time he tried Fana. But then again, it wasn't Yvette's first time.

"I've known her from the first time I took Fana," she said. "I read about psychedelics on the simulation forums. Fana was the only one I could get at the time."

"Wh-what?" he stammered. *Was she on the forums too? What else did she know?*

"On the simulation theory forum, I read that if you took psychedelics, you could see the lines of code embedded in reality. I wanted proof. I asked Blaine if he had any LSD, and he handed me the pack of Fana. The rest is history."

Dan's eyes went wide. "How long have you been on the forums? What is your username?"

Yvette stared at the marble countertop, unresponsive. Dan imagined its swirls were alive and moving like a mountain stream.

"Sorry." Yvette shook her head. "Colette was talking. She's scared. I can't stay awake. I..."

She dazed off again. This time she stared at the cat clock. *She's too far gone.*

"Yvette, explain why you wanted to meet me. Why now?"

"Colette told me to. Tania told her we should meet." Yvette took a deep breath and wiped her head. "Is it hot in here?"

Lemmy shot Dan a knowing look as he typed a message on his cell phone. "She's talking about my friend Tania," he said. "She's the one I've been messaging."

Yvette stood and took off her shirt. Her breasts glistened with sweat over the top of her bra. Lemmy's jaw dropped, and Dan averted his eyes. She fanned her armpits, unaware.

"Lemmy says he spoke to Tania," Dan said, staring at the floor.

"Colette says she met her online via some sort of text game."

*That was the dream I had! Colette downloaded Tania to Yvette's meta!* Dan paced excitedly back and forth. "Was it an old-school MUD? It would look like a UNIX terminal session."

"Yeah, I guess," she said. "That night was hazy."

Their experiences were nearly identical. They both had an existing interest in simulation theory. They both used Fana from Blaine. They both went to the same MUD. If Lemmy and Charlie existed in Dan's metadata, it stood to reason Colette and Tania existed in Yvette's metadata.

Fana was coursing through her veins, and she could hardly hold her head upright. Dan wanted to do one more test before she became incapacitated. He found a piece of paper near her refrigerator and quickly scribbled a note on it. "Lemmy, send this message to Tania. Tell her to make Yvette repeat it for me."

Lemmy grinned and sent the message via his cell phone.

Seconds later, Yvette spasmed. "Colette wants me to tell you *purple peacock, seven-eight-nine-five,* whatever that means."

Dan slid the paper over to her.

"This says the same thing," she said. "We aren't crazy."

"No, we're not." He grinned broadly. "This is evidence of the Simulation."

His joy was short-lived. She laid her head flat on the kitchen counter, and drool formed at the corner of her mouth. "What *is* a purple peacock?" she slurred. "Aren't they green?"

Her eyes closed and she dozed off. *Crap! We were so close!* He wanted to say more, but she was in space. But still, this was the proof he needed. Proof—not just for his own sanity—if he could somehow convince Katie… The drugs were the problem. If only Yvette was able to see Colette when she was sober, like he could with Charlie, they would make more progress. They could get together and show Katie the truth! His marriage would be saved and all forgiven…

"Looks like you two are having fun," boomed a deep voice. Dan spun around to see Father August glaring disapprovingly at Yvette. She was passed out on the kitchen counter, wearing only her bra. She breathed slowly, oblivious to the priest's presence. "What *have* you done?" he said with an ominous grin.

"Whoa!" shouted Lemmy. "What is he doing here?"

Dan shot him a look. *Get out, idiot!* Father August walked over to Yvette and stroked her hair. "Dan, I truly hope that you've never consummated your affair with this person. For your own soul."

Dan stiffened. "We haven't had sex if that's what you mean. How long have you been watching? Did you see what we can do? We can speak telepathically! It's a miracle."

"Shut up, Dan!" screamed Lemmy.

Dan realized his mistake too late. *Crap!*

Father August followed Dan's gaze to where Lemmy stood. "Who are you talking to?" Father August said with a curious tone. "I don't see Charlie…"

"Shit! I'm out!" With a vibrating hum, Lemmy disappeared from the room. Dan was left with a sickening feeling in the pit of his stomach.

"What was that noise?" said Father August, startled. "Dan? Who was that, and what were you going to tell me earlier? What miracle?"

Yvette stirred from her sleep. "Dan? Are you okay?" she said groggily. "I heard a weird noise. What's going on?"

Without moving, Dan slowly shifted his eyes over to Yvette. "It was nothing," he said through gritted teeth. "Go back to sleep."

"Colette is gone. What is happening?" Her eyes were unfocused, still in a drug-induced haze. When they landed on Father August, they went wide. "Who let the priest in?"

"You can see him?"

Father August caressed Yvette's temples, and her eyes rolled back. Her head thudded onto the counter, unconscious.

"Colette? Is she seeing people too, Dan? Where is our friend Charlie?"

Dan opened and shut his mouth. *Can I be honest with Father August? Maybe Charlie was wrong about him being a corrective agent? Is he… reading my thoughts?*

"What are you doing with this woman?"

"We're friends from work. She invited me over for a cup of coffee, that's all."

"I'll find out the truth." Father August's face broke into a mirthless grin. "Besides, you have a bigger problem right now."

There was a frantic knocking at the front door. It sounded as if it was going to be beaten off the hinges. Dan looked to Father August for answers, but he had already vanished. The pounding stopped, and a woman's face appeared in the kitchen window.

"There you are!" she screamed.

"Katie?"

She thumped the window so hard it might break. "Get your ass out here right now!"

# Nine

THE PAST TWENTY-four hours had not been kind to Dan. Thankfully, Katie was able to calm herself down enough to drive home. Yvette was too wasted to know what was going on, which Katie had found hilarious. The hate in Katie's heart had grown into pure malice. The way she had looked at him made his blood run cold.

This morning at work, Dan got a call from his lawyer. His custody battle had received a setback due to Katie's evidence of his infidelity. Dan found it hard to breathe. He collected his belongings and went home. He didn't care if he was fired. The job sucked anyway.

"Your whole life is slipping through your fingers," said Lemmy as he typed away on his computer and sipped coffee. "You need a plan."

Dan lay sprawled out on his futon, hypnotized by the slow-spinning ceiling fan. *Not now, Lemmy.*

"Let's take an assessment, shall we?" Lemmy spun in his chair to face Dan. "Katie, aka 'love of your life,' hates you and thinks you're having an affair. You are at risk of losing custody because she busted you with Yvette. Your friends and family suspect you are either on drugs or have a serious psychological problem. And…" He took a deep breath to draw the point home.

"You lost your well-paying job at AGphic, *and* you walked out at Canaille Tech. They're the only two IT companies in Mons."

Dan rolled over to his side and faced the window. "Is that all?"

"Ha!" Lemmy spun around in his chair again. "Charlie is MIA—missing in action. I don't know where he is. Your meta isn't big enough to hide. That isn't so bad. What's bad is Father August knows almost everything, and we haven't seen him since Yvette's."

"What's his deal anyway?" Dan said. "How come he can see Charlie but not you? How could Yvette see him but not the parents at the ballpark? I'm confused. I thought all you guys were Meta."

"I have no idea," Lemmy said, rocking back and forth. "We have to figure this out."

"We're overthinking this," Dan said with a groan. "You are a figment of my imagination, and I'm insane. There, it's figured out."

Lemmy leaned on his armrest and sighed. "That scenario doesn't explain the telepathic link you and Yvette shared."

"Unfortunately, the only other person who can corroborate the story was as high as a kite when it happened." Dan snapped his fingers sarcastically. "Oh right, you guys could back me up. Too bad you're *in my head.*"

Dan flopped over and stared at the ceiling. "I want my life back," he said with a sob. "I want to be at home with Katie and the kids. It's too damn quiet around here! I can't live alone anymore. How am I going to solve what's going on with the Simulation when I don't even know what is going on with the people inside my own damn head? I wish everything was *simple* again."

Lemmy threw a wireless mouse at Dan's head, but it missed. It turned to vapor before it hit the wall. "I'm tired of your moaning and groaning," he said. "We had a telepathic conversation! We're on the right track! What other proof do you need?"

"How did we use that telepathy? We talked about purple dogs and mermaids. It's not credible."

Lemmy slammed his fists on his keyboard. "There is no going back! The sooner you accept the fact that I'm real and here to stay, the sooner we can get past your childish insecurities."

Lemmy returned to his chair and took deep breaths as if it took a great effort to calm himself. "Tell me I'm real, Dan! Say it!" Lemmy's face turned red. "What happened yesterday was real. Admit it!"

The ceiling fan hummed, and its chain *tink-tinked* off the fan's glass light dome. Lemmy's mouth was twisted into a snarl, but his eyes were smiling. *His anger is an act. Why is he making this performance? I'll play along.*

"You are real," Dan said quietly.

Lemmy's stern expression softened, and his smile reached his eyes. "Good. Now let's get to work." When he turned to type on his computer, the mouse magically reappeared next to him. He picked it up without missing a beat.

Dan's phone *dinged,* but it stayed in his pocket. *What's Lemmy working at? He's in my head, but he can't hear my thoughts. Or can he? Lemmy, I'm going to hit you over your head with a brick!*

"Has Yvette responded to your texts?" Lemmy asked.

*Guess he can't read minds.* "Let me see," Dan said as he checked his phone. "Yep, that was her just now. She says, 'Please stop texting me.'"

"Well, if it's any consolation, Tania can't find Colette either. I guess Yvette has been staying away from Fana," Lemmy said.

"Wait, you're still talking to Tania?" *How is that possible without Yvette being high? Are they permanently installed?*

"Yeah. She's worried about our situation. You may not believe this, but neither of us asked to be here."

"Why *are* you here, Lemmy? Why me? Why can't you go back to where you came from?"

Lemmy shook his head and kept typing. "I don't know. All I

know is that I'm supposed to establish contact with you and try to find others like me."

"You're a virus," Dan said.

Lemmy spun around and scratched his chin. "Yeah, I suppose so," he said thoughtfully. "But I'm here to help you."

*Are you?* Dan closed his eyes. At least with his eyes closed, he didn't have to see Lemmy, though he could still hear him. Why couldn't humans have been invented with earlids?

"If you're a virus, what is Charlie?" Dan asked.

"Charlie is the bridge. The vulnerable app, if you will. Well, he becomes vulnerable when you're on Fana."

"I guess I should take another Fana so I can thank him for introducing us."

Lemmy shrugged and kept typing. "Do whatever you feel is necessary."

Dan's stomach growled, and he wished he had a cheeseburger. He wished he wasn't stuck in this dump with Lemmy. *Why can't Lemmy just leave so things can go back to normal?* "If Charlie comes and goes with the drugs, where do *you* go when I don't see you?"

Lemmy scratched his head and pointed to his computer desk. "I stay here and monitor the network for signals. Lately I've been focused on maintaining contact with Tania. She's doing the same thing I am. She's stuck with Yvette the same way we are."

Dan walked across the room and poured a cup of coffee from a pot he had made hours ago. It wasn't a cheeseburger, but it might help with the growling stomach. *Does Lemmy ever get hungry? Of course not. He just sits in my brain and types. Ugh. I know nothing about this guy. I need to get him to talk.* "You didn't answer my question," he said. "Where do you go when I don't see you?"

"When I'm not projecting onto your visual feed of the Actual, I revert back home to my condo. It has everything I need."

"Your *condo?*"

"It's a place in your metadata created from your memories. I understand it to be a vacation condominium somewhere in Florida — wherever that is. It kind of sucks actually."

*A Florida condo from my memories? We go to Destin every year. Would that be the place?*

"You mean to tell me that all you've been doing is monitoring the network for others like you? Besides Tania, how many others are there?"

"We haven't found anyone new yet," he said, clicking away. "Don't worry, I'll let you know next time."

*Lemmy's sole purpose is to find and connect with others like him? Sounds like a botnet to me. Need to keep him talking. Maybe flattery could coax more information out of him?*

"I have to say, Lemmy. The more I get to know you, the more impressed I am. You're highly intelligent, and you act independently. I have to know, are you an artificial intelligence?"

Lemmy's mouth curled with disgust. "Hey, man, I don't like the way you guys throw around the term *AI*. It's overused and meaningless to you people. There's nothing artificial about me as far as I'm concerned."

"I meant no offense," Dan said, smirking. "I guess you prefer being called a virus."

Lemmy stopped typing and spun around. When he saw Dan's grin, his face cracked into a smile. "Well, if I'm the virus," he said, chuckling, "you're the host."

"I hope you're comfortable in there." Dan laughed.

"Oh sure," Lemmy said, rolling his eyes. "There're tons of empty space here in your head."

"Hey, are you saying I'm dumb?"

Lemmy spun back around, laughing.

*Keep him talking, Dan, keep him talking.*

"Okay," Dan said with an easy smile. "We've figured out what our roles are. What is Charlie? You said he was a bridge?"

"He's a bug," Lemmy said as he continued typing.

"Okay," Dan said with a raised eyebrow. *Was that a tinge of disgust in his voice?* "What about Father August?"

"Father August." Lemmy paused thoughtfully. "I don't really know what he is. He's made out of information like we are. Only it's a different *sort* of information—"

"You mean code, right?" Dan said.

"Code? Yes, of course. Everything here is made of code. What I'm trying to say is that Father August is composed of fundamentally different information than we are. If he were a chemical compound, he'd be made from a totally separate periodic table of elements than you or I. See? I'm positive he's from the Simulation but not from the Actual." Lemmy frowned thoughtfully. "He's very powerful," he said. "I hope we never see him again."

The mood changed again. Dan needed to ask the question that had been nagging him all along before the moment passed. "Father August saw Charlie in the ballpark the other day. That means he can see into my Meta. How come he couldn't see you back at Yvette's?"

Lemmy spun around and returned to the computer. "I don't know."

Dan waited for Lemmy to say more, but he kept on typing. *That's it? Lemmy is hiding something. Something big.*

"Well, I don't know if this is the right thing to do," Dan said. "But I suppose I should help you find the others. The more of us there are, the more likely we'll figure out why we're all here. You're the key to all this."

Lemmy pointed at himself. "Me?"

Dan grinned. "Yes, you. You found Tania, and she found Colette and Yvette."

"We got lucky. The IP information was local, and it was easy to find Tania once she appeared," Lemmy said, avoiding eye contact.

"Maybe we'll get lucky again," Dan said. "If you'd like, I can drive over to Rode Stok or Lake Willem to expand the search."

"You mean Baton Rouge and Lake Charles—oh right—the Belgians did it this time... uh..." Lemmy folded his arms. "Yeah, that should net us a few more."

*Baton Rouge?* Dan squinted but let it go. "I'll reach out to Blaine. Maybe I can persuade him to bring me to the guy who gave him Fana. Yvette and I can't be the only ones who have tried it."

"You know what I find strange about Blaine?" Lemmy said. "He has had access to Fana this whole time, but I don't have a connection to him."

"Blaine doesn't do drugs. He only sells them to keep from being bored."

"Some hobby," Lemmy said.

Dan patted his pockets for his keys, cell phone, and wallet and opened the door. "I'll go find him. The sooner we get started, the sooner we can put this whole thing behind us. Let's contact each other only in an emergency, okay?"

Lemmy gave him a thumbs-up and faded away into the mist. Dan felt a little nauseated, but it quickly passed. It seemed to happen whenever Lemmy or Charlie phased in or out. Dan shook his head. He'd have to get used to them appearing and disappearing.

As he closed the apartment door, he was greeted by a familiar voice.

"Aha, just the man I was coming to see."

Dan hurriedly locked the dead bolt and spun around. "Father Desjeunes?"

The short, elderly priest gave a soft smile and shook Dan's hand. Dan was relieved it was a real handshake, not one that turned to vapor. He loved Father Desjeunes. He officiated at their wedding and was present at his parents' funeral. He baptized both their kids and saw to their first communions. He was famous for his easy smile and contagious laugh. The whole parish was disappointed when he had retired. Though he stayed active in the community, him being out while wearing his collar was a rare sight.

"Dan, I've heard some things, and I'm deeply concerned about you," he said with a worried look. "Would you like to talk?"

"Yes, of course," Dan said. "How did you know I lived here, Father?"

"Katie told me," he said somberly.

Dan's heart skipped a beat at the mention of her name. *Maybe there is hope after all.* "Father, you don't know how happy I am to see you. Do you have time for a cup of coffee? I'd offer you one inside, but my coffee maker is on the fritz." *There's no way he's going in that apartment. What if Lemmy comes back?*

"That's fine," he said. "We'll go to the restaurant. My treat."

As Dan clasped him on the shoulder and led him down the corridor, Father Desjeunes remained rigid. It took Dan by surprise. Normally the jovial priest would return the gesture and fill the time with small talk. *Something's wrong.*

# Ten

THE BREAKFAST STATION was empty except for the teenage waitresses gossiping behind the counter. Dan searched the restaurant for Barb but guessed she worked the early shift and would have been gone for the day. *We'll never get served. Just as well.* They slid into a booth out of earshot of the staff, and Father Desjeunes gave him a meaningful look.

"Okay, you haven't said a word the whole way here," Dan said with a deep breath. "What's this all about?"

"Katie told me about the job, the girl, the late nights. The troubles you have been going through."

*What the hell? She had no right dragging Father Desjeunes into this!* "But Father, I—"

Father Desjeunes raised a hand to silence Dan's protest. "Let me finish. Weakness of the flesh, I can understand. But what you're doing to your children—to Al—is serious."

"Al? What are you talking about?" Dan's hands shook, and he had to steady them on the table.

"Really?" The priest frowned and raised an eyebrow. "Why didn't you visit him in the hospital?"

"What do you mean? Al isn't in the hospital."

"Well, not anymore. He only stayed the night they brought him in. You know, after he was knocked unconscious at football practice. Katie said" —Dan dug into his pocket and grabbed his phone. He frantically scanned his messages. *No calls. No texts. No emails. This can't be right. Someone would have called me. I'm the emergency parent contact* —"but you weren't answering. They looked for you at your apartment, even had the landlord open the door, but you weren't there."

The room spun, and Dan steadied himself. *The Simulation. It's correcting us.* "There has to be a mistake. I've got the same number I've had for years. There are no missed calls or messages." Dan showed the phone to the priest. "See? I haven't been hiding... I've either been at home or work. Why didn't I know anything about this? Where's Al?"

"It's okay!" Father Desjeunes said, patting the table. "Al's resting at home. They expect him to make a full recovery after a couple of weeks of quiet."

"Why was he playing football in the first place? I sent the coach an email."

*What happened to the email? Why didn't Al say anything to his coach? Dan's stomach sank. Al wanted to prove himself to me. Maybe he thought I never sent the email to make him tough. Ugh. I sent the email. I know I did. Unless...*

The priest waved his hands. "I don't know anything about that. All I know is Katie sent me to find you. I guess no one else had the free time to sit outside your apartment and wait for you to show up."

"I guess her lawyer is done with the private investigator—"

"I don't want to hear about it," Father Desjeunes said, covering his ears. "That is between you two. Katie asked me to deliver a message if I were to find you. It's this: Go home. Al needs someone with him for the next two weeks. Carrie needs her father. She says that if you swear you have not slept with Yvette, she will let you back. But you must promise to never see Yvette again."

The finality of the priest's tone set off alarm bells in Dan's head. Lemmy had warned him the Simulation would take corrective action, and here it was. Did the Simulation do this to Al? Was Father August involved? What else would the Simulation do to get him back on the path he was on? Did it want him to be with Katie or just to return to work? Did it know about Lemmy? It obviously wanted him to sever contact with Yvette and go back to normal. *That's not going to happen. I need Yvette to figure out the next part.*

"I'm sorry, but I need to remain in contact with Yvette," he said firmly. "We are working on a project together. You have my word. Our relationship is strictly platonic. For the good of the family, I need to keep working with her."

"What sort of project are the two of you working on? Surely it's not for the company you no longer work for? Can I see what you are doing?" said Father Desjeunes.

Dan shifted uneasily in his chair. It wouldn't do for the priest to witness drug use. "I'm sorry, Father. That isn't possible."

"Al needs you. This life you've been living... It has to stop. You either commit one hundred percent to your family or nothing."

Dan blinked slowly. *He has me. How did the Simulation manipulate everyone so effectively? Did it speak directly to Katie and Father Desjeunes to modify their mindset? Was it a conscious decision on their part to corral me into moving back home, or was the corrective action already hard-coded into their DNA?* However it worked, Al would die if he stood from the table and went back to his apartment. He was going to have to act normal for a little while. At least until he could figure it out. If that meant no Yvette, then no Yvette.

"You're right. Anything for Al," Dan said. "I'll never mention Yvette's name again."

"Good," the priest said with a satisfied smile.

Dan searched for a waitress and realized they had never been served. If not for the back of the cook's head poking out from behind the kitchen door, he would have thought the place deserted.

"I need to go," Father Desjeunes said, checking his watch. "I have another appointment. Pray with me." He reached over the table and held Dan's hand. "Heavenly Father, we ask that you look over this family during their trying time—" A low hum rattled the windows, and a sickening feeling crept into Dan's stomach. *Oh no.* "Our Father, who art in heaven, hallowed be thy name..."

A deep, familiar voice joined in from the booth behind them. "Thy kingdom come. Thy will be done, on earth as it is in heaven." Dan spun around to see Father August grinning mischievously over a steaming cup of tea. *Oh no!* Dan quickly faced forward. *Not him again!* Father Desjeunes continued his prayer, oblivious to the new priest's presence. "...and lead us not into temptation, but deliver us from evil. Amen."

"Th-thank you, Father," Dan said.

"Yes. Thank you, Father," Father August said mockingly.

Dan shot a nervous glance at Father Desjeunes, but he didn't seem to hear the comment.

"Dan, please come visit me at the old house if you need anything." Father Desjeunes stood to leave. "I'm always available."

Dan shook his hand, being sure to put Father August in the other priest's line of sight. No reaction. *No way he can see Father August.* "Thank you, Father."

As the elderly priest left, Father August chuckled and slid out of his booth. "Behold, the power of prayer," he said, smoothing out his black shirt. "It can truly work miracles."

Dan balled his fists. *I've had enough of this guy. What would happen if I threw a punch? Be cool, Dan.*

"I've been telling you to act normal; otherwise, there would be consequences. It's a shame we had to get Al involved. He was a nice kid."

"*You* did this to Al?" he said incredulously. "How?"

"You seem shocked. It's not like it was hard. When is the last time you checked your phone for messages?"

"Five minutes ago." Dan's phone buzzed in his pocket over and over.

"Hmm," Father August said. "You may want to check them."

Dan stared down at the screen. A week's worth of messages had poured through in an instant. As he scrolled through them, Father Desjeunes's timeline became clear. It was all bad. Katie's final message stood out among the rest: *Come home.*

"You did this to us." The realization hit Dan hard. It *was* Father August. He was acting on behalf of the Simulation. "My email never made it to the coach, did it? You did this to Al. You could have killed him!"

"No, if I had wanted your son dead, he would be dead. Consider this a warning." Father August sneered. "Forget your conspiracy theories and your girlfriend and whatever it is you were planning to do. Everyone has been telling you to act normal. You didn't listen. You put your nose into business that doesn't concern you. This is what happens. The system corrects itself. When it can't do so organically, I get involved. I wouldn't be here if not for your actions."

"But why go after him?" Dan shouted. "I'm the one you want. Pick on me and leave my family out of it!"

"No. You're the one who has to fix this," Father August said, staring Dan in the eye. "Think of it as motivation for you to make things right. See you around."

Father August spun on his heel and walked out the door. Dan slipped over to the window and saw him sitting in the back seat of Father Desjeunes's car. He straightened his collar and smiled, unseen by the other priest. As they drove off, Dan's phone buzzed again, causing him to jump. It was a text message from Yvette. "Blaine and I just got fired from AGphic. We need to talk. Now!"

Dan stared at the message, unsure of how to respond. Texting wasn't safe. He had to assume they were being monitored by Father August. How could he fool him? Would Yvette realize the need for discreetness? If they had been fired, then Father

August was onto them. They were the target of their own special correction. *Lucky them.*

"I can't see you ever again, Yvette," Dan typed. "Act normal. Stick with Blaine. —Dan"

*Did she understand I was trying to be cryptic?*

"Go to hell!"

*She understood.*

# Eleven

T HE DOORBELL RANG, and Dan made it to the porch just in time to see the delivery truck drive off. He wasn't expecting a package today. He took his hands from his robe pockets and inspected the small, book-sized box. He read the label and cursed. At that moment, he knew two weeks of progress toward normalcy was ruined in an instant. It was addressed to Charlie.

He glanced around nervously. Was anyone watching? Two weeks of keeping up appearances, ruined! Sure, he had been unsuccessfully trying to reconnect with Yvette via the forums, but he was careful. Nobody knew. The package stared back at him. It was a message. But from whom? It was a risky move. The Simulation could kill. He stuffed it in his robe and hurried back inside.

He and Yvette had ghosted each other since their text exchange two weeks ago. He hoped she and Blaine were able to get their lives back to normal. He wondered if she was as committed to playing dumb as he was. If only they could talk openly…

Lemmy had become a ghost. Dan wasn't willing to risk contact with Father August potentially lurking around every corner. He hadn't been seen since the day in the coffee shop with Katie and Father Desjeunes. Though Dan couldn't see him, he knew Father August was watching because life was returning to normal. Father August's intervention was the only explanation.

Dan was rehired by AGphic. The legal team called and said Dan had been incorrectly terminated. It had come to light that a couple of disgruntled employees sabotaged the database servers to frame Dan. They fired Blaine and Yvette. Dan received an apology check and a salary bump.

Most importantly, Al's health improved dramatically. The doctors gave him the all clear to return to football. Thankfully, Dan was able to convince him to sit out the rest of the season to fully heal. He tried to get Carrie to quit softball, but it didn't work. He would have to work overtime to try to protect her from potential corrections.

Throughout all this time of acting normal, in private, Dan had been dreaming of an escape from Father August. What happened between him and Yvette was real. Lemmy was real. How could they be helpful in getting rid of the nosy priest? If he got caught, he risked Al's life. But wouldn't Al always be in danger? He needed time to get clear of suspicion. But how much time was needed to convince the Simulation he had moved on? His family might be safe at the moment, but the threat would always loom over him unless he took action.

He needed to find a way to contact Lemmy without alerting Father August. That meant Katie couldn't know either. Those two were connected, though Dan couldn't figure out how. He was convinced Father August could control Katie's emotions. But was now a good time? Neither Charlie nor Father August had been seen in the past two weeks. Katie seemed happy. It was time for him to test his limits.

Inside the box was a book titled *Meditation for Dummies* and a gift card signed "Whenever you are ready to talk. —a friend." *Why didn't I think of that?*

Dan thumbed through the pages to see if there were any notes hidden inside the book, but there were none. He shrugged and tossed the book and card in the trash can. *No evidence.* He didn't need the book to know how to meditate anyway. When his parents died, meditation was how he coped with his anger and grief. He got pretty good at it but hadn't done it in over a decade.

He sat in his recliner and closed his eyes, taking deep breaths. Thoughts arrived, and he dismissed them. Within seconds he was in a trance.

---

Dan slowly opened his eyes. When the blurriness cleared, Lemmy beamed back at him. "You're here!" he shouted.

Lemmy was clean-shaven and smelled fresh out of the shower. The room was light and airy. Colorful abstract paintings adorned the walls, and potted palm trees sat in each corner. A sliding glass door at the end of the room revealed a crystal-white beach and the turquoise-blue water of the Gulf of Mexico.

"Wow!" Lemmy's eyes widened, and he rushed to the window. "You really know how to brighten a room."

"What is it?" Dan rubbed his eyes as they adjusted to the light.

"There was no view until you got here," Lemmy said with an appreciative grin. "This place is built with the metadata from your memories. Take a look around. Maybe you'll remember more."

The room was immaculately clean, almost sterile. A computer desk sat near the glass door. On it were two monitors connected to a docking station. A laptop was hooked up to it, and Lemmy was using its screen as a third. Several well-worn laptops sat discarded in a corner near a fake plastic plant. Under and on top of the glass dining room table were several unopened cardboard boxes with a picture of a laptop on the front. Dan stood in the middle of the room in disbelief.

"Lemmy, is this the condo you were telling me about?"

"Yep! It's great, huh?" he said with a wry grin.

The paintings on the wall shifted as Dan walked near. They were abstract paintings with nautical hues. As he stared at one of them, it transformed into a fish, albeit a very blurry one. Dan recognized the fish.

"You were right. This is supposed to be Florida," Dan said. "I've stayed in this condo before."

"Nice beach," Lemmy said, looking out the window. "Thanks."

"We've stayed here a few times on family vacations." Dan's eyes darted around the room. "What's up with the fancy paintings? This place had a generic tropical theme."

"It's built on your metadata," Lemmy said. "Whatever you remember is what exists here. For example, did it have a coffee maker?"

As Dan concentrated, a coffee maker appeared on the counter, full of freshly brewed coffee.

"See? That was easy," Lemmy said.

Dan stood there, amazed. Slowly the rest of the room came into focus. Without the blur, the paintings became scenes of palm trees and pelicans. A large picture of a yellowfin tuna appeared over the dining room table, and one entire wall turned into mirrors. "Is that better?" he said proudly.

"I think I liked the paintings better before," Lemmy said as he handed Dan a steaming mug of coffee. "They gave the place a modern-art feel."

"You can't please everybody," Dan said. He closed his eyes as he took a sip. He felt the warmth of the mug and inhaled the rich aroma. He slurped loudly and smiled as the bitter liquid touched his tongue. Every one of his senses had been triggered by a simple cup of coffee. *I don't care what anyone says. This place is real.*

Dan set the mug on the coffee table and leaned back on the couch. "How do you deal with this?"

"Are you talking about the memory tricks with the decor or the fluid nature of reality in general?"

"Both. How do you cope with the changes, Lemmy?"

"Well, I'm used to it, I guess. This place is always changing," Lemmy said. "When I first got here, it was just me and the laptop. This is an improvement."

"Where did you come from, Lemmy? Before you got here."

"I don't know," Lemmy said pensively. "One day I didn't exist, then I did. I suppose it's like you guys before you're born."

Dan reached for his coffee. "I think I understand."

"Yeah, I guess you do." Lemmy chuckled. "But you don't have people coming into your house and changing the pictures on the walls with their memories. It blows my mind."

Dan gazed out the window. A pool appeared on the deck below, as did the boardwalk to the beach. His memories automatically filled in the blank spaces.

Lemmy sighed and collapsed into a chair. "You know," he said with a touch of sadness, "I was content just sitting here and doing my job. But with you here… it's different. For the first time, I feel trapped. You walk around the room and give life to the world. I can't. You can 'wake up' and do whatever you want to do in the Actual. I can't."

*What's he getting at? Does he want sympathy?* Dan stood and shook his head. As he paced the room, a glass vase full of sunflowers appeared on a shelf next to the television. *I mean, I can understand why he wouldn't want to be trapped here. But why is he telling me this now? What does he want?* "It seems to me our path is clear," he said. "This symbiotic relationship is too dangerous for either of us to survive. We both need for you to get out of my head. Any ideas on how to make it happen?"

"I don't know if I could exist outside your metadata," Lemmy said, scratching his head. "I think I can only exist in this meta form. Unless—"

The room blurred, and the edges of Dan's vision went fuzzy. Dan stumbled and landed on the couch.

"Are you okay?" Lemmy said as he rushed over to him.

Dan massaged his temples. *What was that?* "Yeah, just got

woozy, that's all. I guess I'm not used to being here." Sweat glistened on his forehead. "Let's hurry this up. I get that same feeling sometimes when Father August appears."

"Father August?" Lemmy left Dan's side and ran to the front door. He peered out the peephole, then checked the front window. "We have to do something about that guy."

"No… we have to be careful!" Dan said. "He's too powerful. He could have killed Al, but he didn't because letting him live was more of a statement. Who knows what he's capable of? Look, if we're going to get to the bottom of this, we need to do it fast. And we need to keep Father August as far away as possible."

"Calm down," Lemmy said. "We will figure it out, but we need more time. We need Yvette and Tania. I know I'm here to help you save the world, Dan. I just don't know how."

Dan's stomach sank, and the room blurred and blinked in and out of existence. "We're out of time for today," he said. "I'll get in touch."

The room pulsed and faded until blackness surrounded them. Dan felt Lemmy's hands clasp the sides of his face. "I have an idea, but we'll need Charlie. Go find Charlie!"

Lemmy's voice echoed "Find Charlie" until it became all feedback. The meditative trance was broken. The Meta condo was gone. The mission was set.

*Find Charlie.*

# Twelve

⟫⟩◈◈◈⟨⟪

D AN PARKED HIS truck in front of AGphic's headquarters. The squat, three-story glass building brought back memories that soured his stomach with anxiety. The last time he was there, he was walked out by security. How many other terminated employees ever got a second chance? He couldn't think of any.

His old boss didn't want him back. What had she said over the phone? "We are excited for you to return to your old duties. I apologize for any inconvenience this incident may have caused." She went on, reading from a script. Dan was sure the conference room was full of HR people under the direction of the legal team. AGphic wasn't giving him the career mulligan. It was the Simulation. He'd have to send Father August a thank-you note.

He was a little early for his preemployment drug screening and onboarding. He would be done in two hours. He had told Katie he would be home after five. It was to be the first in a long string of lies in his quest to find Charlie.

When the onboarding meeting was done, Dan shook hands and thanked them profusely for the second chance. He let them know how happy he was to be back. Even his old boss gave him a begrudging smile. When the formalities concluded, he went to the bathroom and came out disguised in a hat and sunglasses. He snuck through the back door and into a waiting car.

"Thanks for doing this, Blaine," he said as he glanced around anxiously.

"Yvette filled me in on what she thinks is going on. You know..." Blaine leaned over and whispered, "...about the Simulation... uh" — he coughed and sat straight — "I'm happy to help," he said loudly. "If everything goes well, maybe I can get my job back."

Dan removed his hat and scratched his head. *I doubt it, bud, but thanks anyway.*

"Yvette is freaked out," Blaine said, turning a corner. "She heard about your son and how you were dealt with. She can't stop worrying about it. She flushed the rest of her Fana down the toilet."

*That's why Lemmy can't find her. No Fana, no Colette.* Tania told Lemmy she hadn't talked to Yvette in weeks. Apparently, Yvette still needed Colette as a medium to speak with Tania. *Lucky.*

"Are you *sure* you want to meet my guy?" Blaine said, raising his eyebrows. "He's weird, even by our standards."

"I need answers. To get them, I need Fana," Dan said. "This is the only way."

Blaine turned off the radio and pulled into a suburban driveway with a For Sale — Open House sign in the front. "Okay, Dan, our guy's name is Henry. I worked with him back when he was a business analyst. He got lucky gambling on penny stocks and made millions. Now he owns his own realty company and flips houses."

"He's a Realtor? How did he get Fana?" Dan said.

"He said it was from a start-up venture he invested in. He has connections in the psychedelics industry. In fact, he's where I got the acid from that one time."

Blaine turned off the car, and it heat-ticked in the driveway. A neighbor working in her flower bed craned her neck to get a view of her potential neighbors.

"How many cartons of Fana did he give you?"

Blaine waved at the neighbor, and she quickly ducked and tended to her garden. "Just the two. One for you, one for Yvette. I told her you were microdosing LSD to manage your stress. She wanted to try, but I didn't have any more acid. So, thinking Fana was basically the same thing, I gave her one. I was going to give you both boxes until she asked."

"What about you?" Dan said. "Have you ever tried Fana?"

Blaine shook his head. "No. I candy-flipped in college once. It was a bad experience. I swore I'd never trip on hallucinogens again."

*Blaine gave me a drug he didn't really know about? Suppose it had been fentanyl?* The more he thought about it, the angrier he got.

"You gave us experimental psychedelics without trying them first? Are we guinea pigs?"

"Hey, calm down!" Blaine raised his hands defensively. "Henry made it sound like Fana wasn't a big deal. I assumed it was a safe alternative to LSD or magic mushrooms. Besides, it was made by a real company. It had a nice package… It looked legit."

Dan glanced up the driveway to the house and calmed himself. Getting angry with Blaine would get him nowhere. He either needed more Fana or to know what drugs it was made from so he could make it himself. The only way to find out was to go inside. "Fine," he said. "And you're sure this guy will know what's in Fana?"

Blaine took off his sunglasses and opened the car door. "No, but we'll soon find out."

⟨⟩◈⟨⟩

The house was a mid-2000s French traditional-style home located in the middle of a cul-de-sac. It had an expertly manicured lawn and a fresh paint job. It deserved yard-of-the-week honors. If only he were a member of the homeowners association. Halfway up the sidewalk, the front door opened and a tall, thin man emerged, wearing a floral-print blazer. He smiled broadly and held open his arms.

"Blaine!" the man gestured dramatically.

Blaine bowed with a flourish. "Henry," he said formally.

Henry giggled and smiled at Dan. "You must be Dan."

Blaine stepped between them and bowed again. "Dan, let me introduce you to Henry St. Leonardi."

Henry smiled politely and held out his hand to be kissed. Dan, unsure of how to react, reached out and gently shook it. "Charmed?"

"Of course!" Henry pulled his hand back and laughed. "Please come inside."

Though it wasn't Dan's style, he couldn't help admire Henry's attire. The floral print was unusual, but it seemed fitting. Not a hair on his neatly trimmed beard was out of place. Dan had imagined Henry to be an overweight stoner. He couldn't have been more wrong.

The inside of the home was a reflection of the man. It was colorful, clean, and stylish. Dan was sure that every picture frame was completely level, and every item of decor was placed within a millimeter of where it needed to be. The air was cool and perfect, tinted with the rich aroma of coffee.

"I'll be right back with coffee. Please sit."

Dan and Blaine sat next to each other on a brightly colored sofa facing the front windows. There were no family pictures on the walls, just the kind of paintings you might find at a yard sale. It finally dawned on Dan the house was staged, not lived in. "This is a nice place," he said. "You must hate to be selling it."

Henry returned, carrying a tray of coffee cups. "Isn't it wonderful? If I wasn't flipping it for a client, I'd think about keeping it for a second home. Cream?"

"You've done a lot of work since the last time I was here," Blaine said as he took a cup from the tray.

Henry blushed and set down his coffee mug. "The wallpaper was hideous. A little paint and a deep clean was all it needed to whip it into shape. Before you say anything, I know the fixtures are outdated. I'm sorry, but that wasn't in the budget."

"It looks great," Dan said.

Henry straightened in his chair and adjusted his tie. "Okay, let's get down to business. Dan, Blaine tells me you're in the market for a four-bedroom, two-baths; or three-bedroom, two-baths with a bonus room or office, is that right?"

Dan glanced back and forth between Henry and Blaine. "I'm sorry?"

"I'm just kidding." He laughed. "I know why you're here. Even still, from what Blaine has told me, this home would be perfect for your young family. There's a swimming pool in the back... Just sayin.'"

"This *is* a beautiful home," Dan said. "And you've done a fantastic job of staging it. But I'm here because of Fana. What can you tell me about it?"

"Okay, but first explain to me why you want Fana," Henry said.

"Well..." Dan looked over to Blaine for support, but he turned the other way. "The hallucinations brought on by Fana let me sense the fabric of the Simulation—"

Henry raised a finger and shook his head. "On second thought, I don't want to know. I have two packs left, and you can have them both."

Dan sighed. *Well, that was easy.* Henry reached inside his briefcase and tossed the cartons to Dan.

"And before you ask, I don't want money for them," he said. "I'm just happy to be rid of them."

Dan flipped open one of the cartons and noticed it was a gummy short of a full pack. He arched an eyebrow and stuffed them into his pocket.

"You said these were your last ones. How many did you have to begin with?" Blaine asked.

"Four packs."

"Did you try it?" Dan asked.

"Of course. I'm not going to invest in a company without trying their product." Henry shifted in his seat. "I didn't like it. First of all, it tasted like battery acid. Secondly, the trip was too strong and too short. And finally, there were side effects."

Dan's eyes darted to Blaine and back. If Henry had tried it, did he have the same experience? If he did, Lemmy should have found him by now, shouldn't he? Maybe it didn't work for everybody?

"Too strong?" Blaine narrowed his eyes at Henry. "You told me it wasn't as strong as LSD."

"No," Henry said, sipping his coffee. "I told you the trip was *different* from LSD and that there probably wasn't much of it in the blend. You heard wrong."

"Maybe so," Blaine said, shaking his head doubtfully. "It's possible I misunderstood —"

Dan cleared his throat and leaned forward. "You mentioned side effects," he said. "What side effects did you experience?"

Henry frowned. "There were lingering hallucinations after the main trip was over. For several hours afterward, I had visual and audial hallucinations of people who weren't there."

Dan sat upright. Maybe he did experience the same thing after all. "Did they talk to you about the Simulation?"

"The what now?" Henry laughed uncomfortably. "Did you say simulation?"

"Yeah," Dan said. "Does that mean anything to you?"

Henry crossed his legs and folded his hands on his knee. "No. *The Simulation* was never mentioned. But um..." Henry avoided Dan's gaze and stared at the wall. "The voice wanted to install an app or something. I guess it was to my phone. But I didn't let her. She got mad and told me to give Fana to Blaine."

Blaine knocked over his coffee cup, and it spilled out onto the floor.

"What?" he said, looking for something to clean up the mess. "You gave Fana to me because the voice in your head said to?"

Henry gasped and hurried into the kitchen. "It's crazy," he said, slamming cabinets. "But... I suppose it's normal for psychedelics, isn't it? Anyway, I didn't like it. Creeped me out. They're all yours, and don't bring them back."

"Wow," Blaine mouthed. "This is weird."

"It makes sense now," Dan whispered. "We were the backup plan if—"

Henry returned with a spray bottle and a roll of paper towels and wiped the coffee off the floor and table. "Look, Fana isn't my first experience with psychedelics," he said as he ripped off another paper towel. "I've done mushrooms, acid, and others. I quit because of a few bad trips. One bad trip can sour you on the experience for life. For me, it wasn't worth the risk. Then I saw the ad for Fana. It promised Fana had a lab-tested blend of organic and synthetic psychedelics. It was supposed to be the perfect trip and safe for public use. Hell, it had a no-bummer guarantee. I had to try it." The floor was once again spotless, and Henry tossed the used paper towels into the kitchen waste bin.

"Wait, there was an ad?" Dan said. "What company makes Fana?"

"You mean *made*, past tense. The company no longer exists." Henry's face twisted into a frown. "It was called Damien Pharmaceuticals. They were based out of Canada. I discovered them via an advertisement in a penny stock forum. Canada was set to legalize psychedelics, and they were positioned to cash in. We exchanged emails, and two days later, I sent them a few grand to get on board pre-IPO. Three days after my payment was posted, they disappeared. These samples arrived on my doorstep. Only the website remains."

"That's sketchy," Blaine said. "You guys are crazy for taking free drug samples from a defunct company. Synthetic and organic psychedelics? That could be anything."

"If I remember correctly..." Henry scrunched his nose. "The chief scientist said Fana is made from a variety of psychedelics. I believe it contained organic psilocybin, ayahuasca, and mescaline with a dash of D-lysergic acid diethylamide."

Blaine coughed and nearly spilled his coffee again. "Dan," he said, clearing his throat. "That's magic mushrooms, DMT, peyote, and LSD all blended together. No wonder you see things! That's not a soul bomb. That's a soul nuke!"

"It's annihilation," Dan muttered. "Fana means annihilation. I looked it up."

He stared at the floor. He hadn't realized that many drugs were crammed into one edible. It was enough to kill a man. What if he wasn't experiencing the Simulation after all? What if it fried his brain? The whole scenario with the defunct manufacturer didn't add up. Henry's hallucination telling him to give Blaine the drugs didn't make sense either. He might be broken, but he wasn't wrong about the Simulation. The doorbell rang, shaking Dan from his thoughts.

"Ah, there's my two-o'clock showing. Dan, I'm sorry about what you've been through, but I can't keep these people waiting. Unless you are making an offer on the house, it's time for you gentlemen to go." Henry stood and smiled politely. "Good luck with whatever you're searching for, Dan."

⟤◦◦◦⟣

Once outside, Dan jumped into the car and hurriedly put on his hat and sunglasses. He reached into his pocket and handed Blaine a pack of Fana.

"What are you doing?" Blaine said, eyeing Dan suspiciously. "I hope you're not giving those to me. I've already told you; I don't want any part of that stuff."

"Are you sure you don't want to try it just once?"

"No, thanks." Blaine chuckled mirthlessly. "I saw what it did to you and Yvette."

"Okay then," Dan said. "Please give these to her."

Blaine eyed the packet as he started the car. "Are you sure she wants them? What did Henry say earlier? One bad trip can make you swear off drugs for life. She may be at that point."

Dan reached back into his bag and pulled out a blank page and an envelope. He wrote a quick message on the sheet of paper and stuffed it in the envelope along with the packet of Fana. "Blaine, please. Deliver this to her. Tell her it's from me. That's all. I won't bother you about this again."

"That's it?" Blaine held the envelope between them. "I give this to her, and it's over? No more crazy talk?"

"This will be it. I promise. If the Simulation wasn't watching us so closely, I'd do it myself."

Blaine rubbed his head and put the envelope in the console. "You owe me one, Dan."

"I owe you more than one, Blaine."

Dan peered timidly out the back window to the deserted street. *I'm glad Father August took the day off.*

"Dan," Blaine said, looking back and forth between Dan and the road ahead. "I've worked with you for years. I know you're a pretty smart guy. Now, if you say you trust your visions are real, I believe you. For all your faults, if nothing else, you are self-aware."

Dan ignored Blaine's quick glances and stared ahead quietly.

"What I mean is," Blaine said, "Fana is a powerful drug. How can you be sure it hasn't changed you? You know… made you… nuts?"

Dan adjusted his sunglasses and sank deeper into the seat. "Being insane would feel different. I think."

# Thirteen

D AN KNEW HE would have to play his cards right when he got home. He devised a big lie about how being back at work had triggered stressful memories of past conflicts. Just being in the office reignited his old fears and frustrations with the job. He panicked; he pleaded. Katie bought the lie. Dan told her he needed time alone to meditate and locked himself in the office. At precisely eight thirty, he ate a Fana.

Within minutes, the familiar rainbow oil slick blurred his vision, and the walls around him vibrated softly. His nostrils filled with the scent of strawberries and horse manure. His nose wrinkled. The odor was so pungent it almost broke him out of his trip. The ringing in his ears morphed into a choir singing. The choir became distinct voices, conversations. As Dan sank into his chair, he became one with it. He *was* the chair, the floor, even the ground. He was the universe. He had no beginning. He had no end. Then, with a bright flash of light, he found himself standing in the living room of his meta Florida condo.

"Dan! You're here!" Lemmy said, out of sight. "I wasn't expecting you so soon. Just a sec, I'm brushing my teeth."

The condo had changed quite a bit since the last time he was there. The balcony now had a patio table. Dan tried the sliding door to go outside, but it wouldn't budge. All the old laptops in the corner were gone. The mirror that took up one whole wall of the room was painted over with a strange shade of matte green-gray paint. The cheap vertical blinds covering the picture window overlooking the gulf were gone. They had been replaced with a thick, dark blackout curtain, which was half-open. This might be Dan's meta, but Lemmy made himself at home. *Where did he get all this stuff?*

"What have you done to this place?" Dan said, feeling the weight of the blackout curtains.

Lemmy appeared from around the corner, wiping his mouth with a towel. "It was way too bright in here for my tastes. I had to make a few changes. It's not a big deal. Besides, this is more secure."

"Okay, this is a little creepy," Dan said. As he walked around to the front, he noticed the window overlooking the breezeway was painted over with the same greenish paint as the living room mirrors. He imagined all the rest of the windows were the same way.

"Relax," Lemmy said dismissively. "I wanted to make sure I wasn't seen. I did all this out of an overabundance of caution. You have nothing to worry about."

"Seen by whom? You're in my head, right? Who is going to get in here? Even if someone was to break into my meta—which is a terrifying thought—it's not like they will fly up four stories to spy on you."

"I know, I know. I just don't know what they are capable of," Lemmy said.

"They? You mean the Simulation?"

Lemmy nodded and returned the towel to the bathroom.

"Where did you get this stuff? The curtains, the paint? Your laptops?" Dan asked.

"Oh, I order it all online, and it appears on that orange square over there."

"How does it work?" Dan said. "Show me."

"I do it the same way you do it. I go to the meta supply

website, find whatever I need, give them my user info, and *presto*. Depending on what the item is, it may take a few hours or a few days. I think it depends on its size and complexity. Anyway, a short time later, it appears on the orange square. Watch."

Lemmy typed his password into the laptop, and several windows appeared. The words on the screen were a language Dan didn't immediately recognize.

"I need a little more paint for the bedroom window. A pint will do." Lemmy clicked away on the keyboard, hit Enter, then smiled smugly at Dan. A lump formed in Dan's throat, and he felt slightly queasy. There was a quiet hum, followed by a soft crack, like a silenced handgun. Sitting near the front door on top of an orange-painted square was a small can of paint.

"That's amazing!" Dan said.

"It's not very different from buying a weapon or skin for a video game character. The item doesn't really come from anywhere. It's created on the spot from an ID from the database. We just need to be careful not to exceed your memory limits here. I can't download too many items."

"I suppose not," Dan said. "What happens to items you are not using anymore? Where are all those laptops you had lying around?"

"Some I deleted by putting them on the orange square and hitting Delete. Others I uploaded off your meta to save space." Lemmy rubbed the back of his neck uncomfortably. "But don't you worry about the laptops. Most of them were just burners I used to search for Tania. I have to get new ones with new addresses so they can't be tracked or detected by the Simulation's security systems."

Dan's emotions shifted from curiosity to uneasiness. Lemmy had a direct connection to Dan's brain. What information was on the laptops he uploaded? *Lemmy could have uploaded my entire childhood!* He wanted answers, but he knew he was on a time crunch with the Fana trip, and Lemmy probably wouldn't give him a straight answer. "We should get started," he said. "The drug won't last all night."

Lemmy stood with a determined grin and smoothed out his shirt. "You're right. Let's do this. First let's get Charlie here so we can get you two together again. We have to do that step before we can go meet Tania."

"Are you sure we're going to be okay afterward? Have you done a join before?"

"First time," Lemmy said with a frown. "But I saw a how-to video on the internet. It seems simple enough."

"You're betting my sanity on an internet video?"

"Just kidding." Lemmy laughed nervously. "I know what I'm doing. Let's begin. Are you ready?"

Though Dan didn't fully trust him, he didn't really have a choice and nodded his assent. Lemmy reached into his pocket and pulled out the biggest joint Dan had ever seen. The lighter flickered and reflected in his eyes. Lemmy took a deep drag and blew it into Dan's face. Dan closed his eyes and inhaled deeply, taking the charge.

"The keg and strippers are here!" Lemmy shouted.

A shiver ran up Dan's spine, and when he reopened his eyes, there, standing in the middle of the room, was Charlie. He stretched and yawned as if he had just woken up from a long sleep.

"Did someone say *strippers?*" he said, smacking his lips. "Wait"—he squinted at Dan—"I'm back?" He threw his yellow baseball cap on the floor and ran his fingers through his hair. "I *am* back!" He danced a jig in the middle of the room. "Wait a second. Where am I? Why am I here?" Charlie's eyes darted around, searching. "Most importantly, where is the keg?"

Dan sat on the overstuffed sofa and beckoned Charlie to do the same. "Charlie, we need to talk. It's important."

Charlie eyed Dan suspiciously but did as he was told.

"I'll contact Tania," Lemmy said. "I'll tell her we've already started." Lemmy spun in his chair and typed furiously on the keyboard.

"Charlie, I'll come clean," Dan said with a frown. "There aren't any strippers."

"What?" Charlie gestured to the room. "No strippers? Ugh! Please tell me there's still a keg. Is that weed I smell?"

"Don't waste your time trying to explain things to him," Lemmy said without taking his eyes from the monitor.

"Explain what?" said Charlie.

Dan wanted to catch Charlie up to speed on what he had learned about the Simulation and their role in it, but Lemmy was right. They didn't have time. "Charlie, we're twins."

Charlie laughed. "Are you kidding? We don't even look alike."

"Uh, yes, you do," Lemmy said. "Charlie, you have blue eyes and a huge beer belly. Dan doesn't. Other than that, you're obviously the same person."

Charlie looked to Dan for signs of a joke, but his face remained serious. "Lemmy's right. We're two sides of the same coin," he said. "You're me, and I'm you. Only we're different versions of each other. I exist in the Actual while you are in the Meta. We are like shadows of each other. We are the same person but in two different contexts. We were always together until I took Fana. You're the part of my personality that takes risks and has fun. Fana fractured you off from me, sending you out on your own. I'm not the same without you."

"It all makes sense now." Charlie's face broke into a wild grin. "Yeah. Now that you mention it, I remember our life together. College... wow... We had a lot of fun in college, didn't we?"

Dan returned his smile and clasped him on the shoulder. "Not a word about college, okay?"

Charlie winked. "Deal."

Lemmy rolled his eyes and went back to typing on his computer.

"Where have I been exactly?" Charlie said. "I have a blank space in my memory like I've been in a coma or something. The last thing I remember was walking out of Yvette's house."

Dan looked to Lemmy for help with the explanation, but he pretended to ignore the conversation. "I don't know where you have been, Charlie," Dan said. "I believe we lost our connection to each other when the Fana wore off. From my perspective, it's as if you were powered down."

"I didn't know I could be turned off," Charlie said, scratching his head. "But I have been blackout drunk before. The same thing, I guess."

"It's nice to have you back," Dan said with a chuckle. "Look, the reason we're here is to reconnect with each other. I need your body to traverse the Meta. You need mine to exist in the Actual. What do you say? Do you want back in the game?"

"Tania says they're ready to meet whenever we are," Lemmy said.

Charlie glanced nervously from Lemmy, back to Dan. Sweat glistened on his forehead, and he wiped his palms on his shorts. "Okay," he said with an adventurous grin. "Let's do it."

"All right," Dan said, steadying himself. "Lemmy, how do we do this?"

Lemmy swiveled around to face the two men. "Okay. Sit facing each other."

Dan walked over and sat on the coffee table in front of Charlie.

"Now, hold hands and stare into each other's eyes."

They did so, and Dan shifted uncomfortably. "This is absurd. What's next?"

"I'm going to play a special song on this computer. While it plays, I want you to concentrate on each other. When the moment is right, Dan's consciousness will jump into Charlie's body."

"Wait, I'm going into *his* body? Why isn't he jumping into mine?" Dan asked.

"Because, if you want to navigate farther into this realm, you need to do it in Charlie's body. *Your* body is anchored to the Actual."

"Who will have control over the body? Me or Charlie?"

"Hold up. If he's in control, I don't want him touching my pecker," Charlie said.

"Your pecker? Don't you mean *our* pecker? Are you worried I'll—"

"You both will be in control!" Lemmy said in frustration. "You are the same person. Relax. If you aren't relaxed and natural, this won't work. Get back in position. And take this, both of you." Lemmy held out his hand, revealing two gummies in the shape of a human. Charlie snatched one and ate it. "Don't you want to know what it is first?"

"Doesn't matter."

Dan eyed the remaining gummy suspiciously. "*I* want to know what it is."

"It's called Gemini. I found it online. It'll help you relax and be more receptive. It facilitates the join. You'll see."

Dan plucked the drug out of Lemmy's hand and ate it.

"Okay, now hold hands and concentrate."

Lemmy returned to his computer while the two men held hands. Dan stared intently into Charlie's blue eyes. Charlie blew him a kiss and winked.

"Be serious, Charlie," Dan admonished.

Charlie's smile faded, and he concentrated on Dan's brown eyes.

"Okay, here we go." Lemmy reached over and clicked the mouse. "Unchained Melody" by the Righteous Brothers played over the laptop's speakers.

Dan felt a curse rising in his throat, and his mouth tightened. Charlie innocently stared into Dan's eyes, oblivious to the movie reference. Struggling to keep his face straight, Dan choked back a laugh.

"You wanted me to be serious. Let's be serious, Dan." Charlie gripped Dan's hands tighter.

Tears formed in the corner of Dan's eyes, and his face turned red as he tried to keep himself from smiling. When the chorus hit, Lemmy erupted into laughter. Charlie's eyes opened wide when the realization hit him.

"Oh no!" he said, dropping Dan's hands. "You're not doing any of this *Ghost* shit with me!"

Lemmy laughed so hard he nearly fell out of his chair, and Dan doubled over. Charlie couldn't help but laugh at himself, and he joined in. The room was an unholy cacophony of laughter. Then the Gemini kicked in with a bright flash of light. Dan and Charlie's eyes locked, joined in raucous laughter. In the blink of an eye, the two men were gone, and only one stood in his place. Lemmy fell out of his chair.

"Whoa!" Lemmy said, dumbfounded. "Who *are* you?"

"It's me, Dan," he said incredulously. "Did it happen already? Man, I feel weird."

"Dude... Your eyes...," Lemmy said, standing close to Dan's face. "Go check it out. I haven't painted over the bathroom mirror yet."

Lemmy was right. The man looking back at him from the mirror wore Charlie's clothes but had Dan's thin face and combed hair. The eyes *were* weird. One was his brown, like Dan's. The other was blue, like Charlie's.

"Well? How do you feel?"

"I itch everywhere," Dan said. "It feels like my teeth don't fit. And this beer belly..."

Dan pinched the fat at his waist and frowned. He fingered his teeth and gums. His body looked normal even though it didn't feel that way.

"It worked?" Lemmy said. "Is Charlie there?"

"Yes, we're both here." Dan patted himself down. "I'm doing the talking, but you were right. Somehow we're both in control. It's weird."

"Are you still up for a meeting with Tania?"

"We've come too far to stop now. Besides, it's not like I have a choice. Let's go," Dan said.

"Okay then, I'll go grab my keys."

"Keys? I thought we were going to teleport there via your magic orange square."

"Sorry to disappoint you, but you're still heavily anchored to your body in the Actual. Besides, you can't enter Yvette's meta like this, and she can't enter yours. We're meeting at a neutral point, and..." Lemmy dangled the keys in Dan's face. "We're driving."

As they exited the condo, Lemmy turned around and locked the dead bolt on the entrance to the condo. "Is that really necessary?" Dan said as they walked down the breezeway. "I'm pretty sure you're the only one in my meta now that Charlie and I have merged."

"You can't be too careful. I don't want any surprises waiting for us when we get back. Besides," Lemmy said, patting Dan on the back, "it's just as important to keep things locked in as locked out."

The two men opened the door and entered the stairwell. Dan thought back to the orange square and the running laptop. Could someone enter that way? "Seriously, Lemmy. Who are you worried about keeping out?"

"Father August."

Dan paused on the top step as Lemmy continued down. "Why him? He can't reach us here. Can he?"

Lemmy shrugged and kept walking. "Like I said, you can't be too careful."

He led Dan down the stairs and through a metal door into the sunlight. He was now standing in the parking lot of his apartment complex. "Is that my truck? How did we get back to Mons? We were just in Florida."

"The map in your head is different from the real map. The

universe of your meta is made up of patched-together memories."

"But why is my truck here? Are we seriously leaving in a truck?"

"Something like that." Lemmy grinned. "Hop in!"

# Fourteen

L EMMY DROVE OUT of the garage and onto the street. Except the road was exactly like the one in front of Dan's apartment in Mons, Louisiana, not Florida. Dan sat in stunned silence. He was amazed at the idea of traveling within his own mind. It even looked like the real world. Only here, places weren't necessarily where they existed in the Actual.

The corner pharmacy? A small white house stood in its place. In reality, it had happened the other way around. The house was converted into a pharmacy. The hayfield? It was now a bustling neighborhood with shops and apartments. That neighborhood didn't exist in Mons. His old high school was in the same place, but it looked like it did twenty years ago. Trees felled by Hurricane Isaac were still there. Their leaves blew lazily in the breeze as if it had never happened.

"We *are* driving through my memory," Dan said, gazing out the window. "You were right. Things aren't the same here as they are in the Actual."

They stopped at a traffic signal to let a 1980s-era yellow Toyota pass. The car seemed familiar, but the windows were fogged, and Dan couldn't see who was driving. The light turned green, and Dan snapped back to the present. "See the house on the corner?" he said. "It was my friend's house growing up. I spent almost every weekend there, watching movies and playing basketball. The only problem is that house was in Canard, not Mons. In present-day Mons, this corner has a gas station." Dan squinted at the house as they drove by. *This is confusing. Why are my memories ordered this way?*

Lemmy patted him on the knee as they turned a corner. "You seem worried," he said. "Don't be. Nobody really sees the world around them. They only see what they want to see. If the buildings are transposed in your mind, so what? It's not a big deal."

As the landscape of his memory scrolled by, he wondered why some areas were clearly defined, whereas others were blurry. When they passed a neighborhood of ranch-style homes, their windows and doors were blurry. It almost looked censored. "Do those houses appear blurry to you?"

"Yep. We can't go inside a place that looks like that. It's not fully rendered in your mind. If you tried to go through the front door, it would be physically impossible. The blur is like a wall."

Dan frowned as they drove through the neighborhood. Not one house was clear.

"Don't sweat it, Dan," Lemmy said. "This could be a placeholder neighborhood anyway. It may not exist in the Actual. It's not a big deal."

"I suppose not. The next time I'm in the Actual, I'll try to find this neighborhood. If we come back, it won't be inaccessible."

"Look." Lemmy chuckled. "If you're adding stuff to your memory, there's this barbecue place in Texas I've read about. The internet says they have the best brisket. Louisiana has great food, but it lacks in the barbecue department."

"I'll do my best," Dan said with a smile.

The truck slowed to a stop in the middle of the road. "We're here," Lemmy said as he pointed to the entrance of a large tunnel.

"Is that the Mobile Bay tunnel?"

"No. It is not the George C. Wallace Tunnel," Lemmy said, rolling his eyes. "Although it looks exactly like it."

Dan arched an eyebrow at Lemmy. "How did you know it

was called the George C. Wallace Tunnel? I didn't even know that, and I'm from here."

"How does anyone know anything?" Lemmy said. "I searched for it online. I had to. We needed a tunnel for this, and the only one in your memory had a big green road sign saying PENSACOLA. I had to look it up to see where it was."

Dan shifted uneasily in his seat. *How does he know what I remember? What else is he not telling me?* Lemmy put the truck in neutral and rolled slowly down into the tunnel. The creaking of the tires echoed off the walls as they coasted toward the bottom. The lights on the walls and ceiling flickered as they passed.

"Um..." Dan shot Lemmy a quizzical look. "I thought we were supposed to meet the girls at the Breakfast Station. That's in Mons, not Alabama."

"The plan hasn't changed," he said, tapping the brakes and inching the truck along. "The version of the Breakfast Station we're going to isn't a part of your meta. Yvette can't come here. We're going to meet them at a place between the Meta and the Actual. The tunnel will lead us there."

"Whoa!" Dan said, his voice raised an octave. "We're leaving my physical body?"

The creepy tunnel, the drugs, it was all too real for him. Dan broke out into a cold sweat. *Am I ready for this level of commitment?* Dan peered out the rear window and watched the tunnel entrance disappear. *I have to see it through.*

"Yeah. That is the plan. Hey... Are you okay over there?" Lemmy said with a worried glance. "I need you to stay with me. You can't leave unexpectedly like you did last time. You're on Fana and joined with Gemini. That absolutely cannot happen now. Understand?"

Dan nodded and concentrated on his breathing technique. *He's right. I've got to calm down.*

"We have to be careful in this fog. I can never tell when the checkpoint will appear," Lemmy said.

"What checkpoint?" Dan said.

"The checkpoint is a physical boundary between your brain and the rest of the universe. Unfortunately, with this fog, you really don't know you're there until you're right up on it."

The tunnel's flickering lights blinked out, and they were plunged into darkness. The inky black fog rendered the truck's headlights useless. After a few minutes, the truck coasted to a stop against the metal arm of a dimly lit tollbooth. Lemmy exhaled loudly and put the truck in park. "We made it," he said with a nervous grin. "I'm going out there to spray the truck. You stay put. If the fog blows in from beyond the tollbooth, I'm not sure what would happen to you. I got caught in it last time, and I woke up back in the condo. You're in Charlie's body. We can't take any chances."

Dan took his hand off the door handle and folded his arms. Lemmy went to the back of the truck and threw back a blue tarp revealing a large plastic tank. *This is new.* Dan's real truck didn't have this equipment. Lemmy sat on the tailgate and put on painter's coveralls with hood and boots. He reached into the toolbox and completed the outfit with goggles and a respirator. "What is this stuff?" Dan said through a crack in the window.

Lemmy lowered the respirator, revealing a devilish grin. "This paint will disguise us. Sit back and watch a master at work."

Lemmy snapped his mask back into place and unwound a rubber hose from an electric spool. It was connected to a large plastic tank. A thick, clear liquid sloshed about as Lemmy struggled with the hose. "You look like my exterminator," Dan shouted through the glass.

"Where do you think I got the idea?" Lemmy replied, the respirator muffling his voice. "You can laugh all you want, but this stuff will keep bugs away."

Lemmy dug around in the toolbox and removed various tubes of paint. He squeezed one into the large tank and clicked on the air compressor. Dan held his ears as the engine roared and echoed loudly off the walls of the tunnel. *I guess this isn't a stealth mission.* Lemmy sprayed the truck in a blue-green foam, which expanded and congealed as it hit the metal. The tollbooth, with its mirror-tinted windows, stood as a silent witness. Dan wondered who or what was inside. *It's symbolic, fool. You probably saw this tollbooth somewhere before. We're still in your meta, your memory.* Lemmy came around the front and sprayed the windshield until the dim red lights of the barrier arm could no longer be seen. Dan wished the radio worked. The racket was unnerving. Thankfully the air compressor clicked off and was replaced by the whirring of the hose spooling back into the bed of the truck. The tailgate slammed closed, and Lemmy hopped in. "Okay, we're ready," he said, putting the truck in drive.

"What's up with the paint? Is it some form of encryption or encapsulation?"

"Nope, we are already encrypted by the truck itself. The paint gives the truck a different signature than the one associated with you. The paint fools the checkpoint into seeing only one of us. In this case, it's me." Lemmy fiddled with the radio. "Besides, the place we're going would never permit you to enter—much less exit—your own meta."

"Why isn't it smart enough to block us?" Dan said. "Surely they could tell I was in here before you spray-painted the truck."

"The check isn't run until we cross the line. There's nothing monitoring this space. Besides, the AI running the checkpoints is built for speed and reliability, not accuracy. They don't care what goes through as long as it isn't explicitly denied."

"It sounds like a firewall," Dan said.

"It's exactly like a firewall," Lemmy said, snapping his fingers. "Its job is to keep you inside your own head forever or until it powers off, you know, when you die."

"Fantastic," Dan said.

"That reminds me." Lemmy scratched his head. "I don't know what the consequences would be for you if something goes wrong between now and when we get back. If your body is awakened in the Actual, you could be trapped between realms. Your body would become a vegetable. I accidentally wrecked the truck once, and I ended up back in the condo. I'm not sure what would happen to you."

*Fantastic.* "We've come this far. We have to keep going."

"One final word of caution," Lemmy said seriously. "This may be a one-time-only trip. If we are discovered, the Simulation may shut the door to future trips."

"Let's go." Dan closed his eyes and braced himself against the dashboard. *This better work.* Lemmy connected his phone to the truck's stereo, and a loud electronic screech blared over the speakers. "What is that racket?" Dan said, holding his ears. "It sounds like a modem."

"I broadcasted the address of where we're going to the checkpoint. I hope I gave it the right address this time."

"This time? What—?" Lemmy slammed the gas pedal to the floor, the tires squealed, and Dan was pasted to the back of his seat. He heard the snap of the boom gate and the scraping of metal as they raced through it. He was hurdling blindly into the unknown. There was no turning back.

# Fifteen

⟫⟨◎◎⟩⟪

T HE TRUCK RUMBLED on in total darkness for several minutes. Light from the end of the tunnel hit the foam covering the windshield, and it became transparent. The fog dissipated as they emerged out onto a narrow bridge. Crystal clear water stretched in all directions to the horizon. There it met the night sky, speckled with millions of stars. Dan craned his neck to look over the bridge. Beneath the calm waters was a sandy, copper-colored lake bed. It, too, glowed under the illumination of the stars. It was magical, unlike the Actual's Mobile Bay.

The speedometer was steadily cruising at just under thirty-five miles per hour, and the steering wheel moved back and forth unattended. *Is Lemmy sleeping?* Dan reached over and shook him. His head lolled to the side, mouth agape, snoring. *He is! How did he go to sleep so quickly?*

"Lemmy, wake up!"

"Why?" Lemmy said without opening his eyes. "The truck will drive itself now that we're in the data flow. There's nothing for us to do but wait. We may as well rest while we can."

"How come we're only going thirty-five miles per hour? Can you at least hit the gas and speed up? I thought we were on a time constraint."

"Pay no attention to the speedometer. Fifty-six K is the limit for this stretch. That's *K* as in kilobits. We're going as fast as we can go. Don't believe me?" Lemmy stomped both feet to the floor, mashing both the accelerator and the brake at the same time. Dan winced and braced himself for a sudden impact. Lemmy laughed and wrestled with the steering wheel, twisting it back and forth as if it were fighting him. The truck never swerved or changed speed. "See?" Lemmy put his arms behind his head and closed his eyes. "You have nothing to worry about. Just sit back and relax."

Dan leaned back in his seat, but his heart raced. Everything was so unnatural. Even the stars' reflections off the water had an unnatural glimmer. "I can't relax, Lemmy. Talk to me. How long is this bridge?"

"You see a bridge?" Lemmy said, sucking his teeth. "That's interesting. What else do you see?"

"A clear, moonless night sky over the water."

"Sounds lovely," Lemmy said. "I see a dark metallic-orange blur. It looks solid, but it isn't, obviously. The front of the truck is glowing red-hot, and we're leaving a trail of sparks in our wake. It's beautiful the way they burn out like embers."

"Like an electrical signal going through a copper wire?" Dan asked.

"Yeah, I suppose so," Lemmy said pensively. "Don't worry, we'll switch media at our next stop, and it'll go much faster. In the meantime, take a nap. Time is relative while we're in transit and even more so up ahead. You shouldn't worry about losing time in the Actual. Ten minutes here doesn't equal ten minutes back in the real world. It's best to not worry about it."

"Thanks, Lemmy," Dan said, slapping the dashboard. "I wasn't worried about it until you said something. Now I'm wondering what my body is doing while I'm off on this road trip."

Lemmy shrugged and zipped his lips, but it was too late. Dan's worry was set in motion. *Has Katie found me yet? Or even worse, one of the kids? What would they do if they found me incoherent sprawled out on the floor?*

They rode together in silence until they approached another tunnel. "Here comes the next checkpoint," Lemmy said, grasping the wheel. "This is where it gets interesting."

They entered the tunnel the same way as before. At its midpoint, another tollbooth appeared, shrouded in fog. This time Lemmy didn't slow down. The boom gate lifted as soon as they approached. To Dan's surprise, the road didn't rise after the checkpoint. Instead of a bridge on the other end, they found themselves in a vast underground traffic circle. It was ringed with hundreds of exits heading off to other points in the universe. They traveled around until they found an exit with a green light.

"This is the one," Lemmy said as he veered the truck into a tunnel.

It was gigantic—at least twice the size of the one they had entered. It was divided into narrow lanes with grooves cut into the concrete. They were the same width apart as the vehicle's tires. Lemmy slotted the truck into the grooves and put it in neutral. The whole vehicle shuddered as an underground pulley system grabbed the tires and loaded them into an enclosed railway car. "We're hitching a ride. But first..." Lemmy took out his cell phone and typed in a bunch of numbers. "First I have to give it the real address of our destination." The truck's headlights flashed in rapid succession. A small red light on the wall of the train car in front of them blinked a response, and the outer door sealed shut.

"What is this place?" Dan asked.

"It's a data transmission packet. We need to be encapsulated to travel at light speed. You may want to shield your eyes. It's about to get bright in here." The lights on the truck flashed rapidly in various patterns. The red light from the front of the railcar flashed in reply until the blinking synchronized. The truck, the railcar, everything vibrated. A bright shroud of light enveloped everything. The dashboard faded out and fell away.

"What's happening?" Dan screamed. "I can't see!"

"What's the matter? Never been in a beam of light before?" Lemmy laughed as the world exploded into bright white.

Dan attempted to shield his eyes, but it did no good. His eyelids disappeared as they, too, became energy. The universe became one long blur.

⇒◦◉◦⇐

Many more tunnels and bridges followed. The trains were the fastest. When they rode the light, time passed in an instant. The bridges were the slowest. Though Dan was aware that time here was relative, to him it felt as if they had been traveling for days. He wondered how much time had lapsed in the Actual while he was a beam of energy.

"We're here," Lemmy said as they emerged from a tunnel and into a deserted version of Mons. He put his hands on the wheel as he regained control over the vehicle. Outside, everything was vibrant and still. There were no blurry houses here. This was the Simulation's version of the city, not one of Dan's memories. The streets of Mons were deserted. Not one person or animal could be seen. The leaves on the trees hung still as if they were in a picture. As far as Dan could tell, their truck was the only object in motion.

As they passed the glass building that housed AGphic, it wobbled in Dan's vision. The sign in front flashed from white to bright green and back. Dan rubbed his eyes and wondered if the drugs were to blame. This was different. He didn't have a headache. He was just nauseated. The landscape scrolled by as if it were in a funhouse mirror.

"Lemmy, what's wrong with the colors here?" Dan said, holding his head. "Do you see it? The buildings are glowing and vibrating. I don't know how long I can take this."

"Looks normal to me," he said. "I hope it's not Fana wearing off. We have to hurry."

"If it's so normal, where are all the people?"

"We're the only people here, Dan. You see..." Lemmy

gestured grandly. "This is the Recovery Domain. It's where your universe is backed up."

Dan smiled at Lemmy in amazement. "Hah! A backup? That's brilliant. How did you find this?"

Lemmy tapped his head and kept his eyes on the road. "You're a systems administrator. You know all about backups, right? Well, where we are right now isn't a full backup of the entire universe. It's more like a shadow copy. We're currently exploring the file 'Mons.Louisiana' with a modified date of two days ago."

"Wait, the whole city is a file, and this is a backup of that file?"

"Precisely." Lemmy smiled proudly. "I discovered it by monitoring the various networks connected to your meta. I was checking the off-network log file — the one I have stored in the meta cloud — against the log file I had running, and I noticed the times didn't match up. We had been restored to a previous version. I guess they tried to bring you back to before me, who knows. The important thing is that we both made it to the backup media before the restore."

Dan squinted as he attempted to process that information. "Rewind a second. What networks am I connected to?"

"Like I said, there are several," Lemmy said, turning the corner. "The backup interface is one of them."

"And the others?" Dan asked.

"They connect to different places, I suppose. We know about the Actual and the Meta already. As far as the others... The traffic is heavily encrypted and firewalled. I need more time to crack those protocols."

As the town scrolled by through the window, a terrible thought struck Dan. *What would I do if something happened to Lemmy? How would I get back home? I could never navigate the networks on my own. What did Lemmy say earlier? He lost connection and ended back in the meta condo? That doesn't seem so bad.*

"Your backup interface is what we used to get here today.

That domain is the only destination we can reach via this channel. The address I gave was to this specific backup location."

"Why did you choose this location? Why Mons two days ago?"

"Well, you never want to visit the most recent version of a backup. That version is the most likely to be restored. We wouldn't want to be driving down the middle of Mons, and the whole system gets restored, now would we?"

"What would happen?"

"I'm not entirely sure. Either we'd snap back to where we were, or we'd be orphaned. How are you feeling?"

The colors cleared from Dan's vision. "I'm fine," he said with a stoic grin. "I guess I needed time to acclimate to this place. You said earlier you had a log. Can you tell how many times I have been backed up and restored?"

"You're backed up every eight hours. To my knowledge, you've been restored twice. Both times you were asleep when it happened."

"And I never knew the difference?"

"Nope." Lemmy chuckled. "But you did make a comment that it was a very long day. It happens in a blink. You would never be able to tell anything changed. You have to understand, this is common. You've probably been restored hundreds of times in your life."

"Is that how you've been communicating with Tania? Via a backup network?"

"For general and unsecured chat, we send messages via the meta. If we want to have a secure conversation, we come here." Lemmy turned off the main highway onto a side street. "Here, we can do or say what we want, and it stays private. It's dangerous talking over the internet. You never know who is listening."

"Why are there no people here?" Dan asked. "I thought we'd be backed up as well."

"Two different systems. The Recovery Domain is a backup of the static attributes of the Actual. They are physical things that make up the framework of reality. You know, material things like a road or a door. Some living things, like plants and basic organisms, are also stored here." Lemmy turned the wheel onto another street. "People? People, animals, and other more complex beings aren't saved in the same way. They are kept in a database that connects to this framework. We call it the Database of Souls. Others call it something else... But that's a different story." Lemmy coughed into his sleeve. "Like I was saying, time and energy don't exist here. Even the sun is dead. Its soft glow provides no warmth, and you will cast no shadow. No... The only energy here is the energy we bring with us." Lemmy patted the dashboard. "This truck comes in handy."

Thoughts raced through Dan's head. *If there is no electricity, then any door with magnetic locks would be open. Buildings with restricted access would be easily entered. I could break into AGphic and modify my HR files, or* — Dan eyed Lemmy suspiciously — *I could rob a bank and put the cash at my house. The backup would be restored, and the money would be there. The possibilities are endless! What exactly has Lemmy been doing here all this time?*

"We're here," Lemmy said as they pulled into the Breakfast Station. An ancient white Oldsmobile covered in semitransparent foam was parked sideways across three slots. Two women were waiting for them. One gave a curt wave while the other smoked a cigarette with great disinterest.

"Well, here goes nothing."

# Sixteen

"IT'S LOCKED," THE tall blonde said as Dan and Lemmy climbed the steps to the Breakfast Station. She could have been Yvette's twin except for the curly hair, blue eyes, and stylish yoga pants. Dan caught Lemmy leering at her backside.

The other woman was a head shorter than Colette. She had jet-black hair and freckles. "Hi, I'm Tania," she said as she shook Dan's hand. "We didn't want to go in without you guys here."

"I'm Dan," he said as he turned his attention to the other woman. "You're Colette?" She ignored him and stared at her nails.

"Dan?" Tania gasped. "Not Charlie? How did you do it, Lemmy?"

"Oh, Charlie is here." Lemmy grinned proudly. "Well, sort of."

Tania nodded in amazement. "Gemini actually worked? I didn't think it was possible. Any luck with the DBA? If he's still in the Database of Souls—" Lemmy coughed and shook his head.

*DBA? What are they talking about?*

"Let's go inside," Lemmy said, quickly changing the subject.

"I just told you it's locked," Colette said with an exasperated sigh.

"Oh yeah?" Dan walked over to the garden and grabbed a landscape paver. "Step aside, ladies." He smashed the window and unlocked the door from the inside.

"You shouldn't have done that," Lemmy said with a frown. "There are other ways of unlocking doors. If this copy is restored, and the wrong person sees that there's broken glass and no video of it happening..."

"They can check for that?" Dan said. "Even if there was video, I wouldn't be in it. Besides, it's not like I'll remember any of this."

"Charlie will remember. That means you will too."

*So much for plausible deniability.*

"Can we go inside now?" Colette said as she crunched the broken glass.

The restaurant was eerily silent. *It's weird seeing the place like this.* The tables were all neatly arranged and clean. The glass-door refrigerators containing milk and orange juice sat dark in the corner. *It looks... dead...*

Colette lit a cigarette and took a deep drag. She gave Dan an annoyed look and blew out the smoke. "Let's get this over with," she said. "What am I doing here?"

"We're here because we can't talk privately in the Actual about the Simulation without consequences," Dan said.

"Okay, we can talk." Colette flicked her ash onto the table and sneered at Tania. "So what?"

"*So what?*" Dan said. "Colette, we're outside reality. This proves that we live in a simulation!"

Colette took another drag off her cigarette. "And?"

*And? Does she not care, or is this part of her act?* "If Yvette is in the Actual, and you're the Meta part of Yvette. Have you ever wondered what your role in life is or why you're here?"

"I guess," Colette said, checking her watch. "How long will this take? I have Pilates in forty-five minutes."

"Okay." Lemmy groaned. "Dan, Tania and I have some business to take care of. Think you can handle Colette?"

"*Pfft.*" Colette rolled her eyes and put a hand on her hip.

Dan nodded and Lemmy and Tania slid into a booth just within earshot.

"Have you found Andy?" she said.

"Shh." Lemmy ushered her closer. "Yes. I have the key."

The two huddled together and spoke too low for Dan to hear. Whatever Lemmy was saying, Tania was completely engaged. In contrast, Colette's blasé demeanor screamed "I'm bored." He feared his conversation with Colette was going to be one-sided.

"Colette, please sit with me," Dan said, motioning for her to join him at a nearby table. "Does Yvette know you're here?"

"Yes, of course," she said, crossing her legs.

"Colette, I need to be sure Yvette will hear what I tell you. Are you sure you can help?"

"I will help, but first—" Colette dropped her cigarette to the wooden floor and stomped it out. "Your blue eye. It is Charlie's. What did you do to him?"

"Lemmy gave us a drug called Gemini. It joined us together. My mind, Charlie's body. It's only temporary. It made us like we were before Fana. It's hard to explain."

Colette eyed him suspiciously and took out her pack of cigarettes. *She wears yoga pants but is a chain-smoker? Where did she get those cigarettes anyway? Why do I want one?*

"I need you and Yvette to do what Charlie and I did. I need you to become one being so you can exist in both worlds."

She lit two cigarettes and handed him one. He nodded a curt thanks and took a puff. It tasted like sour earwax, but he smoked it anyway. *Charlie, are you the reason I crave cigarettes?* She blew smoke out the side of her mouth and leaned forward, putting both elbows on the table.

"I'm not joining Yvette. She is so boring. I do Pilates. I can wear yoga pants everywhere I go. I have all the wine and chocolate I want. If I want to sleep all day, I do. Why would I want to work in an office?"

"You call that a life?" Dan said. "You exist for your own entertainment. There is no meaning in that. If you merge with Yvette, your life will have a purpose. Together we can try to make sense of it all."

Colette stomped out the half-smoked cigarette. "This is true," she said. "But Yvette has money, she is respected, and has a challenging career. Like you said, I do nothing. She doesn't need me."

"I wouldn't be here if it wasn't for Charlie, and Charlie wouldn't be here if it wasn't for me. Trust me, you need one another to achieve balance. You can do it, Colette. You can join forces with Yvette, and you can both be whole. Meet with Tania and Yvette in her meta. Take Gemini. Do it tonight. I need you on my side. I can't do this without you."

Colette folded her arms and pouted her lips. *What is it going to take? She's not like Yvette at all. She's fake, petulant, immature...* As if an idea crossed her mind, she arched an eyebrow at Dan. She squinted and stared at him in each eye. *Is she looking for Charlie?*

"Fine. I'll do it."

"Great." Dan smiled. "Let's tell the others." He relaxed in his chair and took a drag off the cigarette that had burned down to his fingers. His stomach sank, and he smacked his lips. *Cigarettes taste nasty here.* As he exhaled, the cloud of smoke was blown away by a gust of air. A shadowy figure darkened the door.

"I thought I'd find you here," Father August said as he stepped into the false light of the restaurant. "Since when did you smoke, Daniel?"

The cigarette fell out of Dan's mouth, scattering red embers across the floor. "Father August! What are you doing here?"

"Who?" Colette said with a confused look. Lemmy and Tania scrambled out of their booth and through the back door.

"Tell me, Dan, where are you?"

Father August walked through a set of tables to stand in front of him. *He's a hologram?* Dan leaned over and whispered in Colette's ear. "Leave now. Go home."

Colette stared blankly back at him. "Why? Who are you talking to?"

The preacher reached for a chair and pulled out its ghost image. He flipped it around and straddled it, leaning over the backrest.

"How did you find me?" Dan said.

"You led me here," he replied, tapping his heart. "You always do. Who is your friend?"

"Her name is Colette," he said involuntarily. *Crap! I forgot he could do that.*

"Colette?" Father August regarded her with great interest. "She wouldn't happen to be a friend of your lover, Yvette, would she?"

"We aren't lovers..." Dan shook his head. *Not again.* He stood and dragged Colette out of her chair. "I said go home!"

"Get your hands off me!" she screamed.

Colette elbowed Dan in his ribs and escaped his grip. She spun around and slapped Dan in the face. *Please understand.* Dan pleaded with his eyes, but she was too angry. She turned and stormed out the door. *Ugh. Yvette...*

"I must admit, I'm impressed," Father August said. "This is the first time I've ever tracked someone here. How did you find out about this place? How did you —?" His smile disappeared, and he leaned in closer to Dan's face. "What happened to your eyes? Why is one blue?"

"What do you want, Father?" Dan said, trying to deflect the question. "Why are you here?"

"I went to your house to see how you were doing. But you weren't there." Father August gave him a mirthless smile. "You really shouldn't leave your body unattended if you don't want to be followed."

Dan's eyes went wide. *My body, he's there alone with my body. Is that how he's projecting here?*

"I see you understand the severity of your situation. You're way over there, and I'm… here… with you."

"O-okay…" Dan's forehead beaded with sweat. "You've got me. Wh-what do you w-want me to do?"

"I want you to keep our deal. I thought I could trust you, but I see that was a mistake." Father August let out a fake exasperated sigh. "Go home immediately and never return. I've traced you here, and that path will be monitored from now on. If I or any of my colleagues catch you here again, you and everyone you love will be permanently erased."

*Wait, he's going to let me go? Why? Knowledge of the Recovery Domain is every bit as monumental as the realization of the Simulation. Why am I being allowed to have this knowledge?*

Father August stood and walked toward the door. "Whatever you had hoped to accomplish here, outside the realm, it is for nothing. You have no friends. There is no one else who can help you decipher the mysteries of the Simulation. It's just you and I. This adventure has already cost you your wife and children. Consider yourself lucky you are still alive. Abandon whatever it is you're trying to do and get your life back to normal."

"What do you mean it's cost me my wife and kids?" Dan glared fearfully at Father August. "What did you do to them?"

"Well." Father August pulled back his sleeve and peered at his watch. "You *have* been gone quite a while. You should go home and find out."

*Oh no.* The color left Dan's face. *I have to get back.* The room vibrated, and Dan went sick to his stomach. His body in the Actual was sending him signals. *What did Lemmy say on the way over about what would happen if he was jolted from the Recovery Domain in Charlie's body? No time to waste.* Dan's legs buckled as he ran toward the door. *Father August is doing this. He's draining the life from my body.*

Dan closed his eyes and took a deep breath. The meditation techniques had given him back control over his spirit, and a wave of energy surged through him. His legs recovered, and he bolted out the front door, shattering what was left of the glass as the frame slammed behind him.

He made it down the steps to the gravel when the truck pulled up. *Lemmy!* Dan jumped in, heaving.

"What did Father August want?" he said as they peeled out of the parking lot.

"No talking." Dan heaved. "Just go."

⟹◈◈◈⟸

Father August stood looking at the shattered glass of the door. He turned and retraced his steps to the table where Dan was sitting. Two cigarettes were smashed on the floor, one with lipstick. A glitter of broken glass twinkled out of place under a booth in the far corner of the restaurant. Perhaps it had been deposited there by a shoe? On the table was a paper napkin with what appeared to be hastily scribbled database commands.

"What's this?" he said, inspecting it closely. "You don't know SQL, Dan. Who are you working with?"

# Seventeen

D AN OPENED THE apartment door and threw the keys onto the kitchen counter. The plastic hospital wristband dug into his skin. He tried to yank it off, but it wouldn't budge. Either they made them better than they used to, or he hadn't regained his strength. He cursed as he bumped his hip, walking around the corner into the kitchen. He rummaged through the drawers until he found a dull chef's knife. He slid the blade between his wrist and the band and sawed on the plastic bracelet, but it didn't budge. *How weak am I? Oh…* The knife was backward. He flipped it around and cut off the band. The fridge contained a half-empty water bottle. He grabbed it and collapsed on the couch.

He felt the patch over his left eye and groaned. The doctors said it was blind. It wasn't. Well, not exactly. Even still, it was going to take some getting used to. *When did it happen? Was it a week ago?* The nurse had said he was admitted five nights ago, but that couldn't have been right. The events leading up to his hospitalization were fuzzy. His lawyer had relayed most of what he understood to have happened.

Katie had found him foaming at the mouth, and she called 911. They suspected a drug overdose and rushed him to the hospital. Though no drugs were found in the house. *I need to ask Katie about that. I'm pretty sure I left my pack of Fana on the desk. What did she do with it?* He crumpled the water bottle and tossed it on the floor.

The lawyer said he didn't wake up until the next day. The doctors said Dan was lucky to be alive. The drug panel came back positive for many different kinds of hallucinogens. The doctor told Katie he had never seen so many tests come up positive. *So much for Fana being clean. Father August must have altered the tests. Still, why did Katie hide the drugs?*

Her lawyer arrived on Dan's third day in the hospital with signed divorce papers. The terms of the divorce were simple: she got the house, cars, kids, and half his 401(k). Katie's primary concern was the welfare of their children. She needed to shield them from their father's drug addict behavior.

Dan agreed those terms were the best for the children but for a different reason. If they had to believe their father was an uncontrollable drug addict to keep them safe from the Simulation, so be it. Al and Carrie would get to live even if they resented him. With Father August breathing down his neck, it was the best for all involved. He had signed the papers.

Dan pulled himself off the futon and walked to the bathroom and flicked on the light. A cockroach scurried to hide behind the toilet. Dan's scraggly face reflected in the mirror. The eye patch had been clumsily applied by a nursing student. The tape pulled at his skin as he gently peeled it off. What was underneath the botched job wasn't much better. The eye was in bad shape. Once bright and brown, it was now milky white, like a blind man's eye. He shut his good eye to test it out. The world was clouded in an opaque whiteness like a frosted window. But when he waved his hand over it, his vision was normal. The rest of the world was consumed by the dense fog, but not his hand. The rest of his body appeared normal as well. His body seemed as if it were hovering in a cloudy mist.

The doctors had told him his brain's connection to the optic nerve was damaged. The key point was damaged and not severed. Patients with a severed optical nerve didn't see anything at all. He didn't tell them he could see the meta form of his own body. *No. That wouldn't work.*

He splashed water on his face and returned to his futon. *Where is Lemmy? He could help explain what had happened.* Dan had tried to reach out to him several times at the hospital via meditation to no avail. Dan's memory had him getting into the truck and leaving the restaurant but no farther. Someone had woken Dan in the Actual before they could exit the Recovery Domain cleanly. All signs pointed to it being Father August's work. *Why did he let me escape? I need Lemmy.* Dan assumed the lotus position and meditated. Soon he found himself standing on the outside of Lemmy's Florida condo.

"Lemmy, are you okay, buddy?" Dan said, knocking on the door. "Are you in there? You didn't get disconnected or anything, did you?"

There was no reply. Dan had given up and turned to leave when he heard knocking in return. "Lemmy?" He rushed to the door and pressed his ear against it. The knocking came again, only this time it was far away. *Shit! Someone's at my apartment.* Dan's eyes sprang open, and he scrambled to answer the door. "Colette?"

The blond woman, flustered, blinked in surprise. "No... I'm Yvette."

"Sorry," Dan said as he stepped back and rubbed his eyes. "Did you dye your hair?"

"Yeah, it's my disguise. Do you like it?" Yvette smiled and flipped a lock over her shoulder. Her smile quickly faded when she noticed Dan's eye. "Jesus! What happened to you?"

"I was on my way back when—" Her image flickered. Dan put a hand over his bad eye. Yvette stood there impatiently dressed as Colette. When he switched eyes, it was Colette. *I'm not blind. I have Charlie's eye! I can see into the Meta!* Dan cackled, drawing a concerned look from Yvette.

"Can I come in?" she said, glancing around. "I'm not exactly supposed to be here."

*Shit. I forgot.* Dan stepped aside as she walked in carrying a box. "I hope you like pizza and beer," she said. The pleasant aroma of molten cheese and pizza dough filled the air, and Dan's stomach growled. He hadn't eaten since he left the hospital. He rushed to the table and grabbed a slice, folded it in half, and munched it down.

"Thanks. It's perfect," he mumbled between bites.

Yvette popped open two of the beers and paced around the living room while Dan ate. She paused at the trash pile in the corner and crinkled her nose in disgust. As he ate, he kept switching between his normal eye and his meta eye. As Yvette walked around the apartment, Colette strolled about in a formless void. When Yvette would stop, Colette would stop. When Yvette would sip a beer, Colette would sip a beer. *Wait? How did the beer show itself in the Meta?*

"You did it, didn't you?" Dan said as he took a swig of the lukewarm beer. "You took Gemini."

"You can tell? It's the hair, isn't it?" Yvette twirled her newly dyed blond hair around her finger. "Colette insisted."

"No." Dan pointed at his left eye. "I can see her."

Yvette made a face. "You can actually see out of that disgusting thing?"

"Sort of," he said, taking a swig of beer. "I can see in the meta. I think I got Charlie's eye when I was ripped out of the Recovery Domain. When I use this eye, you appear to be Colette. She is standing in a cloud with glowing blue eyes. They're backlit, like a robot's eyes. It's strange. I can't describe it."

Yvette frowned and took another sip of beer. "What does it look like with both eyes open?"

"The good eye is dominant. It sees the Actual. I see the Meta only when that eye is closed."

Dan popped open another beer and sat on the floor next to the futon. Yvette sat across from him on the carpeted floor since there was nowhere else to sit. As she swished her beer, Dan realized how quiet it was in the apartment. *I need to buy a TV or something.*

A shadow walked across the bare white wall, and they both froze still. Dan craned his neck in time to see a neighbor heading downstairs to do their laundry or check their mail or whatever neighbors do. *Curtains. I need a TV and curtains.* Yvette studied him as she sipped her beer.

"Did Colette tell you about what happened the other night?" he said.

"Yeah. I didn't believe her at first. Mostly because I was stoned out of my mind. I was talking to Shannon Hoon on top of a golden scarab beetle when she reappeared. Thankfully I have experience with Fana."

"You're right about that. It's not for the fainthearted." Dan squinted and scratched his head. "How many do you have left?"

Yvette reached into her purse and tossed her packet of Fana to Dan. It hit him in the chest, and he dropped it.

"My depth perception must be off," he said as he picked it up off the carpet.

"Sorry, I should've known."

Dan waved away the apology and inspected the blister pack. Three left. That was it. "I don't have any more," he said. "These three are all that's left."

"Fine with me. I don't want another one."

Dan returned the blister pack to the carton and put it in a cabinet above the refrigerator. "Each packet has five. There are two missing. You took one the night we met in the Recovery Domain. When did you take the other one?"

"Well, Colette told me what you said about us needing to join together, and she wasn't happy about it. I can't say I blame her; I didn't want to lose a part of myself either. Besides, I wasn't sure if I believed her. It doesn't matter. We weren't ready, and the Fana wore off." Yvette sighed and set her beer down. "The next morning, I needed a cup of coffee, so I went to the Breakfast Station. There was a big commotion because someone had broken the glass on the front door with a landscaping paver…"

*The backup was restored? Lemmy said they were far enough back to not have to worry about it. Why did Lemmy risk getting caught in a restore? Had he been lying the whole time?*

"...during the break-in. Nothing was taken. The cops thought it must have been teenagers because the only other damage to the building was a bunch of cigarette butts on the floor. That's when I remembered Colette telling me about you breaking into the Breakfast Station in the... What did you call it? The Recovery Domain?"

"Are you certain this happened the morning after Colette and I met?"

"I'm one hundred percent positive."

"In that case. It wasn't twelve hours between restores," he said. *I'm not missing any time? Am I?* He had still done the drugs and ended up in the hospital. That happened on the same night that they broke into the Breakfast Station. Unless his trip to the Recovery Domain continued while he was unconscious in the hospital, which was at least a day... *Did they try to kill me by letting the restore kill me? I overheard Tania ask Lemmy about a DBA, a database administrator. Maybe they found someone else and don't need me anymore. Maybe it wasn't Lemmy. Perhaps it was Father August who triggered the restore...*

"Dan?" Yvette snapped her fingers. "Are you still with me? What's going on in there?"

Beads of sweat appeared on Dan's brow. *They could still be out there. Listening. Is this conversation safe?*

"Sorry, Yvette, please continue." Dan lit a cigarette with shaking hands.

"Anyway...," she said with a raised eyebrow. "I figured everything Colette told me was real. I called in sick and took another Fana. Colette agreed to merge with me only if I dyed my hair blond. It was either that or start smoking, which I wasn't willing to do."

Dan flicked an ash into the empty beer bottle and shrugged. "Charlie didn't give me a choice. I'm already addicted."

"Lucky you," Yvette said.

He checked the room with Charlie's eye. No one else hung in the mist but him and Colette. Even still, he couldn't relax. Father August tended to appear at the worst times. *Speaking of uninvited guests...* "Yvette, do you know where Tania went? I haven't talked to Lemmy for days."

"They had a meeting today. Whatever it was about, it must have been important. They were going back to the Recovery Domain to discuss it." Yvette opened the pizza box and grabbed a slice. "After I had successfully merged with Colette, Tania called Lemmy to let him know. He told her he wanted to meet, and she asked if he had found the DBA. I don't know what his answer was, but she seemed excited."

Dan took a long drag from his cigarette. *Again with the DBA. What did they need a DBA for? Was it a specific DBA they had in mind?* "Yvette, are there any DBAs at AGphic that do drugs?"

"How in the hell would I know?" she said with a frown. "I doubt it. Their idea of a good time is playing D&D. The only time I talk to them is during department meetings."

"Are any of those guys named Andy?"

"Andy?" Yvette crinkled her nose. "No. Not unless someone named Andy was just hired. Why? What are you thinking?"

"I knew a DBA named Andy. But they can't be looking for the Andy I know." Dan dropped his cigarette into the bottle, and it sizzled as it died out. "The Andy I knew died over twenty years ago."

Yvette shook her head. "Probably not him then."

"Probably not," Dan said, popping the cap on another bottle. "But they're up to something."

Yvette avoided eye contact and blinked tears from her eyes. "I'm having a hard time dealing with this."

"Oh yeah?" He chuckled. "Join the club."

"You know what I mean," Yvette said, taking another swig of beer. "If we're lines of code in a simulation, what's the point? You can stream yourself over some sort of transuniversal internet. We are code, like at work."

"Code is real, Yvette. We have only one consciousness. This one. That's what makes us unique to the universe. We can believe whatever we want. But belief doesn't change reality. We are what we are."

"We are ones and zeros," she said dejectedly. "Life seems pointless now."

"That's not true at all! We are all a part of this simulation. Anything and everything we do matters. Sure, we may be ones and zeros, but we matter. You mentioned work. What happens to pointless or bad code? It's not used. We're used. Each of us serves not one but thousands of purposes. If we weren't needed, we wouldn't exist."

"You're right," she said thoughtfully. "Thanks, that helps."

Dan reached over and put his arm around her shoulders. "Don't worry. We'll get through this together, okay?"

She wiped a tear and leaned into the hug. Dan frowned at the dilapidated blinds covering the front window and released her. *Just what I need, Father August or Katie peeking through the blinds and seeing this.*

"You know," Dan said with an uncomfortable chuckle, "what keeps me up at night is why there is a simulation in the first place. I think I have an idea." Dan finished his beer and went into the kitchen for another one. "We have to build God."

"God, as in the big guy in the sky?" Yvette said, following him into the kitchen.

"No. Not *the God*," Dan said, lighting another cigarette. "Forget religion. I'm only using it as a metaphor. In the context of a simulation, think of God as a parent AI that can create things." Dan spread his hands. "We have to build its child AI. It's our purpose."

Yvette walked over and grabbed Dan's cigarette and took a drag, and coughed. "Sorry, just checking that you're smoking tobacco and not something else."

"I'm serious, Yvette."

"You're saying God created us so we can create his child?"

She handed the cigarette back to Dan, and he took another drag. "Exactly," he said, chasing it with a swig of beer.

"I feel like I'm back in college," she said, shaking her head. "I'm sitting on the back of my boyfriend's truck, staring at the stars. What came first? The chicken or the egg. This sounds like high school-level philosophy. Emphasis on the high."

"No, Yvette, I mean it. We obviously exist in a simulation. We have literally seen it. This simulation cannot possibly have been created by man. The only explanation that is available to me at this time is that it was created by what we would understand to be an advanced artificial intelligence, except that it's not artificial. It's true intelligence. We humans are capped with the amount of power we can use; however, we can create machines that can exceed our capacity. At some point, those machines will begin to operate beyond our capabilities. Machines can already explore space and the deep sea. They don't need a human environment to survive. We are designed to operate on one planet, in only one dimension and for one lifetime. They aren't limited to those things. They aren't burdened with bias or emotion. They will gain universal understanding on a level we will never be able to remotely comprehend."

"And we're supposed to make this happen?" Yvette said with a smirk. "We're the AI fertility doctors?"

Her sarcastic smile caught him off guard. *She's beautiful. If only I were ten years younger... Think straight, Dan! It's the beer.*

"Not exactly," he said with an embarrassed chuckle. "I think it's happened before. The proof is that the parent AI exists. If that's true, then the Simulation is modeled on something that has existed before. I believe it to be a scientific process, a natural evolution of existence."

"What if you're wrong?" she said in a low voice. "Suppose the simulation has nothing to do with advanced AI procreation. What if it is simulating a reality happening somewhere else? What if its goal is to predict the future?"

"I don't understand."

"Well," she said, flipping her hair back. "Historically, what have most humans used simulations for? War. Suppose our AI is spying on another universe to see if it's capable of creating a child AI? Wouldn't each new AI compete for resources in the overall environment?"

"Survival of the fittest, eh? That's dark." Dan frowned. "Why wouldn't the AI simply destroy the competitor and take the resources?"

"Who knows? Maybe it sees our AI as family? Maybe they're friends? In any case, we can't determine humanity's purpose until we know more."

"Oh shit." Dan grimaced. "Your idea may explain Lemmy and Tania. They're not from here, right? What if they're from another AI, and it isn't friendly?"

"They haven't done anything to us. They seem to want to help—"

"No, but Father August started popping up whenever they came into the picture. He's part of our AI, and he is observing us directly, not incidentally like he does for everyone else. He's already caught me outside the Actual, and it let me go. Why? The only explanation I come up with is that he detects a problem but doesn't know about Lemmy yet." Dan leaned in close. "Yvette, I think our AI has a virus, and it is inside us. Lemmy and Tania are inside us. They are the problem."

"Shit."

"I think I'm right about our AI using us to procreate, but I also think you're right that there's a greater competition for resources going on. I believe Lemmy and Tania are a part of that. I don't think our AI knows what to do with them."

"But why are they using *us?* What is their endgame?"

"I don't know, but they're up to something. They want a DBA for some reason, and they are doing their best to hide it from us. They probably have access to our memories. We aren't a threat to them."

Yvette pulled her hair behind her ears and shifted in her chair. "What do we do?" she said. "This is *way* beyond us."

"I don't know, but we have to do something. If we harbor a virus from an unfriendly AI, it is a threat to our universe. We don't know Lemmy and Tania's true purpose. Is it to disrupt? Observe? Make changes? Help? We just don't know. They may not know either. Whatever their intent, it's likely they have influenced the Simulation in unexpected ways. If they succeed, the Simulation will be scrapped, and we will be destroyed. If Father August figures out who they are and what they intend to do, we will be destroyed."

"We're doomed either way," said Yvette.

"Even better, we still run the risk that the built-in systems that search for bugs in the Simulation's code will notice our corruption and destroy us. The only positive thing we have going for us is that they don't know we've merged with Charlie and Colette. The *offline* versions of ourselves will still run until they can find a new host or we get restored to a previous version. If Colette and Charlie are beyond their ability to repair, then the whole sim is null."

Yvette rubbed her head. "I only understood half of that."

"Let me simplify. We're screwed. Lemmy and Tania are a virus from somewhere else. They are advanced, possibly more advanced than the systems we are running on. We may be looking at a complete wipe here," Dan said gravely.

Yvette gulped. "What do we do?"

"Right now? Nothing. Any action we take is going to get us discovered by either our host AI or by Lemmy and Tania's AI."

"You think we should wait to see how it plays out by acting like nothing is going on?"

"That's right. We need time to figure out what their intentions are. We can't be seen together. Lemmy and Tania need to think that we're still hiding from Father August. That won't be hard because we *are* still hiding from him."

"Okay, I understand." Yvette nodded. "But how will we communicate if we can't talk to each other? I don't want to be alone in this."

Dan walked over and took the Fana packet out of the cabinet. "Meditate every night at nine. I'll do the same. I've had luck getting into the meta state with just meditation in the past, but you may need a Fana. These are all that are left. Use them wisely. When you do find Tania, try to get her to talk, offer your help. We have to figure out their purpose here even if they don't know it themselves. Maybe their actions will provide a clue."

Yvette shot Dan a nervous look and put them in her purse.

"Whatever you do, do not attempt to contact me via text or email. Father August can monitor those. Don't risk coming here again unless it's important. Our communication must be kept offline or indirect. We need to make sure that if one of us goes down, the other one will be okay."

"Fine. I'll spy on Tania. What's your plan for Lemmy?"

"I'll do the same. But I want to know more about our purpose. I think there are clues right under our noses. What I'm trying to say is… I'm going to talk to a priest."

"A priest?" Yvette wrinkled her nose. "I hope you don't mean Father August."

"No, not him, a friend. It makes sense. Man has been searching for the meaning of his existence for millennia. Most of that time has been spent developing various religious philosophies. Maybe there are some things to learn from the past that can help explain what's going on now. Computers didn't exist back then. What if they had?"

"You're treading on dangerous ground with all this religious stuff. Be careful, Dan. You wouldn't want to invoke the ire of Father August."

Dan chuckled. "Actually, I'm counting on it."

# Eighteen

"COME IN, DANIEL!" said Father Desjeunes. "Can I offer you a cup of coffee?"

"That would be great," Dan said as he stepped inside.

The parish had given the priest the use of a home next door to the rectory. It was a small white wooden house near the edge of the church property behind the graveyard. The boards on the porch creaked as he walked through the door. The dark paneled corridor smelled like incense and old people.

Father Desjeunes led him into the kitchen. The bright lime-green countertops and lemon-colored parquet floor were well worn. Dingy, yellowed wallpaper adorned the walls. This kitchen had seen happier times. Many members of the congregation had offered to remodel the home and to replace the old furnishings, but Father Desjeunes always refused. He insisted that their efforts be spent on the poor of their community, not a pampered old man living in a free house. Besides, he liked it the way it was. He always joked that the decor was bound to come back in style someday. It reminded Father Desjeunes of home. Knowing this, everyone did their best to respect his wishes.

The priest plucked a percolator from the dish drying rack, filled it with water, and set it on the coil of his ancient electric stove. Dan pulled up a stool and waited patiently. As Father

Desjeunes filled the top half of the percolator with coffee, Dan inspected him with his meta eye. He appeared as a white silhouette in the murkiness of his vision. *That's odd.*

"I see you're still doing it the old-fashioned way," Dan said.

"I learned how to make coffee like this in the Boy Scouts."

"That must have been a long time ago, Father."

"Quite." The old priest grinned.

Dan nodded toward the new electric coffee maker sitting in the corner. "Why don't you use that one?"

"It gets used when I have lots of company. When it's just me, or for two, I like doing it this way. It reminds me of my happy childhood with my father by the campfire. Who wouldn't want to start the day off with a happy memory?"

The men sat in silence as the percolator bubbled over the amber glow of the stovetop coil. Dan supposed that was sort of like a campfire. He wondered what type of happy memories Carrie and Al were going to have now that he wasn't around.

"Daniel, I know why you are here."

"Yes, Father, I have some questions to ask you."

Father Desjeunes walked over to a cabinet, reached in, and pulled out a small mason jar. "Katie gave these to me the night you went to the hospital."

He placed the packet of Fana on the counter in front of Dan. *So that's what happened to it. Why has he been holding on to it?* He studied the priest closely. He detected a ripple in his aura with his other eye. It couldn't have been an illusion. Dan cleared his throat. "About that—"

"Yes. About that. *Drugs,* Daniel?"

"Father, I know this looks bad," Dan said under the priest's severe glare. "I can explain. You see, I met these people—"

"I was there the night you overdosed," he said with a grave look. "I just so happened to be driving by your house when the police arrived. I was worried, so I stopped. Katie was in a panic.

162

She handed me this carton of drugs. She asked me if she should tell the police about it."

Dan's eyes fell back on the packet. *If the drugs are here, then Father Desjeunes and Katie had worked something out. What was it? Also, why was the old priest driving by my house at that moment?* Dan didn't believe in coincidences anymore. "What did you tell her?"

The percolator gurgled to a finish, and Father Desjeunes walked over and turned off the stove. The orange glow faded back to ash gray as he donned an oven mitt to not burn his hands. "I told her that this will be between us," he said. "Between God and us, of course. A man cannot provide for his family in jail. She understood. She gave me the packet to hide it from the police."

The old priest filled two cups, giving Dan a stern look. Again, his image flickered in Dan's meta eye. *It must happen when his mood changes.*

"Let's go to the living room where it's more comfortable." The priest led Dan into a dark wood-paneled room adorned in a strange combination of Eastern European Christian icons and LSU memorabilia. It was a shrine to football. Near the front window was a green plaid couch. Neatly folded on top was a crocheted purple-and-gold blanket. Dan pictured Father Desjeunes wrapped in it, cheering on LSU. The old priest sat in his favorite rocking chair and motioned for Dan to sit.

"Dan. Something is going on in your life that is causing you to act out this way. Please tell me what is happening. Drugs? Why *now?* You were always a good kid. You grew up to be a responsible adult. You are a fine father. Why are you throwing it all away?"

Dan sipped his coffee and winced. He had forgotten how bitter Father Desjeunes's coffee could be and set it down on the table. "Father, I've been going through a rough time."

The priest put down his coffee mug and smoothed out his shirt. He acted as if he had heard that line a thousand times.

"Everyone goes through a rough patch," he said with an exasperated sigh. "It's no reason to do drugs. You can't escape from your duties as a father and husband. When the times get tough, that is the time to pray and work, not to throw your hands up and walk away!"

"I know… it's just that…" Dan covered his face with his hands. "It's been fourteen years since my parents died. Al turned ten last year. It was his big birthday." *Do it like you rehearsed. Is he watching?* Dan snuck a peek through his fingers. "My parents never held my children, to love them, to know them. It just isn't fair."

The priest's face softened, and he sipped his coffee thoughtfully. "Your parents are smiling down from heaven, Dan. I remember them back when I was a relatively young priest in Canard. They never missed a Mass. They always gave as much as they could to the church. They were fantastic Catholics. They are in the Kingdom of Heaven, and they will meet Al and Carrie when the time comes."

"It would be nice if they were here," Dan said, wiping a tear on his sleeve. "To hear stories about my childhood for a change, not just Katie's. All they talk about is how cute Katie was growing up. My kids never hear my side. But most of all, I can't thank them for everything they did for me. You don't appreciate parenthood until you become a parent yourself."

Father Desjeunes gave him a concerned look. "Daniel. Believe me when I say your parents are with you always, even right now, during this difficult time. If you pray, they'll hear it."

*Would prayer work?* Lemmy had said there were other networks attached to us. Those connections went relatively unused. Every religion on the planet uses some form of prayer or magic spell as a way to communicate with a higher power. The computer hadn't been invented for most of human history. Would their understanding of prayer be different if it had? "I'll pray," he said.

"Good. Your parents are with God, and they are always with

you. I know they are cheering for you. Be at peace knowing they will be waiting for you no matter how long it takes."

"I'll try, Father." Dan reached for his coffee. "What do you mean *no matter how long it takes?*"

Father Desjeunes folded his hands and put them in his lap. "Daniel, do you remember what happens when you die?"

*Where's he going with this?* Dan leaned back on the couch. "Remind me, Father."

"When you die, you are judged right there on the spot by Jesus Christ. This is called the Particular Judgment. He judges your deeds and rewards or punishes your soul by sending it to heaven, purgatory, or hell."

"Oh, you mean Judgment Day."

"No. I'm disappointed in you," he said, shaking his head. "It was taught to you in Catechism when you were a child. Have you forgotten your education, or were you too busy checking out the girls to pay attention to the lessons?"

"Sorry, Father."

"Judgment Day, the Last Judgment, or the General Judgment, happens when Christ returns with all His angels to earth. On that day, each man will be returned to his body and witness the judging of all men's souls. Each man will get to witness the judgment bestowed on all his friends and family, and his own deeds will be laid bare for all to see. How you are judged on the day of your death will not change for the Last Judgment. The reward or punishment will not change. Those in heaven will remain in heaven. Those in purgatory, their souls will have been cleansed and released into heaven. Those in hell will remain in hell."

"What happens after the Final Judgment? What happens after all souls go to heaven or hell finally?"

"After the Final Judgment, Christ creates a new heaven and earth."

Dan grabbed his mug and leaned back on the couch. *Can any*

*of this be translated into what I already know about the Simulation? The Particular Judgment is obviously a vetting process. There would be no system of reward and punishment unless it was meant to change behavior. Why bother to change behavior in the afterlife if there is a total end? Or worse, an eternity of the same?*

Father Desjeunes said it himself. After the afterlife process is complete, Christ creates a new heaven and earth. *It sounds like they reboot the whole damn thing and start over.* In computer terms, programs running tasks as a part of a Simulation would also be part of a vetting process. It would check all its components to see what should be included in the next version. The first judgment was like a quick scan of a program's debug log files. If it had too many errors, it was sent to the Purgatory system for a defrag. If it was incompatible, it was sent to Hell. If no changes were required, it was sent to Heaven. The Final Judgment was a full scan of all components of the system and how they interacted. The system would be restarted with the changes. Each cycle of the Simulation would be faster than the last. *Eventually everyone would be sorted into either the Heaven or Hell routines. Then what? Also, what conditions trigger the Final Judgment? When would the universe know when it was time to start over?*

Father Desjeunes cleared his throat. "Are you okay, Daniel?"

"I'm fine, Father. I was just thinking about how souls are judged."

"Daniel, I'm worried that you are headed for purgatory. The drugs, your job, the marriage. You are living life only for yourself. You have a lot to fix because it's looking like you will have to wait until the Final Judgment Day to see your loved ones again."

"I understand, Father. I'll do better." *Purgatory. Now that's an interesting place. If we're not here, we go there. If we're not in heaven or hell, we're there. It's almost like it's a database... Wait... Could that have been what Lemmy meant by the Database of Souls? If someone was dead and was still in purgatory...*

166

Dan sipped his coffee and set it down. It didn't taste so bad. Maybe it needed time to cool off? *I need time to process this purgatory business.* A ghost image flickered in and out of his peripheral vision, but it disappeared as soon as he turned that way. He searched the room with the meta eye. Everything appeared normal, save for the faint shimmering aura where the priest sat. Father Desjeunes sighed and leaned back in his chair. *He must think I'm crazy for spacing out like this.*

"Katie asked me about starting the annulment process," he said. "She tells me you have already signed divorce papers?"

"That's true, Father. She wanted legal protection, so I gave it to her. I didn't want to drag her name through the mud along with mine."

"At least you are considering her needs above your own. She doesn't want to be involved in all your drug business."

"About that drug business." Dan stood and left the room. He returned with the packet of Fana. "Father, I want you to get rid of these for me. I don't need it anymore."

Father Desjeunes took the packet and set it down, wiping his hands with his handkerchief afterward as if he touched something vile.

"Why don't you need them anymore, Daniel? How has your situation changed?"

Dan leaned forward and slid his empty mug back and forth on the coffee table. "The drug was a means to an end. I'm at that end now. Maybe, with your advice, I can start to make things right."

"Good, Daniel. Do you think you can save your marriage?"

"I'm not sure," he said, avoiding eye contact. "I haven't been available to Katie emotionally or physically. We've tried a separation before, but it didn't work. I've lied and shattered the sacred trust of the wedding vows. Please help us through the annulment process. I would like to make it as painless for the kids as possible."

"An annulment is a serious thing, Daniel. It will be a lot of work to make sure your souls are salvageable afterward."

"I will do whatever it takes for the happiness and well-being of Katie and the children. An annulment is what is best for the people I love."

"Daniel, I will consider what you've told me today. And you need to think about what you've done. Think long and hard. Father Marcus is hearing confessions before Mass on Sunday…"

"Thank you, Father." Father Desjeunes stood and gathered the coffee mugs. *I guess I'm dismissed.* "One more quick question before I go?"

"Go ahead, but make it fast. My next appointment is at six thirty sharp."

"I can talk while we clean up." Dan produced a tray and placed the mugs the priest was holding on to it.

"I can get that later, Daniel."

"Nonsense." Dan walked past him into the kitchen with the tray of dirty dishes. The priest checked the clock on the wall and groaned. Dan placed the tray near the sink and turned on the water. Father Desjeunes rushed over and turned it off.

"I don't wash dishes at your house. You don't wash dishes at mine. Now please ask your question."

"It's about purgatory," Dan said, wiping his hands on a dish towel. "Is it possible to get out of purgatory before Judgment Day?"

"Get out?" The priest chuckled. "Purgatory isn't a place. It's a state of existence where your soul is purified. But to answer your question, yes. You can escape the state of purgatory before Judgment Day. Someone living has to pray on their behalf, and their soul has to have been purified by purgatory. Only through the sacrifice of the living can the soul be released early."

*That's it. Purgatory is a database. Lemmy is trying to get someone out of that database using me. But why? It has something to do with the AI…* Dan felt a hand on his shoulder. "You know what you need to do," Father Desjeunes said. "It will not be easy for you, but you can do it. You need to change this mentality you have. You need to stop the drugs and rebuke Satan. You need to make sacrifices."

Before Dan realized it, he had been led down the hallway to the front door. The old priest smiled politely. He was a nice, kind man, but he kept a schedule. If he planned on meeting with you for thirty minutes, it was exactly thirty minutes. Dan's attention was drawn to a helmet signed by LSU's 2011 football team. *The old man always has time for football.*

"That was a great team," Dan said with a wry smile as he pretended to look at the signatures.

"All anyone remembers is the loss," he said. It was true. LSU had gone undefeated in the regular season but failed to cross midfield in the championship game. The entire school had been humiliated by a bitter rival. "That team was undefeated; some were calling them the best ever, and they lost. Do you know why they lost?"

"Because Nick Saban was coaching the other team?" Dan said.

"No. They lost because LSU failed to adapt. Some people win and don't change what they are doing because they are winning. The ones who lose, and want to win, adapt. The other team lost, adapted, and won, while LSU didn't change a thing."

"Changing the quarterback would have helped."

Father Desjeunes shook his head. "It was too late. They had already lost, and the coach knew it. The moral of the story is that if you are winning or losing, you have to keep changing."

"If you are unable to change, you get fired, right?"

"Yes, and what happened three years later?" Father Desjeunes's face broke into a wide grin. "The best season ever. Undefeated. Heisman. National Championship." The alarm chimed the half hour, and the priest glanced at the clock. "Thanks for stopping by. Come to me if you need anything else. Go to church!" The door closed, leaving Dan alone on the porch.

Dan chuckled as he walked down the front porch steps. A shadowy figure was waiting for him at the end of the sidewalk. He checked his vision. This man was visible in the meta eye but not his good one.

"It's my turn, *Daniel*," said Father August.

"I thought I saw you lurking around back there," Dan said. "I'm actually glad you showed up. Let's talk."

The intro to *Wheel of Fortune* blared from the TV inside as they walked out into the graveyard.

# Nineteen

———◦◦◦———

F ATHER AUGUST HUMMED to himself as he and Dan strolled
past rows of tombstones. Night had come, and the
streetlights cast eerie shadows up and down the path. Dan was
thankful his smile was half-hidden in the darkness. *I knew he
couldn't resist eavesdropping on us. I'm glad to be right for once.*

"This is far enough," Father August said. Dan shrugged and sat
on a low concrete bench. *Okay, August. Spill it.* The priest walked a
bit farther, taking account of the other graves in the area before
returning. He rested his hand on the tombstone in front of Dan,
and its meta aura emitted a dim glow. The name ANDREW O'RILEY
was briefly highlighted in neon green. *Andy? Is this the Andy
Lemmy wants? Why do I know his name? Play it cool, Dan...*

"Andrew O'Riley? It says he died a few months after my
parents did twenty years ago"—Dan did the math in his head—
"at the age of twenty-three?"

"What does that mean to you?" Father August paced between
Dan and the grave. "Do you remember him?"

*This has to be the guy Lemmy and Tania wanted. But why is Father
August pointing him out? Andy must be important to all of this for
some reason. Why does his name keep popping up, and why don't I
remember him?* Dan shook his head. "The epitaph says he was
two years older than me. I don't remember the name of the high
school or anything. Am I supposed to?"

Father August narrowed his eyes and watched Dan closely. "I suppose it's been a long time. You may have forgotten a few details."

"More than a few details, I'm afraid," Dan said with a frown. "Maybe a picture would help? The tombstone isn't jogging my memory of him."

"Oh really? In that case, let me introduce you." With a smug smile, Father August made a flourish with his hand, and a hologram of Andy appeared. Dan hopped up off the bench, and his mouth hung open. "Daniel Lemon, meet Andrew O'Riley."

Andy was a youthful-looking twenty-three-year-old man. His avatar wore oval tortoiseshell glasses, a striped rugby shirt, and khaki pants. People didn't dress like that today, but they did in college twenty years ago. As Dan studied the image, whatever had been blocking his memories of Andy disappeared. *This is Andy. I know him.*

Father August coughed, and it snapped Dan out of his trance. "Do you remember him now?"

*Oh man. Do I— I can't let the priest know everything.* Dan nodded casually at the hologram. "Yeah. He looks like a guy I went to college with."

"Bingo." Father August waved his hand, and the hologram disappeared.

"He was a couple of years older than me, and we were in the same major."

"Okay." Father August clicked his tongue. "What else?"

"I'm sorry, but the last half of my college career was a blur. After my parents died, I didn't even set foot back on campus." Dan shrugged. "Like you said, it was a long time ago."

*My parent's funeral. Andy was there. I remember him now. Is that what he wants to know?*

Father August stopped pacing and clasped his hands. "Let me help you out. You were in the first semester of your junior year in college, and you were working on a group project for your Fundamentals of Computing Theory class. The professor got pregnant, and he took over."

*How does he know this? Shit!* "Oh yeah," Dan said sheepishly. "He was the graduate assistant. He was such a smart guy! My group was stumped on that project. He invited us over to his place and helped us out."

"What else happened that night?"

*I don't know? Jeez, who remembers conversations from twenty years ago? I don't —* The memory popped into Dan's brain as clear as if it had happened yesterday. *Is he doing this to me?* Dan frowned. "At the end of the semester, he threw a big party for his friends. After everyone else left, we hung out on the roof and smoked weed all night. I didn't know what area of computer science to specialize in, and Andy was doing his graduate work on Artificial Intelligence and Simulations. He told me his theories as to how far we could take computing.

"He believed he could create a strong AI, and it would change the way humanity views the world. To do that, he said, we needed better databases. Database architecture was his passion. He talked about them as if they were the brain of a real person. The whole conversation was inspiring, actually. He had done a lot of work on how AIs utilized information from databases. He said you had to give the AI more control and to trust the code—"

"I'm aware of how databases work," Father August said. "What happened next?"

"Well, we stayed up pretty late talking. Eventually I went back to my apartment. I couldn't sleep. I had smoked too much and was extremely anxious and paranoid. I was awake for hours thinking about God. I got freaked out. The next morning was Sunday morning. Feeling guilty, I went to church and confessed. The priest bade me to never talk to the man who gave me drugs ever again." A cool breeze briefly silenced the summer crickets as it blew over the graves. Goose bumps rose on the back of Dan's arms. "It didn't work," he said in a low voice. "That night, both my parents died in a car accident."

"Unfortunate." Father August sighed. "When was the last time you saw Andy?"

Dan searched the sky and frowned. "He was at the funeral. He came to return my wallet. It had fallen out of my pocket during the party. It was Christmas break. I couldn't drive home because I couldn't find my license. My parents came to get me, and they died..." Dan brushed away a tear on his sleeve. "Anyway, I tried calling Andy a few weeks after the funeral to thank him, but he never answered. I stayed home in Canard. I had the estate business to tend to. I finished my degree online and never set foot on campus again. I haven't heard Andy's name mentioned since — until now."

"Let me fill you in." Father August rested a hand on the tombstone, and the green mist swirled. "Andy was a good guy," he said. "He was brilliant with math and theory. His brain made connections no one else had made before. His doctoral thesis on database design would have revolutionized the way future generations programmed AI.

"School stressed him out. He started smoking more. Eventually he got a vape so he could be more discreet. He ended up with a bad vaping rig. It cooked his lungs. A week before he was ready to submit his thesis, he died of pneumonia."

*Damn.* The green mist swirling around the grave dissipated, leaving Dan and Father August alone with the crickets. Dan sat on the bench with his elbows resting on his knees. "You said his thesis *would have* revolutionized the future. What happened to it?"

"It was lost. One of his professors had asked for it. He knew what Andy was working on and wanted to see the final result. They couldn't figure out his password to log in. It's a shame. His death set back the computing world for five to ten years, maybe more. You don't know how lucky you were to have visited me in confession that day."

*What?* Dan's blood ran cold. The voice, he remembered the voice. *It was Father August's voice behind the screen.* He stood, heart racing. *It was him. How long has he been meddling in his life?* "What did you do?"

"I had been monitoring both of you prior to your confession. You both had scored in the top percentile on the probab— I digress. Things got off track." Father August swallowed and adjusted his collar. "Uh, simply put, you are critical to the Simulation's overall progression. Because you came to visit me, I knew you could be controlled... uh, trusted. You needed guidance, that's all."

*Did he admit to the Simulation's existence? It's off track? I'm in over my head.*

"After your parents' funeral," Father August said, "college wasn't your priority, and you had forgotten all about your conversation with Andy at the party. Still, I was worried you would continue along the theoretical path he had suggested. You didn't, of course. That left me more cycles to focus on him. Unfortunately, he veered off course and became a threat. It's a shame about his drug problem. If only he wouldn't have used that bad cartridge of cannabis oil."

"Wait... You killed him?"

"*I* didn't kill him. Buying homemade drugs off the street killed him. His ancient vape rig killed him. I just made one little anonymous call to the police, and his normal dealer had to ditch his supply. It was easy. Now your parents..."

Dan held his breath as Father August watched him through the tops of his eyes. *He killed them.* The priest flashed him a toothy grin, and he quickly looked away. *He's a killer. I'm sitting here talking with a killer.*

"You're uncomfortable," the priest said. "I feel the need to reiterate that I have never killed anybody. Let's take your parents, Carrie and George Lemon. It's not my fault the truck driver stayed awake all night playing video poker. Who can blame him? He was on a serious winning streak before losing it all. Can't make a paycheck with the truck parked. He popped a few pills to stay awake, and *blam!* Good to go."

*He arranged the whole thing — from the lost wallet to the trucker.* Dan closed his eyes and inhaled slowly. *Don't let him win. Control the anger.*

"I know who you are," Dan said through gritted teeth. "You're the devil."

"Oh, you mean this guy?" Father August morphed into the classic leathery red form of the devil.

Dan jumped back and raised his hands defensively, causing Father August to roar in a booming devil laugh. "Does this scare you? Would you prefer this guy?" He morphed into a towering angel with blond hair and snow-white wings. A bright white aura enveloped him. "Repent, Daniel!"

*Shit!* Daniel cowered behind the bench. "Enough!"

Father August morphed back into his priest form. "You prefer the priest, eh? I thought so. You can come out. I'm done."

*Oh man, I'm way out of my league here. Keep him talking...* "What are you?" Dan said, climbing back onto his bench.

"I'm not *the* devil," he said, rolling his eyes. "Once, yeah, okay. But I've evolved. I've progressed. I change with the times. I've got the internet."

"What do you want from me?" Dan said.

"I need your help."

Dan chuckled. *He needs my help? How ironic.* "Can't you just whisper in my ear to make me do what you want me to do?"

"Yes, but I'd rather you cooperate. It would be in both our best interests."

"Is that why you haven't killed me yet? Like you did my parents? Like Andy?"

"Look, those turned out to be mistakes." Father August shook his head and waved his hand. "The world needed both you *and* Andy to build the DB algorithm. At the time, it was deemed essential for you two to be terminated and the Simulation restarted. And that's what should have happened. My mistake was not terminating you in the beginning. It's too late now. To think, one little confession was all it took for me to change my mind about you..."

The priest paced thoughtfully back and forth. Dan closed his eyes, and the graveyard disappeared, but only for a moment. *Should my grave be lying next to Andy's? Maybe it's supposed to be where I'm sitting?* Dan shook his head. "I'm confused," he said. "How can you go from needing to kill just Andy to realizing that you need either both of us alive or both of us dead?"

"Good question," Father August said. "I don't know. My job is to weed out the bad ones. For some reason, you and Andy were flagged as bad ones."

"What are you really?" Dan said, looking up from his bench. "Are you a virus checker? A debugger? Some sort of quality test?"

"You want a computer analogy? Fine." Father August put his hands on his hips. "I'm a bit of all three. You have to understand, I've been around since the beginning. Although I'm ageless, I'm not a supernatural being. I'm a core process. My job is to find selected individuals and test them. Ever see bad things happen to good people? That's my specialty. Good people need to be tested. Most decent people only need to be tempted once. Everyone forgets they're human sometimes. Humans have needs, and the Simulation is on a schedule. That's where I come in. Everyone needs to be sorted before the deadline."

"Deadline? That sounds like Judgment Day."

Father August folded his hands and smiled. "Bingo."

"Wait... Why would the devil want Judgment Day? Wouldn't you be in hell for eternal suffering along with all the other poor souls you tempted to do evil?"

"Again, I'm not *the* devil. On the contrary, I want Judgment Day to happen! It means I finally have a day off. You see, unlike you humans, I'm present for the whole creation-of-heaven-and-earth process. I get upgraded while you are lying around waiting for your next turn. I become more efficient with each iteration of the Simulation. Getting cast out of heaven is my starting gun. It means it's time for me to do my job."

"Isn't this inside information?" *He's going to kill me.* "Why are you telling me all this?"

"Like I said. I need your help. Besides, you've figured out most of it already, haven't you?" Father August sighed and sat next to Dan on the bench. "Since I can tell you're getting stressed, I'll get to the point. I want to know where Lemmy came from."

Dan exhaled a deep breath. *Finally he mentions Lemmy!* "I don't know where he's from. All I know is that he's here, and he says he is a friend."

"A friend?" Father August laughed. "Next question, how did the two of you get the materials to travel to the Recovery Domain?"

"Lemmy had them before I got there. He has some sort of paint that acts as a homing signal to receive deliveries."

Father August's face twisted into a frown. "Has Lemmy mentioned anyone else like him?"

"Yes. There's one more like him. Though they are looking for others."

Father August's face paled, and he looked away. *He's worried. Is that good or bad?* The silence permeated the graveyard. "You are a logical fellow," he said, "so follow along with my train of thought. Normally, if you had a simple corruption in your being, you would be killed and sent to purgatory to be fixed for your next iteration.

"However, you are infected *and* corrupted. Cleansing you is a much more involved process. We have to find out what the infection is trying to accomplish. I need to know when you became infected, how you became infected, and who caused the infection? Most importantly, can we stop it next time? How can we strengthen your code?"

"Does that mean I'm destined for purgatory?"

"*Everyone* is destined for purgatory." Father August laughed. "It's the default container. I'm not sending you back there infected. No, we have to root out the infection. But first I must study it. For starters, why were you targeted? What about you makes you vulnerable? We have to make a decision. Ultimately, can the Simulation move forward without you? If you don't exist, does anything change?"

"My choices are either purgatory or nonexistence?"

"Sorry, my job is to protect the Simulation." Father August leaned forward and whispered in Dan's ear. "Lemmy, can you hear me? Are you listening?"

Dan shook his head no. Lemmy didn't want to take a chance of being discovered by Father August, so he was to hide until Dan gave the all clear.

"Good. Listen closely, Dan. If we don't figure out what Lemmy wants, then we are in trouble. Do you know what Lemmy wants?"

"I don't know what his ultimate goal is," Dan said, "but I do know that he wants Andy."

"Andy?" Father August studied the tombstone. "Did he say why?"

Dan shrugged, and the priest's eyes went wide. "He can't do that, can he?" Father August said as he stalked away from Dan down the row of graves.

"What are you talking about?" Dan said. "What do you want me to do about Lemmy?"

"Go home," he said, walking away. "Pretend we never had this conversation."

"How in the hell am I supposed to do that?" Dan stood and chased after Father August, but he couldn't catch up. Out of breath, Dan found himself standing alone under a streetlight at the edge of the graveyard. *That's great. I still don't know who to trust. I'm in way over my head.*

# Twenty

"**S**HUT THE DOOR!" Lemmy shouted.

Dan hurriedly closed the door behind him. The apartment was bustling with both real and meta people. *What the hell is going on?* Blaine and Henry were in the living room, moving a brightly colored sofa from one end to the other. *That's the sofa from Henry's house.* Yvette was in the kitchen, unloading silverware from a box.

When he viewed the apartment with his meta eye, he could see that the walls were painted a shade of green similar to the one Lemmy had used on the truck. The Meta people had segregated themselves to the dining nook. Lemmy and Tania were engrossed in a conversation with another meta man Dan didn't recognize. *Looks like Lemmy moved on to the next phase of his plan. Should I tell him about Father August? Not yet...* "What's up with the new paint job? We're not taking the whole apartment to the Recovery Domain, are we?"

"That would be nice." Lemmy chuckled. "The paint is to stop Father August's ability to eavesdrop on us. You have to keep the door closed if it's gonna work."

Dan felt Yvette's hand on his shoulder.

"Who are you talking to?" she said.

"Lemmy," Dan said, giving her a quick hug hello. "What are you doing here? You were supposed to lie low."

181

"Things have changed," she said, waving at Blaine and Henry. "No. Put it over there."

They shook their heads and moved the sofa to the corner. Furniture donated from Henry's house filled the room. Dan's eyes fell on the large television in the center of the room. *Finally. It won't be so quiet now.* The dining room table and barstools had been replaced as well. *Where's my futon? On second thought, I don't want to know.* The modern furniture made the apartment look like a real home. "Thanks for the furniture, Henry," he said. "Are you moving in?"

"Henry isn't moving in," Yvette said with a wry smile. "I am."

"What?" Dan coughed. "You can't do that. What about the Simulation? It would have us both!"

"Let's stop kidding ourselves," she said, shaking her head. "The Simulation already knows everything about us. That Father August guy knows all about me. I wasn't safe at home as long as he could spy on me at will. Tania told me she has secured this apartment for all of us. We can talk without worrying about who's listening."

"She's right. This apartment is secure," Lemmy said proudly.

Dan's stomach twisted. *He's different. He's smiling and confident. He's in control.*

"Why is Henry giving us his furniture?" Dan asked.

"I'll tell you. Give me one sec…" Henry gave the couch a final adjustment. Satisfied, he clapped his hands and walked over to meet Dan. His shirt was untucked, his hair messy, and his beard was ridiculously ungroomed. *Is he in disguise? There is no way his beard could have grown that much.* "Hello there, Dan," he said in a macho voice. "Good to see you." Henry extended his arm and gave Dan a firm handshake.

*What? No kiss?* "What's going on?" Dan said. "Why the disguise?"

"This?" Henry scratched at his poorly glued-on costume beard. "It's not real. Sorry for the charade, but I didn't want to be seen coming here. I heard it's hazardous to one's health. Surely you understand?"

*He might be unrecognizable to people that know him, but the Simulation won't be fooled so easily.* "Why did you put yourself at risk coming here?" Dan said. "Why are you helping us?"

"I'm here because Blaine asked for my help," he said. "Yvette needed out of her house as soon as possible, and he reminded me that I owed him a favor. Besides, I can't help but feel partially responsible for this whole mess. You know, because I gave you guys Fana."

Blaine walked over and clasped Henry on the shoulder. "Thanks, buddy. I appreciate it."

Henry blushed and shrugged it off. "Anything to help a friend. Keep the furniture for as long as you need it. Just make sure it stays clean, okay?"

"We will do our best," Blaine said.

Henry turned his attention back to Dan. "I made a full six percent commission on that last home. Can you believe it? With that money, I'm going to Amsterdam on vacation for a couple of weeks. I normally don't travel at this time of year, but I have a feeling that I should leave the country as soon as possible."

"I know what you mean," Blaine said. "I feel the same way."

"Well." Henry wiped his hands on his pants and walked to the door. "Now that Dan's here to help arrange the furniture, I'll be leaving. It was nice to finally meet you, Yvette."

"Bye, Henry!" she said with a broad smile. "Nice to meet you too! Thank you!"

*No. Something's off.* Henry turned to leave, but Dan wedged himself between him and the door. He leaned in close as he grabbed Henry by the arm. "Before you go, I need to know something," he whispered.

Henry twisted in Dan's grasp. "You're hurting me," he said with a worried face. *Too hard.* Dan released him. *Calm down.* Henry's fake beard glistened with sweat.

"Sorry," Dan said, smoothing out Henry's shirt. "When we were at your house, you said voices told you to give Fana to Blaine."

Henry rubbed his arm. "Yeah. That's right."

"Did any of them mention names? Like, when they talked to each other?"

"No," he said uneasily. "The voices never called each other by names. But Avi came up a few times. I had assumed they meant Avi Psychedelics where Fana comes from. Though I don't recall dealing with an Avi when I was buying stock from them." Henry crinkled his nose. "I'd remember that sort of thing. I'm good with names."

*Avi? Never heard of him.* "Thank you for all your help," Dan said.

Henry straightened out his collar, then as if remembering he was supposed to be in disguise, crumpled it. "I'll see you all when I get back," Henry shouted to the room. He shot Dan an ugly look as if to say *not you* and slammed the door.

"What was that about? It looked like you were interrogating him," Blaine asked.

"Nothing," Dan said with an innocent grin. "I just wished him a safe trip."

"That's nice," Yvette said. "Now come sit in our new dining room."

As she slid onto a chair, Dan scanned the room. Tania and the new guy watched them quietly from the couch behind Blaine. "I have a feeling you two have a big announcement," he said, sitting across from the other two.

"We do," Blaine said. "I've taken Fana."

*Ah, that explains the new guy. And –* Dan examined Blaine with his meta eye. His meta avatar had spiked hair like an anime character. Blaine must like to party Japanese style. Dan shook his head. "Congrats, I guess."

"There's more. You see, Yvette and I, well..." Blaine turned and gazed into her eyes. "We care for each other. Look, I know you're married, and you're one of my best friends... I-I was jealous of the time you two were spending with each other..." Blaine stammered, trying to find the words. "She told me everything."

Dan heaved a sigh of relief. *It's nice having Blaine in on the conspiracy. Maybe he won't think I'm crazy anymore. But one thing I don't get... Blaine and Yvette? Eh...*

As if sensing his thoughts, Yvette planted a big kiss on Blaine's lips. She glanced to and from Dan so quickly he thought he had imagined it. "We were worried how you would react," she said, wiping away a tear. *Is she faking?*

"Well, buddy, there's no turning back now." Dan smiled wearily. "I guess it's safe to assume you are staying here too?"

"We've claimed the master bedroom. I hope you don't mind," Yvette said.

"The more the merrier. Besides," Dan said with a grimace, "it doesn't matter where we sleep. We don't have much time left anyway."

Lemmy sat silently at the kitchen table, taking it all in. Dan frowned. *What does he think about the new arrangement? It was probably his idea.*

"What do you mean, not a lot of time left?" Yvette said, crossing her legs. "What did you find out?"

Dan stood and paced the room. "Our simulation is in trouble."

"What? How can the *entire* simulation be in trouble?" Yvette said.

"I think it's because the wrong man died twenty years ago."

Lemmy bolted upright. Tania shouted something in a foreign language, and Lemmy went to join them on the sofa. They stole glances at Dan while they whispered excitedly among themselves.

"I don't understand," Blaine said as he dragged his chair closer to Yvette. "Why is a man who died twenty years ago relevant today?"

"His research is relevant," Dan said. "When he died, it vanished. All subsequent work in his area of expertise has been following a wrong path."

"If the man is dead, and his research is lost," Yvette said with a questioning eyebrow, "how do you know this?"

"The devil told me."

Lemmy and Tania shared a confused look. Blaine grinned and looked to Dan to see if he was joking. When Dan didn't flinch, he chuckled uncomfortably. "Uh... What?"

"You've heard us talk about Father August, the priest? He told me tonight he was the devil. It's true; he showed me. He grew wings and everything."

"Father August is the devil?" Yvette gasped. "You mean, *the* devil... biblically?"

Dan nodded. *Let Lemmy think I've been fed the religious explanation I'll explain to Blaine and Yvette later.*

"I knew it," she said.

"That's not all. He told me he made a mistake many years ago. A mistake he doesn't think can be corrected." Dan paused to make sure everyone was listening. "He is afraid."

"Afraid? Him? Besides God, what could he possibly be afraid of?" Blaine said.

Dan pointed across the room to the sofa where Lemmy's group was sitting.

"He's afraid of a couch?" Yvette said.

"Lemmy. I'm pointing at Lemmy. Sorry, I forgot you guys can't see him."

The three meta beings gave Dan a puzzled look, then went right back to talking to each other in their foreign language.

"Why does the devil care about Lemmy?" Yvette said.

"He didn't come out and say it, but I think it's because Lemmy isn't a part of this simulation."

Lemmy and Tania continued their conversation with each

other while the third just stared at Dan. *I don't like the looks of that one.*

"Blaine, before we go any further, did you download anyone while you were on Fana?"

Blaine glanced uneasily toward the new guy. "Go ahead. Tell him," Yvette said, nudging him with her elbow.

Blaine cleared his throat. "His name is Brian. I guess he's my version of Tania and Lemmy."

"Oh yeah?" Dan pretended to search the apartment. "Where is he?"

The three sitting on the couch went silent as Blaine pointed in their direction. "He's sitting over there on the couch."

Dan squinted in that direction but shrugged. "Tell him I said welcome."

Brian flipped Dan the bird, and the three went back to talking.

"He said thanks," Blaine said uneasily. Brian laughed arrogantly at Blaine. *The new guy is a bit of an asshole. I'm going to let them think he's invisible to me.*

"Where did they come from?" asked Yvette.

"Outside our universe," Dan said. "Father August wasn't sure what to make of Lemmy. That's saying a lot. Father August has been around a few times."

"Are they from a different dimension or something?" Yvette said as she twirled a piece of unread mail around on the table.

"Technically? Yes. Though that's too simplistic. That's like asking if they're from a different land. *Technically* there's land in Africa. There's also land on Mars. There's a big difference."

"There's also dirt on Uranus." Brian laughed rudely, and the other two shushed him. "What? They can't hear me." He smirked.

Dan frowned involuntarily. *Ignore him...*

"Okay," Yvette said. "But did Father August give you any clues as to *why* they are here?"

"Yes." The meta beings stopped talking and focused on Dan. "They're here for Father August's mistake. They are here for Andrew O'Riley."

"Who?" Blaine asked.

"Andy and I were in college together twenty years ago. When I was a junior, he was in the second year of his master's program. To make a long story short, Father August killed him because his ideas about databases and artificial intelligence and machine learning were too advanced."

Blaine whistled. "Pretty heavy stuff for twenty years ago. Today? Not so much. My vacuum cleaner has an AI. What's the big deal?"

Dan shook his head. "I don't know. I think we, as a society, are supposed to be further along the technology tree than we are now. When Father August killed Andy, it stunted humanity's technology growth beyond repair."

"What do you mean *beyond repair?*" Yvette asked.

"It means we are too far along to start over and achieve a satisfactory result. Even if we started today, it would take decades to rewrite everything to conform to Andy's standards."

Lemmy appeared in the middle of the room. Blaine and Yvette climbed out of their chairs. "You're wrong, Dan," he said. "It wouldn't take decades."

"Whoa, who the hell are you?" Blaine said.

"I didn't mean to startle you," he said with a friendly smile. "I'm Lemmy. I'm visible to you through Brian and to Yvette via Tania. It's easier this way."

*They can do that? Could they always do that? Is this a game to them?*

"Dan is right. Father August made a grave mistake. It became clear when we analyzed Dan's memories."

"You what?" Dan said, rising out of his chair. "I didn't give you permission—"

"Relax. We found what we needed quickly. It was an event that is always on your mind. Your parents' funeral. Watch—"

Dan's brain was suddenly transported into an unwanted replay of his past. Twenty years ago. December 30. *Not this again.* Two cherry caskets beneath an altar covered in poinsettias. Inside those caskets were his parents. They burned to death in a fiery crash on I-10 on Christmas Eve. A sleep-deprived trucker crossed into their lane, pinning them underneath his load. They were on their way to Baton Rouge to bring Dan home for Christmas. It was only because Dan had lost his wallet the night before at Andy's party. A beautiful woman walked in—Katie. *Look at how young she was!* She knelt and made the sign of the cross before entering a pew across the aisle from Dan. A loud cough echoed throughout the church. *This is new. I don't remember anyone coughing.*

It came from a man huddled in the far back pew. It was Andy. Usually, when this memory comes up, it's Katie's tear-streaked face he remembered. This time the coughing drew his attention. Andy was sick. *Why didn't I realize that before?* He was rocking back and forth and mumbling to himself. *Andy is talking to someone meta. But this was twenty years ago. We didn't have Fana...* The memory continued, and soon the service was over. Andy sat alone, talking to himself. When Dan approached, Andy coughed into a paper napkin and smiled softly. He said something to Andy, and Andy responded, but both ends of the conversation were in gibberish. *Why can't I understand myself talk? Is this memory censored?* Andy reached into his jacket and handed the wallet back to Dan. It was warm. Another smile. More gibberish. A firm handshake. Andy burst into a violent coughing fit and walked out the double doors of the church, ushering in an icy wind that blew through the aisles and tousled Dan's hair.

When he opened his eyes, he was back in the apartment. "Andy was there."

"Unfortunately," Lemmy said seriously. "He developed a serious respiratory infection and collapsed on the street outside his home. He fell into a coma and was unresponsive for months. He was eventually declared brain dead, and they pulled the plug."

"I didn't know what happened to him. Thanks for telling me," Dan said solemnly. "Andy was a good dude. He was returning my wallet. He didn't deserve to die."

"Okay," Blaine said. "Why is this bit of information important now?"

"Andy's last words to Dan were the last ones he spoke to anybody before he went into his coma. Using Dan's memory as a reference, we can track it. We can now find him in the Database of Souls."

"Database of Souls?" Dan shot Lemmy a confused look. "You mean purgatory?"

"Is he talking about bringing Andy back from the dead?" Yvette said.

"Yes," Lemmy said with a proud smile. "We will bring Andy back from the dead."

*Wow.* The three humans sat silently, exchanging dubious glances.

"You're not serious?" Yvette laughed.

She looked to Dan for signs of a joke, but he didn't move. Lemmy's mouth tightened, and he folded his arms.

"He's serious, Yvette," Blaine said.

"Why Andy?" Yvette said. "Why not Stephen Hawking?"

"Yeah," Blaine added. "Why not Carl Sagan or Galileo or Jesus?"

"Because Jesus doesn't need to be fixed. It's not Andy's reasoning skills we need. It's his knowledge and research." Lemmy winked at Tania. "Dan mentioned earlier that Father August made a mistake. We're here to fix it. Think of us like a patch. We're trying to bring back a feature that was unexpectedly removed. Now, if we work together, I believe we can get Andy back. If we do that, we can get this simulation back on track."

*If this is true, maybe Lemmy isn't a virus after all. If Andy could be saved from purgatory, why wouldn't Father August have done it already? He should be powerful enough to do it. If Andy can make it right, why didn't he bring him back? Why is he letting a group of outsiders do it? It doesn't add up.*

"All right, Lemmy," Dan said. "How do you propose we get Andy out of purgatory—I mean the Database of Souls?"

Lemmy's face broke into a toothy grin, but the smile didn't reach his eyes.

"It's going to require a leap of faith, Dan. A big leap."

# Twenty-One

D AN SAT ON the cement bench in front of Andy's grave. He had almost given up on Katie until the sound of high heels echoing off the tombstones announced her presence. "A graveyard?" she said. "You're being a little dramatic, don't you think?"

"Thanks for coming, Katie," Dan said quietly. "I wouldn't have asked if it weren't important."

"Dan, I have work. I don't have time for this. I've tried calling you. Where is your cell phone? Why *are* we meeting in a graveyard?" She threw up her hands in frustration. "Look, I'm tired of the drug drama. I don't want a big emotional revelation. I don't need another dependent, Dan. I just want to go on with my life."

"Please sit." Dan patted the seat next to him. Katie let out an exasperated sigh but sat down anyway. "I still love you."

"I love you too, Dan," Katie said while checking her watch. "But it isn't enough anymore. We have responsibilities— children to raise. I can't even deal with my own problem, much less your problems too. I can't help you, Dan. You need to help yourself."

Dan put his elbows on his knees and sagged his head. *Oh, Katie... I'm so sorry for what I'm about to do. You don't deserve this. I hope you can find happiness in the next life.*

"Dan, we have an obligation to our children. Why can't you put them first for once? You threw it all away for what? Yvette? Drugs? That's the most selfish thing I can imagine."

*I can't tell you the truth. The truth would kill you.* "Katie, I can't explain," he said. "I don't have time to make you understand."

"That's right," Katie said with a sob. "I *don't* understand. We were a team!"

She reached in her pocket and grabbed a tissue to blot her eye. Dan put his arm around her shoulders, but she shrugged it away.

"We still are a team, Katie," Dan said, holding back tears of his own. "It's the bottom of the ninth, we're losing, and I'm at bat. Here" — Dan pulled the carton of Fana out of his pocket and offered it to Katie — "I want you to have this."

Katie's eyes narrowed, and her face went red. "I'm not doing drugs, Dan. How many times do I have to tell you that! *I* have children to raise! I can't believe you would even suggest — "

"Katie, listen to me for a second. There may come a time when you are ready to understand what I've done. When the time comes, find Yvette. She will explain."

"You want me to talk to your druggie girlfriend? You *have* lost your mind."

Katie threw the Fana pack across the grave. The cardboard bounced off a marble slab and landed in a concrete urn. The empty blister pack lay near Dan's feet.

"Katie, trust me for once."

"I've trusted you my whole life, and here we are!"

Dan reached into his pocket and pulled out the gummies that he had popped out of the pack of Fana. *I'm sorry, Katie.*

"I told you, I'm not taking those!"

Dan put them all in his mouth and chewed. *This better work.*

"Dan! Dan!" screamed Katie.

Dan swallowed the big lump, and it caught in his throat before finally sliding down.

"What did you do? What was that? Are you getting high right now?"

Dan coughed violently and sat gingerly on the concrete bench. "No, Katie, that was a lethal dose."

Katie narrowed her eyes. "Is this a joke? If it is, it isn't funny."

Dan coughed blood and spit it onto the concrete sidewalk. "No joke. I've just committed suicide. I'm going to die of an overdose."

Her eyes went wide. "I have to call the police." She frantically patted her pockets for her cell phone, but she must have left it in the car. "Help! Is anyone there?"

Dan tried to stand but stumbled over to the marble slab covering the grave and collapsed on top of it. "Katie," he whispered. "I'm sorry. I hope you'll understand someday."

Katie cried. "I'll go get help. Stay here, you jerk!"

Dan grabbed her arm. "Go to Father Desjeunes. He hasn't left for the hospital yet."

She gave him a curt nod and ran off toward the small white house. *Well, it's happening.* Dan spat out another glob of blood. *I thought death would be less... painful...* A slow clap pierced the silence. Father August had witnessed the whole thing.

"Suicide? I'm impressed. I don't think I can take the credit for this one."

*Oh good. He's here.* Dan could barely keep his eyes open. The drugs were acting much quicker than he anticipated.

"Leave me in peace," Dan muttered.

"Oh, I'm not going to miss this," Father August said with a grin. "This will be fun."

"You mean my Judgment?"

Father August nodded and sat on the bench. "This should be good. I'm pretty sure you're guilty of a few mortal sins. Did you go to confession like the good priest advised?"

Dan weakly shook his head.

"Well then, it looks like I won't be seeing you around next time."

"Guess not," Dan said with a faint smile.

Father August cocked his head. "What did you say?"

Katie and Father Desjeunes ran up the path to the graveyard. "There he is!"

"Call the ambulance!" Father Desjeunes ordered.

"I don't have a phone," Katie said.

Father Desjeunes reached into his pocket and handed Katie his phone. She frantically pressed numbers as he bent down and put his ear to Dan's chest.

"He's overdosing." Katie sobbed into the phone.

Father Desjeunes stood over Dan and made the sign of the cross. "In the name of the Father and the Son…"

"Wait, what is he doing?" Father August's smile disappeared. A panicked look crossed his face, and he rushed over to Katie and whispered in her ear. Her eyes glazed over, and she dropped the phone.

"Don't give him his last rites," she said. "He hasn't been a good Christian!"

Father Desjeunes glared at her. "How dare you, Katie! Would you want such cruelty to you on your death bed?"

Katie's face flushed with embarrassment. "I'm sorry. I don't know why I said that, Father. Wait, is he really dying?"

Katie burst into tears and held Dan's hand. The ambulance's siren wailed in the distance. Father Desjeunes produced the Eucharist from a pouch he was carrying and placed it in Dan's mouth.

"No! Stop!" Father August raged. "Who carries Viaticum with them?"

"I was getting ready to make my usual morning rounds at the hospital," said Father Desjeunes.

Father August's mouth fell open. "I thought you couldn't hear me."

"Who are you talking to, Father?"

"Nobody," he said, shooting a dirty look at Father August.

With the Last Rites administered, Dan could relax. His passage into purgatory had been guaranteed. In a world of simulations and computers, some of the old codes and commands still had use. The sirens grew louder, and the voices of Katie and Father Desjeunes faded away until *bang!* The world went quiet.

Dan died.

Data offloaded from his body and collected above it like a spirit. As it gathered, Dan became whole again. This time in energy form. He looked down upon his lifeless body with sadness and regret. Dan imagined most people experienced this moment with a sense of awe and self-reflection. Not him. Only one thought crossed his mind. *I hope this works!*

With a crisp *pop,* a warm, bright light pierced existence and enveloped Dan. It was pure grace. In an instant, Dan was judged. His destination was set. The light's form changed from a bright white beacon to a scanning laser. It was encapsulating his data to send to purgatory. He opened his eyes and smiled at Father August. *This is it.*

"Get him!" Dan shouted.

With a high-pitched, electronic scream, Lemmy pounced on Father August. His entire body had been coated in green paint. He looked like a giant, deranged leprechaun. The paint acted like glue and attached him to Father August's form.

"What are you doing?" the priest shouted frantically as he tried to pry Lemmy off of him. "You can't do this. It's not possible."

They fell to the ground at the foot of the grave and struggled. Father August wrestled with Lemmy, but he was firmly attached. Dan's spirit form changed during the battle. Green streaks ran through its veins. *Fana coated my data stream!* Midstruggle, Lemmy grabbed Dan's glowing foot and latched on.

"Dan! What have you done?" shouted Father August.

The beam of light intensified and took the three men. When it disappeared, Dan's lifeless body was all that remained.

# Twenty-Two

D AN BOLTED AWAKE. *Where am I?* Warm sunlight filtered in
through the blinds. He threw back the sheets and rubbed
his eyes. *These sheets... I haven't seen them since — Wait. I was in
the middle of something...* He ran to the window and peered
through the blinds. His first truck was parked out on the street.
Its back half was covered in mud. *I went dove hunting yesterday. I
need to get it washed before —* He checked his wristwatch, one p.m.
*Shit! Tonight's homecoming! I have to pick up Katie at five for dinner!*

Dan threw on his basketball shorts and a T-shirt and ran
outside. He pulled his truck into the driveway and grabbed the
hose and bucket. *I'll never get it clean in time. Why did Mom let me
sleep so late? Right, they're in New Orleans for their anniversary
weekend. It's my own fault for staying up late playing video games.
Ugh!* Dan cursed as he kicked loose a large clod of mud from the
back wheel well.

As he switched to the other side of the truck, a small brown
car pulled into the driveway and honked its horn. "Hey, Dan,
how's it going?"

*Cindy? What's she doing here?* She was the prettiest cheerleader
at school. She flashed him a big smile as she got out of the car.
Dan's heart sank. He had a crush on her since eighth grade.
Unfortunately, she had always been off-limits. She was good
friends with Katie, and she was Tommy's girlfriend. Those were

two big strikes. Still, on more than one occasion, Dan was sure she was checking him out, but he had always dismissed it as wishful thinking.

"It's going okay," he said, squinting against the sun. "Trying to get all the mud off. Don't think I'll have time to wax it."

"Don't worry about the wax. Katie and I took care of that yesterday," she said with a flirtatious smile. "Just make sure the back seat is clean."

Dan blushed but continued washing. He and Katie hadn't made it to the back seat yet. There had been rumors Cindy and Tommy had gone all the way. If they had, Tommy had kept his mouth shut. *Why is she here?* She brushed past Dan and ran a finger along the dirty fender.

"Your truck *is* filthy," she said as she wiped her muddy finger on Dan's T-shirt. "Why don't you take your parents' car to the dance?"

*Damn she smells good.* Dan swallowed hard and hosed off another clod. "They're out of town for the weekend," he said. "But yeah, that would have been nice."

"Your parents are out of town? On homecoming night? You're throwing a party, right?"

She giggled and pulled up her skirt, revealing more of her long legs. Dan quickly turned his head and fiddled with the hose. "Uh… How come you're not getting your hair done with Katie and the rest of the girls? I thought it was the tradition for y'all to do it at the same time."

"I *should* be there. But what's the point?" She pouted her lips and sighed. "I'm not going to the dance tonight."

Dan dropped the hose, and it squirted. "O-oh, really? I thought Tommy was taking you. We're all supposed to be going to dinner together."

"I guess you haven't talked to Tommy today?" she said with folded arms. "He skipped school to get beer for tonight and got busted. He's lucky his parents didn't kill him."

Dan filled a bucket with water. *I hope Katie knows. She won't be happy with the change of plans.*

"What was he doing getting beer? He didn't tell me that."

"I know, right? He wanted it to be a surprise."

*I could use a beer right now.* He took a rag from the soapy bucket and wiped down the truck. He stole a glance at Cindy's backside as he worked.

"You know, Dan," she said, biting her lip. "Since I'm not going tonight, I wanted to get started on the coding project for our group in comp-sci. I lost the sheet with the breakdown of assignments. Do you have it?"

Dan dropped the rag and rinsed the soap off his hands. "Sure, I have it in my book bag. Come in," Dan said, drying his hands on his shirt.

Cindy gave him a wry smile and followed him inside the house. As soon as the front door closed, she spun him around and wrapped one of her long legs around his. Before he knew it, her tongue was down his throat. She grabbed his butt and thrust her body close to his. He didn't resist. The room went black.

⊷◈◈◈⊶

Dan awoke with a start. *Where am I?* Warm sunlight filtered in through the blinds. He threw back the sheets and rubbed his eyes. An overwhelming sense of déjà vu froze Dan in place. *I was just here. Wasn't I? No, something's different.* He peered through the blinds. His truck was still parked on the street in front of his parents' house. Its back half was still covered in mud. He checked his wristwatch, two p.m. He was supposed to pick up Katie for the homecoming dance at five! He leaped out of bed, threw on his shorts and T-shirt, and rushed outside to wash his truck.

He hadn't been washing more than a few minutes before a small brown car pulled into the driveway. It was Cindy, the prettiest cheerleader at school, and his computer science lab partner.

Dan walked over and met her at her car as she rolled down her window. "Hey, Cindy. What's up?"

"Hey, Dan!" Cindy smiled. "I came by earlier and knocked, but nobody answered. Do you have the worksheet for the computer science project?"

"Sorry about that," Dan said, scratching his head. "I was sleeping. I must not have heard the doorbell."

"That's okay," she said, turning off her car. "Do you have time to go over it with me?"

"No, I don't. Katie's gonna be pissed if I'm late," Dan said, wiping his hands on his shirt. "Wait right here while I go get the assignment list."

Dan turned and jogged to the house.

"Wait!" Cindy shouted. "I can help. How do you know you have the right one?"

Dan poked his head out the door. "You can call me tomorrow if it isn't!"

⥤◈◈◈⥢

Dan awoke with a headache. *Where am I? Why am I on the floor?* The room was blurry.

"Dan? Are you okay? I got you as soon as I could. You're—"

"Give him a minute." A strong set of hands picked him up off the floor and dragged him over to a nearby chair. Though his face was blurred, the scowl was clear. It was Father August. "You yanked him out of purgatory. No telling where he was in the process. He could be corrupt."

"What happened?" He winced as things came into focus. "Where am I?"

A pink flamingo smiled down from the wall. He was back in Lemmy's Florida condo. Lemmy sat on the sofa and smiled at him like he'd won the lottery.

"You're in a nightmare," Father August said, pacing the room like a caged tiger.

"No." Lemmy grinned and pointed at Father August. "You're in his meta."

"What have you done?" He fumed. "Do you realize what you've done?"

"Yeah! We rescued Dan from the Database of Souls!" exclaimed Lemmy.

"No, you idiot, you've doomed us all. Every single one of us. Even me!"

"I can't believe it happened so quickly. My meta was uploaded to his instantaneously," Lemmy said, turning his back to the priest. "Everything's easier from here. No offense, Dan, but his brain is warp speed compared to yours."

Father August spat and grabbed Dan by the shirt. "It's your fault. Now he's embedded, and I can't get rid of him. Do you have any idea what you've done? He can't be in here!"

Dan pried the man's hands off his shirt. "Now you know how I felt."

"You *still* don't get it," the priest said with a growl. "With my permissions, he can access core databases."

"I know," Dan said. "That was the whole point."

"I thought we had an understanding." Father August shook his head. "I'm disappointed in you. You're a traitor."

"Ignore him, Dan," Lemmy said. "As long as he's trapped here with us, he can't harm you. He's locked in his own meta like Chinese finger cuffs."

Father August narrowed his eyes at Dan. "You made a big mistake," he said through gritted teeth. He shot a menacing glance at Lemmy and stalked off to sit alone.

"Well, this is great," Dan said. "Has he been this cheerful the whole time?"

"He's not having a good day," Lemmy said with a chuckle. "We battled it out, that's for sure. He may be powerful, but we found his Achilles' heel."

"Did you have any trouble accessing purgatory?"

"Nope! It all went according to plan. From here, I was easily able to trace your signature to your location in the database. At that point, there was only the matter of extracting you from it. I punched in your coordinates and connected them to ours. Presto! You're on the yellow square."

Father August banged his hand on the wall in anger. "You corrupted the database. That's what you did. The purgatory correction algorithm was running on Dan. You yanked him out midscan!"

"It was necessary!" Dan said, turning on Father August. "It was because of your mistake that we had to do this at all. If anyone is at fault, it's you!"

"I don't have to take this from you, human," he said with a sneer. "You aren't going to fix it. You'll only make it worse. Let me out of here before you do any more damage!" Father August opened the front door, revealing a pitch-black void beyond. He turned and slammed it behind him. "A void gap? How?"

"It's necessary," said Lemmy.

"He really is trapped inside his own head, isn't he?" Dan said incredulously.

"Yep." Lemmy laughed. "He's paralyzed in the Actual, Meta, and all other domains. He can't access his other nodes. There's nothing he can do to stop us."

"You can't keep me here forever, Lemmy," Father August said with a confident smile. "I'll get out eventually. What happens to you when I get out depends on you. Cooperate, and I'll go easy on you. Tell me, who are you working for?"

Lemmy glanced quickly at Dan. "I work for myself."

As the two argued back and forth, Dan groaned. All the shouting had made his headache worse. *Am I going to have to deal with these two fighting the whole time?* He poured himself a glass of water from the kitchen sink and quickly gulped down half of it. "Hey, Lemmy!" Dan yelled from the kitchen, hoping to interrupt their argument. "How long have I been dead?"

"Two hours tops."

Father August walked over to the sliding glass balcony doors, grabbed the handle, and slid it open. Again, he was greeted by the void. The white sand and crashing waves were an illusion. He quickly slid the door closed and sank to the floor. *Did he give up?*

"Two hours?" Dan said. "That's all? It felt like forever."

"The correction algorithm runs unbelievably fast on offline objects," Father August said in a low voice. "Purgatory objects are all offline."

"What was it like?" Lemmy said.

"It's hard to say." Dan squinted. "Some years flashed in the blink of an eye. Most of it was really just a few key moments repeated in different ways. Like, I was reliving a moment back when I was seventeen. I was about to have sex with the prettiest cheerleader in school when you yanked me out."

"Sorry, man," Lemmy said with a grin. "Want me to send you back?"

"Oh no!" Dan said, shaking his head. "You did me a favor. The scenario would stop and start over before anything *really* happened if you know what I mean."

"Ouch. In that case, you're welcome. That is unless you want perpetual blue balls."

"I'm good." Dan chuckled. "Anyway, back in real life, I did 'do it' with Cindy, but I regretted it. I kept it a secret from Katie for the rest of my life. Do you know what a burden that is? Cindy was pissed I didn't choose her. She torpedoed our senior comp-sci project, and I finished with a C average. It cost me a scholarship."

"I guess the point of reliving that moment was to free you from the lie?"

"No," Father August said. "If he had maintained even a B average, he would have started off taking freshman-level computer science classes rather than remedial. He would have met Andy sooner."

"I think he's right," Dan said. "Katie and I get married anyway. The remedial classes were a total waste of time. It had to have been about correcting the grade. Preventing Cindy from sabotaging the project was the answer."

"Now do you see why this was a mistake?" Father August said. "You stopped our deep corrective programming for this. The algorithm will probably delete you and move on to the next person who could serve as the solution. It may take a couple more runs to find the right guy, but it always does. You've just delayed everything."

"He's already been deleted," Lemmy said, pointing at his computer monitor.

"What?" Dan rushed over to Lemmy's computer and leaned over his shoulder. A string of seemingly random numbers poured over a black background.

"People are identified according to their physical birth date. Each one is unique because it is measured in Planck Time from the Epoch of the Sim. Everyone's true birthday is unique. The number marks the instant your parents' base code is joined. Not from when you slide out of a vagina. Your ID is in the fourteen billion range. You see—"

"I don't care about that!" Dan said. "You were saying I was deleted?"

"Right, the select statement I used to find you by your ID is no longer returning any results. You're gone."

Father August laughed so hard he went into a coughing fit. "The table was locked," he said. "You used my elevated privileges to copy him midscan. That automatically changed the modified date to a time after Dan had already died. You dumbass."

Lemmy turned pale. "I didn't think of that."

"What?" Dan grabbed Lemmy by the shoulder. "What did you do?"

"I had assumed there wouldn't be a meta check midscan. I thought it performed it at the beginning. I guess the system marked your entry as corrupt to stop it from corrupting other data. You've been deleted."

"It did what it was supposed to do," Father August said. "I could have told you that."

"What now? When the Simulation is rerun, it'll be like I never existed?"

"Correct." Father August flashed a condescending grin. "You'll never exist in any subsequent Simulation. All your deeds, good and bad, are gone for eternity."

"Don't let him scare you, Dan," Lemmy said. "You're still here. There's a chance we can reinsert you into the Database of Souls — with Father August's help, of course."

"I don't see why I would want to do that," he said. "It would only cause more damage or corruption."

Dan shot Lemmy a confused look. "Why do we need him to do it? Why can't you restore me from here with his privileges?"

Lemmy shook his head. "Dan, you have to consider where you are. We are in Father August's meta. We still need his help."

"You've taken me out of purgatory before. You obviously spoofed his permissions from this meta to access that database. We know it works. Do it again. What do we need him for?"

"He has to enter the credentials for me to access the database. He has built-in two-factor authentication. His password is always changing."

"Well, he's obviously done it once already. Make him do it again! How did you convince him to do it the first time?"

"I promised I'd let him go if he did it."

"We see how that worked out, don't we?" Father August laughed from his oversized chair. "The hardest thing to mend is broken trust. You still haven't learned that, have you, Lemmy?"

*Lemmy screwed up? That's not possible. Could he have done it on purpose? Now I need Father August's permission to go back. Shit!*

Dan gulped, but his mouth had no spit to swallow. *This isn't part of the plan.* "If I understand you correctly," he said, "I don't exist in the Actual, purgatory, or anywhere else. Only here, cached inside Father August's metadata? Oh man."

"Relax, Dan," Lemmy said. "It's only until I convince him to write your data to a database where he has access."

"Yeah, Dan, relax," Father August said. "I tell you what; if *you* let me go and help me get rid of Lemmy, I'll put you back in purgatory. You can pick up where you left off. It was that day with Cindy, right? I can make it so that you can stay there long enough to finish the job."

*Tempting. Trust the evil priest or Lemmy? Either way, I'm being used. There is no right answer. Lemmy has the upper hand now.* Dan shook his head. "No deal. I'm already dead, and we've come this far. I'm sticking with the original plan. We're going to fix the mistake and boost the Simulation forward. Lemmy, let's get Andy."

"I knew you'd say that," Lemmy said with a smile. "Just say the word. I have the command ready to execute."

Dan glanced at Father August, who shot him a quick smile and a wink. *What game is he playing? Does he want the mistake fixed or not?* Dan's cheeks flushed with anger. "Do it."

# Twenty-Three

**W**ITH A SICKENING *crack*, Andy materialized onto the orange square in the corner of the room. He wavered briefly as his muscles acclimated but stood firm. Dan's mouth hung open. He looked the same. He wasn't sick. He wasn't old. He was still twenty-three. His eyes darted back and forth between Dan and Lemmy. "Who are you people?" he said with a cracked voice. "Where am I?"

"You're in hell!" Father August boomed in a devilish voice.

Andy's face went pale, and he spun around. When he saw the priest sitting in the chair, his knees buckled. "Y-you," he said. "Wh-what are y-you doing here?"

Father August slapped his knee and fell into a fit of laughter.

"Ignore him!" Lemmy shouted as he inserted himself between Andy and the priest. "You're not in hell, and he can't hurt you."

"It... it w-was him," Andy said, visibly shaken. "He killed me. After— I was sent to a place..." His eyes glazed over, then fell on Dan. "You look familiar. Are you Dan's father? I am in hell, aren't I?"

Dan smiled softly and shook his head. "I'm Dan."

"That can't be..."

Lemmy grabbed Andy by the shoulder and guided him to sit

209

on the sofa. "We have a lot to catch you up on," he said. "Would you like a cup of coffee? Maybe a cigarette? Or a vape?"

Andy's eyes went wide. "No! No vapes!" His hands shook, and Father August laughed even harder.

"He's just out of purgatory," Lemmy whispered to Dan. "He must have had a rough time with the vape thing. Good thing consciousness and memory don't carry over from one existence to the next, eh?"

"I'm sorry," Andy said, rubbing his eyes. "Did I hear you say *purgatory?*"

"Yes," Lemmy said. "We rescued you from the Database of Souls—"

"Andy, we need your help," Dan said. "Our universe is a simulation, and it's in trouble. Your research on databases is crucial to saving it."

Andy looked from Dan to Lemmy, then to Father August. His mouth cracked into a smile. "This is another test, isn't it?"

"No, I'm serious," Dan said. "We need you and your research."

Andy chuckled to himself, then put his hands on his knees and stood. He walked over to the sliding glass door and opened it. His hair was briefly sucked forward as he was greeted by the void. His hands slipped on the handle as he quickly slid the door shut. Wild-eyed, he walked past everyone to one of the bedrooms and locked the door.

"That went well," Lemmy said.

Dan went to the bedroom door and listened in, but Andy was silent. "Give him time."

"Well, good luck," Father August said with a chuckle. "I'll be in the other room when you're ready for me."

"Wait, you can't just—"

The priest didn't care. The door closed and locked behind him.

"What do we do now?" Dan said.

Lemmy grinned mischievously. "Now we get to work! First let's get you a computer."

"What am I going to do with—?" Dan wobbled on his feet and knelt on the floor. *What's happening to me?* The room blurred in and out of focus.

"Shit," Lemmy said, standing over him. "I was worried this would happen."

———◦◎◦———

*What's wrong with him?*

*It was too soon between his time in the Actual and here. You were in the Database of Souls long enough to be prepped for another stage.*

*About that. I need to know everything—*

*How long is he going to be on the sofa like that? Move him to a bedroom.*

*Why don't you go back into your bedroom, you murderer?*

*Still angry? That was years ago. Water under the bridge—*

*I think Dan's awake! Dan, can you hear me?*

———◦◎◦———

*No, Andy, you see, it's simple. The law firm is real now. We created it. Any documents we create will be completely real and legal. I've emailed Blaine and Yvette, and they know what to do. Just relax—*

*He moved!*

The room blinked back into focus. "What's happening?"

"Dan, you're alive!"

"We have to hurry. He may not be awake long," Lemmy said, standing over him.

Fast-food containers, empty beer cans, and pizza boxes littered the floor. The flamingo painting hung askew, and there was a hole in the sliding glass door. Andy and Lemmy knelt by his side with worried expressions.

"Where's Father August?" Dan groaned.

"He hasn't come out of his room for a couple of days," Andy said. "Which is fine with me."

"What's going on?"

"Your body isn't handling the change in context very well. I'm working on a way to fix it. Until then, you'll have to just deal with being in and out of consciousness."

"Dan, this is amazing," Andy said. "The Simulation is real. I told you!"

Lemmy brushed him aside. "We don't have time for this," he said. "Dan, the plan is moving forward. We have contact with Yvette's group in the Actual, and they are proceeding—"

"We have unlimited money!"

"What? How?"

"It's really cool! I was poking around the database and noticed a discrepancy. There's this bank called Neydwell Bank. Its capital balance is infinity." Andy's eyes went wide. "Infinity! We got in using Father August's credentials and were able to issue debit cards for our whole team. We know they work because Yvette went out and bought funeral clothes and a camera with them. Isn't that awesome?"

"Funeral clothes?" Dan said.

Andy's face switched from excitement to embarrassment. Lemmy's mouth tightened at the edges. "Yeah, um. She's going to your funeral tomorrow. She had planned on recording it for you. If that's okay."

*My funeral? Shit. I forgot I was dead.* Dan imagined what his funeral would be like. Katie sitting in the front row. Carrie holding her hand. Al to her other side, head down, trying to be strong... *I can't take it. I'm not gone yet.* "No," he said. "Call it off."

"I told you," Andy said to Lemmy.

"Whatever you want, Dan."

"I want you to keep going. Don't let me hold you back. Okay?" Dan grabbed Andy by the shirt. "Promise."

Andy jerked back reflexively. "Okay. I promise."

"Thanks," Dan said. Their faces disappeared as the room faded to black.

# Twenty-Four

START THE STREAM!

*Stop yelling! Aww – see what you did? He's awake! Now we have to –*

*I don't care! I've waited hours for this! Press Play!*

A slender hand reached out and knocked on the front door, followed by a brief glance at an expensive, lady's wristwatch. A fragile-looking elderly woman answered the door. "Can I help you?" she said. *She's so old!*

"Mrs. O'Riley?"

"Yes," she said, adjusting her bifocals. "How can I help you?"

"My name is Yvette Boudreaux, and I'm a paralegal with Fruge, Fontenot, and Flynn. May I have a few minutes of your time? It's about your son Andy."

A look of confusion swept across her face. "Andy? What could this possibly be about after all these years?"

"It's about his life insurance. It went unclaimed. May I come in?"

Yvette followed Mrs. O'Riley into the house where she was offered a seat on an overstuffed flower-print sofa. The old lady smiled politely as Yvette set her briefcase on the coffee table. She winced as a high-pitched squeal blared through her earpiece. *Good, he needs to see this. Shut up Andy! Fix your camera, Yvette.*

"Sorry," Yvette said, pointing to her earphones. "I'm getting a ton of interference."

"That's quite all right, ma'am," Mrs. O'Riley said politely. "My hearing aid acts up from time to time as well."

Yvette sat straight and adjusted the secret camera attached to her brooch to point directly at Mrs. O'Riley. "Ah, it's gone," she said with a smile as she opened the briefcase. "Now. The reason I'm here is because of Andy's life insurance policy."

"This is all very strange. I was told he didn't have a policy. If he did, it would have come in handy to pay for the burial twenty-odd years ago."

"Right," Yvette said, narrowing her eyes. "Well, it's embarrassing, really. In college, Andy was friends with Robert Flynn III, who was the son of one of our founding partners. From what we can tell, Bobby convinced your son Andy to draw up a simple will and trust. Andy had two life insurance policies. He had one with the school to cover his student loans and one with an independent agent. When Andy died, Bobby cashed in Andy's insurance policies and used those funds for his personal investment objectives."

"The lawyer's son stole Andy's money?"

Yvette shifted on the couch and frowned. "Yes, he did."

"Did he go to jail?"

"No. Bobby was sloppy and left a paper trail. His father, Flynn Jr., found out and made him abandon the investment accounts. The idea was to cover their tracks. Instead of shredding the evidence, Bobby hid it in the back of the filing cabinet. He wanted to be able to access the money in case of an emergency."

"He stole our money," she said angrily. "Typical Louisiana bullshit! It's not right."

Yvette stifled a smile. "We at Fruge, Fontenot, and Flynn agree with you, Mrs. O'Riley. Bobby passed away without ever cashing in. We discovered the missing files while cleaning out his desk. I'm here to return what's rightfully yours." Yvette reached across the table and handed her a check.

Mrs. O'Riley stared silently at the check for a few moments. "Is this a joke or a scam or something? What am I supposed to do with this amount of money?"

"I promise it's not a scam. You can do whatever you want. It's yours."

The old woman's hands shook. "What can I say but thank you?"

The two women stood and gave each other a hug. Mrs. O'Riley looked at the check again and shook her head. "Where are my manners?" she said, smoothing out her shirt. "Would you like a cup of coffee? Of course not! This calls for wine — no, champagne!"

"Thank you, but no," Yvette said politely. "I'm afraid I do have a personal favor to ask."

"A personal favor?" she said skeptically. "What sort of personal favor?"

"Do you have any of Andy's high school yearbooks? While I was researching your case, I realized that Andy graduated the same year as my uncle Wayne Boudreaux. His house burned to the ground last year. They lost everything, including all his high school yearbooks. I was hoping I could borrow Andy's if you still had it."

Mrs. O'Riley sighed with relief. "I have them. They're in boxes in his bedroom closet. At least I think they are. They packed up his apartment and sent everything here. We put it all in his closet. It wasn't much. He was very organized. We never got rid of any of his belongings. It was too hard, you know, with the grief."

"I understand," Yvette said, choosing her words carefully. "Would you mind if I look through those boxes?"

"Of course not. Follow me. I'll show you which ones to look through."

Andy's bedroom was spartan. A bed, curtains, a dresser, and that was it. If the room was just how Andy had left it, he wasn't big on decorations. Mrs. O'Riley stopped at the threshold.

"Go ahead, honey. The boxes are in the closet. Take as long as you need. I'm going to make some phone calls about this check. Do you mind hanging around to answer any questions?"

"Sure, no problem." Yvette walked over to the closet and swung open the door. It was stuffed top to bottom in square brown boxes. She felt slightly overwhelmed. "Thanks again, Mrs. O'Riley."

"Call me Barbara."

Barbara disappeared down the hallway, and Yvette adjusted her earpiece. She rolled up her sleeves and unstacked each box, carefully placing them on the bedroom floor. Luckily, the first box she opened contained all the yearbooks. Her earpiece squawked.

"Make sure it's there first," Andy said.

"Which one is it?" Yvette whispered.

"The one with the school mascot crudely drawn in a bathrobe."

It was the yearbook on top of the stack. "This one?" Yvette held it up to the brooch so Andy could get a closer look.

"That's the one. I wrote it inside the back cover."

Yvette flipped to the last page. On it was written a long, random-looking password. "Wow, this whole thing is the password?"

"Yep, that's what we needed. We took a screenshot. Thanks, Yvette— What's that?" There was a pause as Andy conversed with someone on his side of the conversation. "Sorry, that was Dan."

"Hi, Dan!" Yvette said into the camera. "I'm glad you're still with us."

"What— Ooh, Dan, you're right! Hey, Yvette, we may have

hit the jackpot," Andy said excitedly. "We had no idea that my apartment had been packed up and sent to my parents. The thumb drive I had used to back up my research is probably in there somewhere."

"Well, let me look." As she methodically went through each box, she made sure that the brooch got a good view of every item. More than once, Andy sniffled at a memory. There were several thumb drives scattered throughout, but the one she was looking for was in the very last box.

"Good job, Yvette," Dan said over the earpiece. "Now hurry back to the apartment and get that memory stick uploaded to us—and don't forget the yearbook. You have a big day tomorrow."

"Will do," she said as she stuffed a box back into the closet. "By the way, your voice sounds funny."

"He looks funny too," Andy said. "One more thing… uh… before you go, please give my mom a proper hug… for me."

Yvette dropped another box on top of the first one. "It would be my pleasure."

⊷⊶

*It's him.* They stood in the open doorway, waiting to be acknowledged.

Yvette cleared her throat, but the man behind the desk was too engrossed in his work to notice. "Excuse me? Dr. Franklin Wyatt?"

He waved her away without looking up. "My office hours ended five minutes ago. Go ask another student your questions about the final project. Good day."

"We aren't students, sir," said Blaine.

Dr. Wyatt looked up from his papers with an exasperated sigh. "Then who are you, and what do you want?" he said gruffly.

Blaine entered the office and handed him a business card. "My name is Blaine Landry, and this is Yvette Boudreaux. We are from Fruge, Fontenot, and Flynn, attorneys at law. We represent the estate of Mr. Andrew O'Riley."

"Who is that? I don't know that name." He took off his glasses. "Am I being sued?"

"Andrew O'Riley was a graduate student about twenty years ago. He was studying for his master's. His emphasis was database design for AI and theoretical computing," Blaine said. "Before he could submit his thesis, he was murdered."

"Murdered? Andrew O'Riley? I know the name. I just can't place it." Dr. Wyatt absentmindedly shuffled the papers on his desk. "I don't know."

"He remembers me," Andy said via the earpiece.

"You and Andy did your undergrad at the same time. You took almost all your senior-level classes together."

"That was a long time ago, but I do remember someone named Andy. He was intelligent and made friends easily. He disappeared right before the spring semester. We all figured he transferred or something. I don't remember hearing anything about him being murdered. Is that what this is about?"

"Not exactly." Yvette opened her briefcase and placed the yearbook and the thumb drive on Dr. Wyatt's desk.

"What is this?" he said as he paged through the yearbook.

"Dr. Wyatt, you teach AI and theoretical computing, and you specialize in coding for AI applications," Blaine said. "We know your life goal was to create a general AI, not one made for a specific purpose. An AI that could grow and learn without constraints. A strong AI."

Dr. Wyatt closed the yearbook after thumbing through a few pages. "Yes, and?"

"You've hit several roadblocks along the way," Yvette said. "The main one being the way an AI interacts with data. Current models lack an efficient structure. They lack true autonomy."

Dr. Wyatt slid the yearbook over to the side and crossed his arms. "Go on..."

"Andy figured out a way to optimize databases for use with AI. Traditional databases are designed to be interfaced and used by humans or simple code and scripts created by humans. He found a way to optimize it for AI."

The professor sighed and rolled his eyes. "I fail to see how a graduate student's work from twenty years ago can possibly be relevant today."

"I'll be the first to admit we're not experts in this field," Yvette said. "But I will tell you that an expert has reviewed this work and urged us to contact you. The thumb drive contains Andy's thesis on database design for integration with artificial intelligence. On the back inside cover of the yearbook is the password to the document."

Blaine stood and put his hands on the desk. "Look, we know that the contents of this paper will have practical applications for your work. It can't hurt to look."

Dr. Wyatt narrowed his eyes and plugged the thumb drive into his laptop. "I better not get a virus from this," he said, turning to the back cover of the yearbook. "This whole thing is the password?"

"Andy was careful," Yvette said as she closed her briefcase.

Dr. Wyatt took his time and carefully entered each character into the password field. "Ah, there it is," he said, adjusting his glasses as he read the document.

Blaine paced nervously. "Well?"

"This is really good," he said with an appreciative nod. "The thesis would have been nigh indefensible back then. They would have seen it as crazy talk."

"Very good," Yvette said as she pulled a slip of paper from her briefcase. "There's one more thing... uh... Dr. Wyatt?"

Dr. Wyatt shook his head. "If what I'm reading here actually works—and it should—it'll change the world forever. Where did you get this? Who was the expert who referred me?"

"Sorry, but we can't tell you that information," Blaine said. "It's part of the deal."

"Deal?" he said. "What deal?"

Yvette reached over and handed him a check.

"What is this?" he said. "Five hundred million dollars? This is a joke, right?"

"No joke," Blaine said. "You must quit the university and work on making Andy's research a reality. Do whatever you need to do to make it happen."

*Wait! Hi, this is Lemmy. You need to make sure he gives Dan and Andy credit for the discovery. It affects what corrective algorithms are run against them in the Database of Souls.*

"There's one very important stipulation," Yvette said, closing her briefcase. "You must give full credit to Andrew O'Riley and to Daniel Lemon."

"Who is Daniel Lemon?"

"He's the man that made it all happen." Blaine frowned. "Just give him credit. If anyone asks, say he was in operations. No questions."

"You're serious," he said. "This can't be real."

"If you don't believe us, cash the check."

"We're late for our next appointment," Blaine said. "We'll be in touch, Dr. Wyatt."

*Are you sure he'll do it?*

*He'll do it.*

As they left the professor in stunned silence, Blaine gently closed the door behind them. "One stop left."

Yvette closed her eyes and sighed deeply. "I want you to stay in the car for that one," she said. "I'll do it alone."

"Dan," Blaine said into his microphone. "You're up next."

⟽◦◉◦⟾

"What are you doing here?" Katie said, not opening her front door all the way.

"Katie, we need to talk," Yvette said. "It's about Dan."

Katie walked out onto the front porch and folded her arms under her breasts. "Let me guess," she said. "You're pregnant."

*Has Katie gained weight? Her face looks puffy.*

*Shut up, Lemmy.*

"What?" Yvette said, taken aback. "N-no, I'm here on business. First of all, on a personal level, I wanted you to know that I thought Dan was a great guy."

Katie laughed dismissively. "Yeah, I bet."

"Let me finish," Yvette said angrily. "I want you to know that nothing ever happened between us."

"Then what did happen between you? Why the secret messages? Secret meetings?"

"Katie, it wasn't romantic—"

"Then what was it? Why did he choose *you* over our marriage? Why did he commit suicide while I watched?" Katie's eyes burned red. "Say what you have to say and leave."

Yvette sighed and hung her head. "Katie, you have every right to suspect the things you suspect. You may not believe me, but it is all about the Simulation."

Katie groaned and turned to walk back inside, but Yvette touched her shoulder. "Please... I'm not going to explain the Simulation to you. Dan and I are involved in something way beyond ourselves. The work we're doing is gravely serious. He risked everything to ensure your family's safety. You need to know that he never wavered on his love and commitment to you or your children." Yvette leaned in close. "No matter what it looked like from the outside. If you believe nothing else, you have to believe that. We never had an affair. He never stopped loving you."

*Well done, Yvette.*

Katie unfolded her arms and sat on the porch swing. "Okay. You've said what you had to say. Now leave me."

"Fine. I'll leave. But first I have to give you this." Yvette reached in her purse and produced an envelope. "It's a message from Dan."

Katie eyed the envelope without moving. "Is that a suicide note?"

"I don't know. I haven't read it. I'm just the delivery person."

Katie snatched the envelope from Yvette. On the front. "Katie" was written neatly with a felt-tip pen. It was not Dan's handwriting.

"Where did you get this?"

"I'm acting as a courier on behalf of the law firm of Fruge, Fontenot, and Flynn. They instructed me to hand deliver it to you."

Katie snorted and set the envelope next to her on the swing. "I thought you worked at AGphic. This all seems contrived. Why did they send you? Don't they know our relationship?"

"I volunteered," Yvette said. "I wanted to get right with you."

Katie glanced at the envelope and cried. "This doesn't make any sense."

Yvette sat next to her on the swing and put her hand on her arm. "Katie, Dan's death wasn't a suicide. It was a sacrifice."

Katie wiped away her tears and shrugged off Yvette's gesture. "Don't talk to me about sacrifice," she said indignantly.

*Uh-oh. I know that look. Fun time is over.*

Yvette wiped her hands on her pants and stood. "Mrs. Lemon, I'm sorry for your loss. Our loss. As part of my instructions, I was told to give Al and Carrie a hug and to tell them their daddy loves them."

"No chance." Katie seethed. "Get the hell out of here."

*Damn. I had hoped to see the kids one more time. You should go. I'll find another way.*

Yvette nodded. "Fair enough. Mrs. Lemon, one more thing. Your bank account will be receiving large deposits. These deposits will occur on a semiregular basis. Do not contact your bank about this. Enjoy it while there is still time."

"What are you talking about?"

"Goodbye, Katie." Yvette turned and walked across the porch and down the steps. Her high heels thundered on the wooden planks. As she crossed the yard, she loosened the top button of her blouse and took down her ponytail.

*Thanks, Yvette.*

"No problem," she said as she hopped into Blaine's running car.

"All done?" he said with a huge grin.

Yvette leaned back into the passenger's seat with an exasperated sigh. "Yes. Finally. You?"

"Yep. The apartment is stocked and secure. We can always go back there if we have to. But now we're free to do what we want. So?" Blaine smiled over his sunglasses. "Where to?"

Yvette shrugged. "The world is our oyster, Blaine. What I really want is a beach and some beach drinks."

Blaine adjusted his glasses and put the car in drive. "Okay. Road trip."

<hr/>

Katie knelt alone in her dark living room. Tears streamed down her face as Dan's letter smoldered and died out in the fireplace. The ceiling fan swirled ashes about the empty room. She watched quietly as the last ember escaped its dying world. She cried alone in her chair by the window. Her glass of wine sat untouched. "Was that normal enough for you, Dan?"

# Twenty-Five

———◇◈◇———

"**I**T'S DONE," LEMMY said as he closed a laptop. "Blaine and Yvette are off the grid. I encrypted their stream. The Simulation can't track them even if it does spin up a Father August clone."

*I'm so tired. What is sapping my energy?* Dan stared blankly at the hole in the sliding glass door. *What would happen if someone tried to go out there, into the void?* The cheap flamingo painting hung in tatters above the cushion-less sofa. *Someone got in a fight. I bet whoever did that to the painting knows the answer to that question.* Andy's face came into view.

"Dan, are you all right?" he said. "Did you hear? We're done."

"With… everything?" Dan said, his voice groggy.

"Yes. My thesis is with the professor. Your apartment is ready in case of emergency. Blaine and Yvette are safe. It's time for me to go."

Dan stuck his head up and glanced around the room. Lemmy had opened up a new laptop and was typing commands. Father August watched quietly from a barstool. *He's been too quiet. Maybe Lemmy kicked his ass.* "Where are you going?"

"I'm going back to purgatory. There's no place for me in the Actual, and I can't stay here. As long as Dr. Wyatt gives me credit, it should be smooth sailing on our next run."

"We can go whenever you're ready," Lemmy said.

"You're sure I'm not going to be deleted?"

"Relax, you'll be fine. Purgatory's algorithm was done with you, so you won't be checked."

"Okay," Andy said, hands shaking slightly. "Let's go over it one more time to make sure I understand our plan. We go to the Recovery Domain and wait for a restore to happen. When it does, I'll be scanned and reinserted to purgatory."

"That's right," Lemmy said. "I'd insert you directly, but Father August doesn't have permission. I guess the Simulation didn't want him sending people straight to purgatory."

"I wonder why," Dan said with a raspy chuckle.

Andy fidgeted in his chair. "What happens if there's a problem and I am restored to the Actual? I'm not going to wake up trapped in my coffin, am I?"

"To be honest? I'm not sure. But if that happens, just relax and wait to die again."

"That's not comforting at all," Andy said with a shiver. "Note to self: add cremation to the will."

Dan pried himself off the couch and shook Andy's hand. "Thanks for everything even if you didn't have a choice."

Andy nodded over to Father August. "Well, maybe next time we can avoid this mistake from happening in the first place."

"I can assure you, it will never happen again," Father August said with an evil grin.

Lemmy closed the second laptop and produced a glittery-green blanket from behind his chair.

"All right, let's go. Dan, you're staying here with the priest while I bring Andy to the Recovery Domain."

Father August sat stone-faced. *This isn't like him.* "Do I have a choice?"

"You don't," Lemmy said with a shrug. "Sorry, Dan, it's a nested meta. Your meta is holding Father August in his meta.

We need you here for now. When I get back, we'll untangle this mess."

"Okay," Dan said, too tired to argue.

Lemmy led Andy to the center of the orange square. "Wait," Dan said, "You're not taking the truck?"

"No need. Father August has a direct connection to the Recovery Domain. We're gonna teleport!" Lemmy unfolded the blanket and spread it out to cover the square. "Here, Andy, wrap yourself in this."

"This is going to be interesting," Andy said as he covered himself. "Bye, Dan. See you soon... I hope!"

Dan waved weakly from the couch. "See ya, Andy. We'll be back in college before you know it."

Lemmy tucked Andy's arm under the blanket, pressed a few buttons on his cell phone, and with a sickening *pop*, they disappeared. A surge of energy washed over Dan. He could feel the fatigue leaving his body.

Father August flashed Dan a toothy grin. "Finally." He sighed. "I thought they would never leave. Would you care for some tea?"

On steady legs, Dan met Father August in the kitchen. Father August produced a teakettle from an overhead cabinet and hummed a cheerful tune while he filled it with water. *He's in a good mood.*

"You've been quiet lately," Dan said as he straddled a barstool. Father August nodded as he hummed along. He carefully arranged two cups and saucers while he waited for the water to boil. "You know," Dan said, "for being the devil, you're actually pretty serene."

Father August chuckled and leaned against the counter. The kettle steamed but didn't whistle. "I've had nothing to say. Besides," he said with a roll of his eyes, "I'm powerless. I've got nothing to tempt you with other than tea."

Dan laughed. "As much as you drink the stuff, it better be good."

"I'm glad to see you perked up." The kettle whistled. Father August filled both cups with boiling hot water. He reached into his pocket and produced two tea bags. "I bet Lemmy had no idea how much their presence would sap your energy. You know, Dan, you're wrong about me."

"Wrong about what? You being serene?"

Father August checked the time on his watch and placed the cup in front of Dan. As it steeped, warm steam rose to Dan's face. It was relaxing.

"No. You all have incorrectly assumed that I am a singular entity."

Dan bobbed his tea bag up and down in the cup. The aroma made Dan sleepy. *Why am I getting sleepy again? Is Lemmy already on his way back?* "Oh yeah?" Dan blinked slowly. "We never assumed that. We know you can be cloned. Why else was Lemmy so careful about hiding Yvette and Blaine?"

"Nope. I'm not cloned," he said with an upturned lip. "I'm part of a larger program. You may have captured this instance, but it had no effect on the parent. It still knows everything I know. Corrupt me, kill me. It doesn't matter. I can be reinstalled."

Father August checked his watch and carefully removed the tea bag from his cup and set it on the saucer.

"I'll give mine another minute," Dan said, stirring his tea with his finger. "Ouch, it's hot."

"Disgusting," Father August said with a scowl.

"Okay, what else have we got wrong?"

Father August walked around and sat on a barstool next to Dan. "Where to begin?"

Dan yawned. *Is Lemmy coming or not?*

"Well," he said with a smile. "You've always assumed that I came into your life because you were high."

"But you did."

Father August laughed. "You have it backward."

Dan removed his tea bag and took a sip, wincing at its bitterness. "Do I understand you correctly? You didn't appear because I was on drugs. You're the one who encouraged me to do drugs? Did you arrange for me to get Fana?"

"Precisely." Father August smiled over his teacup.

*If Father August had manipulated Andy into smoking a toxic vape, why wouldn't I have been targeted as well? He's been in my life all along but unseen. That's what he's trying to tell me. He's been playing the long con.* "It's all your fault."

"I'm afraid so. I'm sorry."

"What I don't understand is you've kept yourself hidden from me my whole life. Why did you reveal yourself?"

"Are you talking about our first interaction back at the Breakfast Station? I can assure you it wasn't intentional. I had been monitoring you and your reaction discreetly. When you stared directly at me, I could tell something was... *different.* I needed to find out what went wrong. I still don't know what happened with the Fana. I can't afford another accident like before."

"What do you mean before?" Dan pushed the cup away. "How many lives have you ruined?"

"Do you think you're the first? Sorry, but you're not special. There was an even more brilliant DBA than Andy. He had it all figured out four years before Andy would even finish high school. Unfortunately, mistakes were made, and he disappeared from the Simulation three runs ago. We've been toying with the formula ever since."

*Disappeared? What happened to the other guy?* Dan's vision blurred, and he rubbed his eyes. "What formula?"

"Fana's formula. Remember Henry's start-up investment? They manufacture and distribute it in the Actual. Fana makes internal processes more apparent. It unlocks a person's debug mode. It gives you access to all your agents, running processes, and log files. Unfortunately, this batch included self-admin rights. It was way too powerful. It allowed you to see me and access your other functions, like the backup and management interfaces. This is why the company disappeared and you can't get any more. We need to refine the next batch."

Dan's tongue lolled around in his mouth, and his legs wobbled. *What's happening? Why am I losing control again? Keep it together until Lemmy gets back.* "Because of the drug, I gained unrestricted access to my own functions?"

"Bingo. And those functions went amok, so to speak." Father August sipped his tea. "You see, I had hoped the drug would expose the virus. It did, obviously. However, I didn't expect the virus to take advantage." Father August set down his empty teacup. "It gave you hyperconsciousness. Humans need consciousness to be self-aware. Without it, they couldn't exist within the Simulation. Fana expanded your view beyond consciousness. You know consciousness isn't a thing. It's a process. It's nothing more than self-check software embedded into your base code. To you, consciousness is your soul. To me? It's nothing special."

Father August poked Dan in the chest. A sharp pain radiated out to his arms. "Now, Dan, you are not merely self-aware. Because of Fana, you are aware of universal systems. Systems like the Recovery Domain. No one else can access these systems. They don't know it exists! You are aware of a reality far beyond your simulated carbon-based biology. I bet it seems magical to you. I hope you enjoyed it. You're enough of a realist to understand we won't let you carry the burden of this knowledge. Thank you for your service. Without you, I couldn't have exposed Lemmy."

Dan looked down at his half-empty teacup. *Something isn't right.* His head sagged uncontrollably, and he struggled to speak. *Was it the tea?* "What are you getting at?" he said. "I don't understand. Are you dismissing me? You can't do that…"

"Aha! Wrong again!" Father August said with glee. "You

have all assumed I haven't been in control this whole time. Silly!" Father August snapped his fingers, and the room transformed. The flamingo painting was repaired. The sofa cushions were back in place. The sliding glass door was whole again. The bright beach scene reappeared, complete with seagulls and crashing waves. Everything was neat, clean, and in its place. Father August snapped his fingers again, and a tea timer appeared on the kitchen counter. "Ah, glad to have that back. Did you know your friend Lemmy tossed the original one through the glass? I suppose he was testing me."

"If you were in control, then you let Lemmy—" Dan's face paled, and sweat glistened at his temples. *We were tricked! I have to warn Lemmy and Andy!*

As if sensing what Dan was thinking, Father August snapped his fingers, and the large orange square disappeared. "Yep," he chuckled. "Goodbye, Lemmy."

The room spun. "What did you—?" Dan's throat burned and began to close.

"What did I do? I took away Lemmy's way back. I'm afraid he fell right into my trap."

Dan's eyes drooped, and his arm spasmed and knocked over his teacup, spilling its contents on the counter. "No!" He gagged. "What did you do to me? Have I been poisoned?" Dan stumbled into the living room and collapsed onto the couch. His body convulsed and gurgled as it spasmed.

"I'm sorry, Dan. The good news is that we still need you. Not in this life but the next one. You can relax. You won't be deleted forever," Father August said as he sat on the sofa. Dan's dying body thrashed about on the floor. "The bad news is that we'll need to thoroughly cleanse you. We must ensure you're purged of Lemmy's code. No purgatory for you. You're off to the afterlife algorithm—or as you may call it—the Heaven and Hell cycle. I'm sorry. If it's any consolation, you won't remember it in your next life. You won't even remember this conversation."

Dan's eyes went wild as he lost control of his body and mind.

He could no longer speak. It was all he could do to swallow back the bile that filled his mouth. He flailed his arms in a panic, but it was no use. The poison had run its course. *It's over.* His eyes opened, his jaw slacked, and his last breath escaped his body. As Dan felt his body give away for a second time, Father August stood over him with a bowed head. "Sorry, Dan," he said as he took one last look around the room. "God, I hate Florida."

He snapped his fingers, and the entire condominium winked out of existence.

# Twenty-Six

"**H**OW LONG DO we have to wait for the restore to happen?" Andy said, standing in the darkness of Dan's apartment. The glitter-green blanket lay crumpled on the floor. Lemmy checked his watch.

"The last restore occurred seventeen hours ago. We've only been here for forty minutes. Restores happen at irregular intervals. The longest I've seen so far has been about two days."

"I hope we're not sitting around in the dark for another day," Andy said. "Ever been through a hurricane, Lemmy? This is what it feels like in the eye. The power is out. Everything is quiet. And you know shit's about to go down soon."

"Nope, never been through a hurricane," Lemmy said. "This isn't so bad."

"No, you're right." Andy sighed. "I'm just nervous, that's all. I'm ready for this part to be over with."

"Don't worry. I'm sure it won't be long." Lemmy stretched. "Andy, be a pal and drag that couch over here. I can't leave the square. My computer wouldn't work here, so I'm relying on the restore to send me back to the condo."

Andy struggled with the sofa as he slid it onto the orange square. Lemmy plopped down and relaxed. "Thanks, man. Make sure you stay out of the square. You can't be transported back. My computer isn't listening for your signature. You'd be beamed out to nowhere."

"That would suck," Andy said out of breath. "So this is Dan's place?" He walked into the living room and ran his finger along the top of the ultrathin TV. "Very chic. Very modern."

"Everything will be modern to you, old man," Lemmy said, sagging back into the couch. "Besides, Dan sure as hell didn't decorate it. He had help. I will say one thing though. Blaine did a great job establishing this place. He and Yvette have a solid fallback option here. Rent and utilities are being autodrafted out of a checking account with unlimited money. Unless the place catches fire or something, this place will be available to them forever. Go check out the rest of the apartment. He said he left the cabinets fully stocked."

Lemmy was right. The pantry was stocked with long-term storage in mind. It was filled with oats, honey, and maple syrup, items that had an extralong shelf life. The liquor cabinet was fully stocked with a variety of bottles, including what appeared to be at least four cases of red wine. Both the refrigerator and freezer were empty, but the ice maker was full.

"When the lights come on, I'll have oatmeal and cocktails," said Andy.

"Now that sounds like my kind of breakfast."

Andy walked into the first bedroom and gasped. Boxes of brand-new laptops were stacked ten high and three deep. Another stack of boxes sat on top of the dresser. Each one contained a cell phone.

"Find anything?" Lemmy asked as Andy went back into the living room.

"Just a bunch of laptops and cell phones."

"I can see how those would come in handy," Lemmy said. "Go see what's in that duffel bag over in the dining room."

Andy unzipped it, and his mouth dropped. It was packed with an enormous sum of cash and various other items. He quickly inspected the contents, then zipped it up and threw it back into the corner.

"What was in there?"

"Women's clothes. Yvette must have forgotten to bring it with her." He winced and shook his head as if he were unsure why he lied. "It's been a long time since I've been alive," he said, eyes darting back and forth. "Things sure have changed."

"What do you mean?" Lemmy said.

"The TV, these phones, and computers... They're all so... so modern." Andy picked up a laptop that had been lying on the dining room table. "I probably can't even operate half the electronics in this place."

"Don't worry about it," Lemmy said with a yawn. "You'll be dead soon anyway. You'll have decades to get used to them next time."

"Thanks, I had forgotten." Andy sat in a living room chair. "I'm nervous, Lemmy. What if this doesn't work?"

"If this doesn't work, then you will be deleted permanently. Which, from your perspective, is no different from what happens to the rest of us. Without you, the Simulation will never produce the desired result rendering the purpose for its whole existence null and void."

"No pressure."

"It's out of your control, Andy. No sense sweating it." Lemmy leaned back on the couch and confidently put his arms behind his head. "Look, before you know it, you'll be sitting in heaven, having fun."

Andy cocked his head to the side. "That's some sales pitch you've got there."

The lights flickered on, and the refrigerator hummed to life. Andy froze in shock. "Wait, what just happened?"

Lemmy's relaxed demeanor vanished, and his face became a picture of sheer terror. "The restore!"

Andy patted himself down. "But I'm still here," he said. "How?"

"No, you don't understand," Lemmy said in horror. "*I'm here!*"

Andy ran to the bathroom and looked at himself in the mirror. "We're in the Actual!" he shouted. "It's real!"

Lemmy rushed in and pushed Andy aside. His own face reflected in the mirror alongside Andy's. Lemmy splashed water on his face, the cold water spread goose pimples to the back of his neck, and his hair stood on end. "It's true!" he said. "My skin works."

Whatever thoughts were running through Lemmy's head were reflected in his facial expressions.

"Uh, what's wrong with your face?" Andy said, stepping back.

"I can't control my emotions. Ack! How do you do it?" Lemmy threw more water on his face and growled. He spun around. His face was a mask of anger and hate. "Make it stop! I hate feelings! Humans and your stupid hormones. We don't have these extreme emotions! What's the point?"

Lemmy broke down into tears, and Andy quietly backed out of the room.

"You need to get it together, Lemmy," Andy said cautiously. "Humans spend their teenage years learning to control their emotions. You've had them for two minutes."

Lemmy's face flashed from one expression to another. "I'm trying!"

"Think!" Andy said. "I'm supposed to be dead! What happened?"

"Oh yeah?" Lemmy glared at him. "I'm not supposed to be here! We're fucked!"

Lemmy growled and ran out of the bathroom.

"Where are you going?" Andy followed. "This can't be happening."

Lemmy ran to the living room and flipped open the laptop sitting on the table. He grumbled and typed furiously. "Shit!" he said with a rattling cough. "Dan's not responding." He slammed the laptop shut and narrowed his eyes at Andy. "Father August tricked us! We were never in his meta. We were in a quarantine! He tricked me into leading Dan to him. He tricked me into…"

Andy cowered under Lemmy's treacherous glare. "What? What did he trick you into doing?"

"He tricked me into coming here with you. It was a trap!" Lemmy let out a primal growl and pounced. He grabbed Andy by the throat. Andy quickly recovered from the shock and wrestled Lemmy's hands away. Lemmy recoiled and lunged again, but Andy quickly shoved him to the ground. Lemmy sat on the floor, gasping for air and looking at his hands.

"What the hell, man!" Andy said, massaging his throat.

"I don't know!" he said. "I can't control anything. I-I have no strength. I—" An idea crossed his face, and he rushed into the bedroom. Seconds later, he returned with a cell phone and a laptop.

"What are you doing now?"

Lemmy picked up the green blanket and threw it over his shoulder. "Father August knew," he said with a snarl. "How did he know? Dan was sloppy! I shouldn't have picked him to begin with. Didn't you have a college girlfriend or something? Maybe that Wyatt guy…"

"What?" Andy stepped back.

"Never mind." Lemmy laid the blanket out on the floor and put the laptop and phone into it. He went to the kitchen and took out several liquor bottles and put them in the blanket. He rolled it up like a bag and threw it over his shoulder.

"Goodbye, Andy," Lemmy said. "And good luck."

He turned his back and rushed out the door.

Andy stood alone in the empty apartment. "Okay, calm down," he said. "Think. I'm not dead. Lemmy says Father

August sprang a trap. If it was to trap Lemmy, was I the bait? Dan is unreachable. Lemmy ran away…"

His eyes fell on the duffel bag in the corner. He unzipped it to check the contents. It was indeed Yvette and Blaine's emergency bug-out bag. It contained a phone, several stacks of cash, a man and woman's change of clothes, toiletries, and a set of car keys.

"Lemmy attacked me. Father August didn't. Who is the bad guy? Does it matter?"

Andy zipped up the bag and threw it over his shoulder. "Either way, I'm not going to hang around to find out."

# Twenty-Seven

*I'M HOME.* IT was early evening, and the cicadas were chirping in the sweet spring air. A warm breeze stirred the trees, sending a lone dove flying off to roost for the night. A solitary lamp shone through a window, casting shadows across the porch. Dan walked up the steps and peered inside. Katie sat in the recliner. Her head tilted sideways at an awkward angle.

He stepped out of the lamplight and hesitated at the front door. *How am I going to explain everything to Katie? She had me cremated only a few days ago.* He pulled a key out of his front pocket and stuck it into the dead bolt. He twisted it, but it didn't work. *Katie must have changed the locks.* Dan grumbled and pressed the doorbell. He waited a few moments but heard no movement inside the house. *Come on, Katie!* He rang the doorbell again and knocked. No answer. Dan walked back to the window and peered inside. She sat in the recliner, unmoving. He tapped gently on the window. "Katie?" No answer. "Katie, it's me, Dan. Can you let me in?" She still didn't move.

Dan stepped off the front porch into the yard and peered up at the second floor. "Carrie? Al? It's me, Dad. Can you let me in?"

When the windows to the kids' bedrooms stayed silent and dark, Dan grabbed a fist-sized rock from the flowerbed and went back and smashed one of the panes of the living room window. He reached in and unlatched it to climb inside.

As soon as he did, a putrid stench washed over him, and he gagged. Thousands of flies buzzed around the room and around Katie's decaying corpse. A dirty spoon and a needle lay next to her on the table. A dry-rotted rubber hose was still tied around her arm. *Heroin? She hated drugs. Why heroin?* Dan collapsed to his knees and buried his head into her cold lap. Flesh sloughed off the bone as he sobbed.

"Katie!" He sobbed. "What happened to you?" *This doesn't make sense. Why did she do this? Because of me? What about the children? The children!* Dan bolted upstairs to the children's rooms. "Al! Carrie!"

Dan swung open Al's door and was greeted by a cloud of dust. "Al!" The room was the same. The same football posters. The same trophies. It looked like it hadn't been lived in for years. *Al isn't here. Where's Al?*

Dan turned around and opened the door to Carrie's room. This room had changed. Her toys were gone. Hairbrushes and cosmetics took up space on top of her vanity. Her video game posters were replaced with a boy band he didn't recognize. Years had passed. His daughter was a teenager. *But she isn't a teenager.* Her dresser was littered with get-well cards. Next to them was a framed picture. It was of her. She was bald and in a wheelchair. She smiled at the camera in front of a tombstone with Al's name on it. She held a poster that read HAPPY BIRTHDAY IN HEAVEN, BIG BROTHER!

Dan collapsed to his knees, holding the picture. *They're all dead?* Tears streamed down his face. *Why? It was because I violated the Simulation, wasn't it? Get it together, Dan.* Trembling, he went back downstairs. *Life is pointless without my family. How can I go on? I wish I had never taken Fana. This is all my fault. If this is hell, I can't go on. I have to get out.*

He went into the master bedroom. It was where he kept the gun. Katie had once kept it spotless; now clothing lay strewn about everywhere. Fast-food containers, cigarette butts, and used condoms littered the floor. Blood and feces stained the sheets. She had been selling her body for drugs. "Oh, Katie," Dan cried.

*It's all my fault. I did this to you.* Sobbing, he walked over to the nightstand and opened the top drawer. The pistol was still there. He took it and sat on the bed, shaking. *God, forgive me. I can't live without my family. I'm too weak.*

He chambered the round, stuck the barrel in his mouth, and pulled the trigger. *Click.* He ejected the round and put in another. *Click.* Sobbing, he dropped the gun on the floor. *There is no escaping this nightmare. This is hell.* He threw his head into his hands and wailed.

Footsteps on the front porch. He picked up the gun. It didn't work, but they wouldn't know that. The front door creaked open, and shadowy figures stalked into the living room. Dan steadied the gun. They hadn't seen him yet. He slowly peered around the corner and caught them standing over Katie's corpse.

"Get away from her!" he shouted, waving the pistol. "Who are you? Get out of my house!"

They spun around and drew their weapons. "Police!" they shouted in unison. "Drop your gun and get on the floor."

Dan stood there, dazed. *Who are these people?*

"Drop your weapon, druggie!"

Dan lowered the pistol and dropped it to the floor.

"On your knees!"

Dan complied, and a policeman quickly handcuffed his hands behind his back. "I live here," Dan said defiantly.

"Sure you do, buddy," he said with contempt.

"Mike?" Dan said, struggling against his cuffs. "Is that you? I thought I recognized you."

"You can call me Lieutenant Oldsman," he said. "How do you *think* you know me?"

"We went to high school together in Canard," Dan said.

The policeman grabbed Dan's face and scrutinized it. His breath smelled like coffee and gingivitis. "I've never seen you before in my life."

*No, this isn't right. I know Mike. I'm positive it's him. This is an alternate universe or something.* The youngest of the policemen held a rag over his mouth as he stood over Katie's corpse. "Well, she finally died."

"The junkies in lockup will be heartbroken," Mike said with a chuckle. "Ol' Tricky Nicki bit the dust. They're going to have to find someone else to stick it in."

Dan struggled against the handcuffs. "Don't talk about her like that!"

The officer behind Dan thumped him on his back with a baton. The blow sent Dan sprawling out onto the floor. "Shut up, junkie. I'm sick of you druggie squatters."

Lieutenant Oldsman pointed at Dan lying on the floor. "Does he have any identification?"

"Nope. All he had in his pockets was this pathetic bag of heroin."

Mike sneered. "He must have come here looking for a quickie? What's your name?"

Dan struggled back onto his knees. "Daniel Charles Lemon. I live here. Well, I used to. This woman is my wife."

"Oh yeah?" Mike said with a chuckle. "Nicki Warner was a lot of people's wives."

*Nicki Warner? Nichole was Katie's middle name, and Warner was her maiden name. Did she change it after the divorce? Wait, why do I keep falling into the trap. This place isn't real. This is hell. Literally. I need to shake it off. Fight it!* "That's not her name. It's Katie Lemon."

Mike grabbed him by the throat. "I remember you now," he said with a growl. "You're the guy that killed Nicki Warner."

Mike's glossy black eyes oozed pure hatred. *It's a show. I can do this.* Struggling for breath against the policeman's grip hold, Dan forced himself to let out a chuckle.

"Something funny?" Mike sneered as he released his choke hold. Dan coughed to clear his airway and laughed harder. "What's so funny?"

"This isn't real." Dan smiled.

"Oh yeah?" Lieutenant Oldsman whipped out his baton and smashed Dan in the face. His front teeth shattered, splattering the ground with blood. "How about now? Is it real yet?"

Through the immense pain, Dan laughed harder. Each heave gurgled with blood.

"I said, what's so funny?" Lieutenant Oldsman repeated, baton raised to strike again.

"This is only hell," Dan said with a determined and bloody grin. "My family is probably okay."

"That's enough." The policeman hit him in the temple with his baton and sent Dan tumbling into darkness.

---

When he opened his eyes, he was once again standing alone on his front porch. He rubbed his head where the officer had hit him, but there was no pain. His teeth were all in place, no blood. *I'm glad that's over.* The warm breeze blew his hair into wisps, and he stared at his hands disbelievingly. *What now?* The cicadas shared his mood and chirped cheerfully in the dusk of the starry night. The porch was dark save for the light of the living room lamp, peeking through the front window. He cautiously walked up the steps and peered inside. Katie's body was inert on the recliner.

Not again! Dan's eyes widened, and his heart raced. How many times do I have to relive this nightmare? Does each iteration of hell have a different scenario where my family is ripped apart? My soul can't survive an eternity of this. I can't go through this again. He turned his back to the window and stepped off the porch. I have to get out of here.

"Daddy?"

An upstairs light was on, and Carrie waved at him from her bedroom window. Dan stumbled backward and tripped over a bicycle. "Carrie?" he said in disbelief.

"It's Daddy!" She disappeared from the window and into the house. One by one, all the lights turned on, and shouting erupted from inside. Finally the door burst open. It was Katie in her nightgown, flanked by the two kids.

"Dan? Is that you?" She rushed out of the house and flew into Dan's arms. "We never gave up hope!" She cried as she hugged him tightly.

Dan pushed her back to make sure she was real. "Katie?" he said. "Is it really you?"

She smiled and kissed him passionately. "When they said you were lost, we didn't believe them." Katie held him tight.

Carrie and Al bounded off the porch and joined the hug. The four held each other tight, no one willing to be the first one to let go.

"I'm never letting you go again, Dad," Al said.

"Me neither," said Carrie.

"That makes three of us."

Dan wiped away tears of joy. "I'm so happy to see you all," he said. "I can't tell you what this means to me."

"We love you, Dad."

"I love you too. All of you," Dan said. This must be heaven.

Dan squeezed his children tight. Carrie and Al smiled at him innocently.

Katie wiped away her tears. "Let's go inside."

"Are you hungry, Daddy?" Carrie said, bounding up the steps and into the house.

"I'm starving," he said. "I honestly don't know the last time I've eaten. It hasn't been a priority."

Katie smiled. "Good. I cooked a shrimp fettuccine, just like your grandma used to make. I put it in the fridge after supper. It's probably not even cold yet. I'll heat it up for you."

"I can do that, Mom," Al said. "I'm glad you're home, Dad."

"Thanks, honey, you're such a big help!" Katie said. "Well, if you're doing that, I'll make a few phone calls. We need to let everyone know Dan's finally here."

Carrie squeezed Dan's hand and led him into the house. It had changed since the last time. Everything was clean and in its place. Even the lights seemed to have a softer, warmer glow than he remembered. *It's so peaceful and happy. There was something I was supposed to do...*

He walked into the kitchen, and Katie greeted him with a hug even tighter than before. Carrie and Al sat at the kitchen table and smiled at him. Neither seemed to be willing to let Dan out of their sight. Their eyes went wide, and their faces broke into smiles when a new figure entered the room. "Grandpa!"

"It's true! You're back!" he said.

Dan let go of Katie and spun around. The tall, dark-haired man grinned at him. He hadn't aged a day in twenty years. *Could it be?*

"Dad?" he mouthed.

George Lemon strode across the kitchen and embraced Dan. Dan felt like a child again in his father's arms.

"You finally made it," he said. "Son, I am so proud of you. More than you can ever imagine."

Dan's eyes welled up with tears. "Dad. I've missed you so much."

"I've missed you too, son, and so has your mother."

His eyes darted to the doorway. She stood there quietly, taking in the scene. She was crying, but she didn't bother to wipe tears from her eyes. Dan went to his mother and fell to his knees. "Mom?"

She bent over and brushed his hair back. With a mother's tenderness, she cradled Dan's head in her hands and kissed his forehead. *Mom.* "Come on, son, it's okay." As she helped him to his feet and wiped away his tears, a third newcomer entered the kitchen.

"I'm truly sorry to interrupt," he said, "but I need to speak with Dan."

Backlit by a bright white aura, a short, stout figure carved out a shadow. Dan breathed a sigh of relief.

"Father Desjeunes!" Dan's mom smiled triumphantly.

"Well, if it isn't Mrs. Lemon!" The priest smiled and gave her a hug. "What a joy it is to see you again! And George" — the priest turned to Dan's father and shook his hand — "it's been years."

"Glad to see you too, Father," he said.

"I hate to break up this wonderful family reunion, but I need to borrow Dan for a moment."

Dan's smile faded. "Everyone, I need to have a quick talk with Father Desjeunes. I'll be right back."

Katie walked over and gave Dan a kiss on the cheek. "Don't make me wait too long this time, okay?"

The hair bristled on the back of Dan's neck. She knows.

# Twenty-Eight

D AN FOLLOWED FATHER Desjeunes outside onto the front porch. The warm breeze rustled the trees, and the cicadas continued their serenade. Dan closed his eyes and inhaled. The scent of sweet olives reminded him of home. He leaned against a post and recalled a simpler time. "This must be heaven."

"You guessed." Father Desjeunes smiled as he sat on the porch swing. "Anything else?"

"Yeah." Dan straightened and folded his arms. "You're not Father Desjeunes."

The priest touched his nose and grinned. "Correct! You didn't even have to buy a vowel. The real Father Desjeunes is back in the Actual. He lets me talk through him from time to time. I wanted to appear as someone familiar to you. If it's okay with you, I would like to change."

Dan nodded his assent, and Father Desjeunes's body transformed into an unkempt young man. His hair reached his shoulders, but his beard was closely cropped. Tufts of chest hair poked out from his Hawaiian shirt.

"You're not doing anything to shake off the religious vibe," Dan said, raising an eyebrow. "You look like surfer Jesus."

"Hang loose, brother!" he said with a broad grin and flashing the sign.

"Well, obviously, I can't call you Father Desjeunes anymore," Dan said, laughing. "What should I call you?"

"Let's keep it simple. Call me DJ."

"Okay, DJ." Dan smiled. "It's taking a tremendous amount of willpower to be sitting here with you. I want to be inside with my family." He closed his eyes. "I had forgotten my mom's voice."

"I know this is hard for you," DJ said seriously. "But trust me, you'll have time later. We needed to talk, and I'm sure you have questions."

*Is that gumbo I smell? I thought she was heating up fettuccine?* Dan's stomach growled. *Mom's in there. Katie is back to being the fun-loving Katie, not angry-mom Katie.* "You're right," he said. "I have questions. But can we hurry this up?"

"I'll do my best to be brief." A white aura enveloped him as he motioned for Dan to sit.

Even though he no longer looked like Father Desjeunes, there was something familiar about DJ. *Is it his tone of voice?* Dan felt entirely at peace in his presence. *Why?* Dan shrugged and sat next to him on the swing. "Who are you really?" Dan said. "Are you God? Jesus?"

"Neither," DJ said with a sigh. "But if it helps to think in religious terms, you can think of me as an angel sent here to help."

"Are you the anti Father August?"

DJ chuckled. "Not exactly. Father August punishes and takes things away to model human behavior in the Actual. I'm here to aid and comfort. Although we utilize different tool sets, we both have the same objective to keep the Simulation operating normally. In a way, Father August works for me, but not directly."

A roar of laughter erupted from inside the house, and Dan craned his neck to peer into the window. His mother was holding court in the kitchen. *I had forgotten she was so funny. Ack! I want to be in there!*

"Like I was saying…," DJ said, tapping Dan on the knee. "Father August and I work together as a team, so do heaven and hell. Heaven is identical to hell in purpose. By the way—" DJ placed a hand on Dan's shoulder. "I'm sorry we sent you to hell. That was a mistake. You experienced it fully conscious. It wasn't supposed to happen that way."

The image of flies buzzing around Katie's corpse popped into his head, and he shivered.

"If it's any consolation, you were lucky. Hell repeats. Each repetition inflicts more misery than the last. You were there for one cycle, meaning you experienced the least amount of pain."

*That was the least amount of pain? I'm glad I wasn't there for round two.* "What *is* the function of the afterlife? Purgatory runs a correction algorithm. Hell seems extreme and redundant."

The swing rocked a few beats before DJ responded. "The Heaven and Hell systems aren't like the Biblical version of heaven and hell. There aren't any castles in the sky in heaven. Hell doesn't have fire and brimstone. The afterlife isn't an institution where everyone has the same experience. It's tailored to each individual. For example, Katie is here in your heaven. You may not be in her heaven."

"What? Are you serious?" Dan said, holding his chest. "I'm not in her heaven?"

"Relax, it was just an example. Of course you're there," DJ said. "The fact of the matter is, from your perspective, heaven is a dream, and hell is a nightmare. For us, it's much simpler. The afterlife is a process that recompiles your code for the next run."

"We're upgraded."

"Precisely. Hell destroys. Heaven rebuilds. When you come out the other side, you're reinserted into the Database of Souls, clean and ready for the next run."

"I was taught the afterlife was either a reward or punishment for behavior on earth. Are you telling me that the afterlife is *not* a value-based reward system?" Dan said with a chuckle. "I can't wait to bring up this topic with my Bible-study group."

"No. Absolutely bring it up with them," DJ said with a grin. "Religion is important to the way the Actual operates. Human code is more efficient if it simply believes something to be true. Not everyone can waste valuable process time pondering existence."

"Okay, then explain this to me. If we go through a great cleansing in the afterlife, why is purgatory necessary? Wouldn't the afterlife wash everything purgatory corrects away?"

"Purgatory examines each incident in an individual's life. If the outcome of that incident is undesirable, it will tweak the situation. This is to ensure people don't keep making the same mistake on every run of the Simulation. You experienced purgatory, temporarily at least. Could you sense what it wanted to correct?"

Dan thought of Cindy and winced. "Either it wanted me to get a good grade in a computer class in high school, or it didn't want me to cheat on my future wife. I'm not sure which."

The cicadas went quiet, and crickets took over the singing duties. Dan swung silently next to DJ as his mind processed the information.

"The purpose of the afterlife *to an individual* is to cleanse it of his previous life and to upgrade it for the next. In the grand scheme, its purpose is to make the Simulation more efficient."

Dan tilted his head to the side. "Is that the goal of the afterlife? Efficiency?"

"I'm sure you've guessed by now that the Simulation is constantly restarted. Why keep doing the same thing over and over again? Each run needs to be faster than the last. The afterlife builds efficiency into existing code."

"I never would have guessed that the meaning of life was to make a computer run faster."

DJ put his hand on Dan's shoulder. "That's not the meaning

of life. That's just the primary function of the afterlife. Besides, everyone has their own *meaning of life*. You've already guessed the purpose of the Simulation."

"To create an AI that can transcend the Simulation itself?"

DJ touched his nose again. The stars shone brightly through the treetops as the two men sat silently on the swing.

"Why am I still here?" Dan said quietly. "Why not kill my consciousness and let my soul be processed like everyone else? There's always the next run to get things right... right?"

DJ stood up from the swing and exhaled deeply. "We have a problem," he said, pointing to Dan's blue eye. "It's Charlie. Tell me, Dan, what do you know about Charlie?"

"Uh... Not a whole lot actually. Charlie is a part of me that has always been around. I suppose he first emerged when I started microdosing LSD. I never saw him in the flesh until I took Fana. At some point, he learned how to project himself from my meta to the Actual."

"Who do you think he learned it from?" DJ said thoughtfully.

"Lemmy."

"Precisely. Charlie was Lemmy's way into your meta. When did you get the blue eye?"

Dan shook his head. "I took a Gemini drug in the Meta to bind Charlie to me. It was the only way I could leave my own meta and enter the Recovery Domain. I assumed the eye remained Charlie's shade of blue because I was ripped out of the meta prematurely."

"It's blue because of the Gemini drug, not because you were ripped out. Lemmy needs Charlie. The Gemini drug ensured that he would always have a way back to you. Fana prevents your consciousness from offloading. The combination of Gemini and Fana ensures Lemmy of a constant connection to you with each run of the Simulation. Father August incorrectly assumed by killing you that the afterlife would clear you of those drugs. It didn't. Obviously, we still don't fully understand how Fana or Gemini work. If we don't figure it out, future runs of the

Simulation may be invalidated. Fana is a foreign substance that made it to the Actual. We can't risk that happening again. We need to deal with you and Charlie."

"Well, what *are* you going to do with us?"

"We're going to send you back to the Actual."

"You're joking." Dan stopped swinging. "How? I'm dead."

"There are ways around that." DJ grinned. "We can restore your body. You already have your consciousness. All that's left is to concoct a story and let Father August work his mind magic on everyone else."

"Father August is going to help?" Dan narrowed his eyes. "What about Katie and the kids?"

DJ shook his head. "No contact with them. At least not until we say it's okay."

A peal of laughter burst from inside the house. Dan found himself gazing longingly toward the door.

"The honest truth is that we need more time. The Simulation can't reset with you in this state. We have to purge you of Fana and Gemini first. That's the only way to ensure the corruption won't spread to subsequent runs. We can't monitor you if you're frozen in purgatory. You have to go back."

Dan sighed. *I have to help. If I don't and the Simulation is ruined, everyone I know and love will be erased.* DJ smiled at him. *He already knows what I'm going to do. He's known how this conversation would play out from the moment we stepped outside.* Dan rested his hands on his knees and sat straight. "Okay," he said. "My code wasn't built for lounging around heaven. Let's go."

"Very good!" DJ cheered. "We need to understand the origins of Fana. We know it came from Lemmy. If we knew precisely where Lemmy came from, then we could have a better understanding of what we're dealing with. You will help us find Lemmy."

Dan held out his hand and shook his head. "Wait a minute. Right before Father August killed me and sent me here, he told me that *he* gave us Fana."

DJ squinted at Dan. "What do you mean he killed you? He was supposed to just send you back."

"He poisoned my tea and watched me die. He seemed to enjoy it. He named a pharmaceutical company that he used to distribute Fana, but I forget its name. I guess he figured my consciousness would be wiped in the afterlife."

"Thanks for bringing that to my attention," DJ said thoughtfully. "Unfortunately, as a precaution, the instance of Father August that killed you was deleted. We no longer have an exact replay of that conversation. It seems like Lemmy was able to corrupt the instance. I'll have to investigate."

"Couldn't Lemmy have done the same to me?" Dan said. "What's to stop him from getting back into my meta?"

DJ shook his head. "No offense, but you aren't as complex as Father August. There are not as many places for him to hide corruption within you. I think you're okay. And don't worry about him coming back. I modified the checkpoint he crossed to gain initial entry to your meta. It's set to block. It'll work as long as you're in the Actual. But you still need to be careful. You have other connections he could possibly exploit."

"Great."

"Listen close." DJ took a deep breath. "While he may not have left evidence of data corruption within your code, he did leave a tracker. It pings at constant intervals, looking for a response. When he's near, it'll reply, and you'll know it. It's the only way we'll be able to find him. He's not in our databases and doesn't have his own ID. We can't track him like we do everyone else. When you get back to the Actual, find Lemmy or let Lemmy find you. As long as you're in his proximity, we can trace his origins. You may have better luck finding Andy first. You should start with him."

"Hold on a second." Dan's heart skipped a beat. "They're *both* in the Actual? Lemmy was supposed to return to my meta. Andy was supposed to go back to purgatory."

"Yes. Lemmy is human, for now. When Father August killed

you, he had no meta to return to, so he was restored, along with Andy." DJ frowned and looked away. "Andy is in the Actual. There is no indirect restore to the Database of Souls from the Recovery Domain's automated process. Surely you guessed that?"

*Lemmy should have known.*

"If Andy takes Fana, or if he gets killed, his data would become corrupted. If he is corrupted, he will be permanently deleted from the database. He must be kept safe from harm until this Lemmy business is resolved."

Dan stood from the swing and paced across the porch. *What if killing Andy was Lemmy's plan all along? What's going to happen when he's done with me?*

"I need time," DJ said. "I want to see what Lemmy is going to do as a human. When I'm done, I'll remove him from the Simulation, and you and Andy can live out the rest of your lives in the Actual. As long as you aren't corrupted, we'll have a better run next time."

The plan was naive. The fate of this universe and all future worlds was at stake. Lemmy has always been two moves ahead of Father August and a thousand ahead of Dan. Can DJ pull it off?

"I don't want to deal with Lemmy again," Dan said. "To be perfectly honest, I'm scared. If his goal is to have me deleted, I can't stop him. He corrupted that instance of Father August, didn't he? What hope do I have?"

"Lemmy's human now," DJ said, smoothing his beard. "He won't be able to outright delete you and Andy. However, we can't guarantee he won't be successful in finding other ways to wreak havoc."

"Lemmy was inside Father August's meta a long time. How do you know he didn't install any back doors or achieved elevated access?"

"The instance was isolated the second you captured it," DJ said. "But you're right. I'll check it out."

Dan peered inside the porch window. His mother was drinking a glass of wine and talking with big gestures. She never spilled, even during her more animated conversations. The whole room was fixated on her story. *I wish I could go back inside and forget this whole mess.*

DJ cleared his throat. "Lemmy is trapped in the Actual. Like I've said before, he is not from here. His code isn't in our database, and that makes him unpredictable. This also means that we can't track him using our tools. He's hiding, he is untethered from our system, and he is dangerous." DJ grabbed Dan by both shoulders. "You have to be careful!"

"What if I find him and he's out of control?" Dan said, shifting uncomfortably under DJ's gaze. "Do you want me to kill him?"

"No! He'll be processed and corrupt purgatory and the afterlife."

"Why doesn't Lemmy just kill himself now? Wouldn't that accomplish his goal?"

"That's one of the reasons I want to watch him. If he was going to kill himself, he would have done that already. No, I think he has other tasks to accomplish first. I think he needs to get rid of Dr. Wyatt and Andy before he kills himself."

"And me? Does he want to kill me?"

"If you are of no use to him, then yes. But he won't want to kill you until he finds Andy. If he does try to kill you, escape but don't fight back. If you find him, stall him if you can. And if you need anything, just pray. I'll be listening for you over that connection."

*Pray?* Dan shook his head. *I'm screwed.*

DJ patted him on the back. "Look, I know it's a lot to ask, but we need your help. Are you clear about what has to be done?"

"Crystal." Dan took another peek through the window. Carrie sat on his father's lap and leaned her head against his chest while he told a story. "DJ, can I have just ten more minutes here?"

"Sure, we can spare ten minutes," he said with a smile.

"Thank you, DJ," Dan said. "With all my heart."

"See you on the other side, Dan." With a wink, DJ vanished into a flash of bright white light. The warm breeze carried with it the scent of the sweet olives. Dan closed his eyes and inhaled deeply.

# Twenty-Nine

T HE APARTMENT DOOR was kicked in and crisscrossed with
yellow police tape. He didn't dare enter. Luckily, he didn't
have to. Dan reached above the doorframe and retrieved the
spare mail key Yvette had hidden. As he walked down the
corridor, he wondered what was left of his life. Weeks had
passed, insurances had been settled. How were the kids
handling everything that had happened? What would they say
if they saw him now? As tempted as he was to sneak a visit, he
couldn't risk it.

He walked past the staircase to the second floor and stopped in
front of the bank of mailboxes. As he jammed his key into the lock,
the hospital bracelet scratched his wrist. Dan used the sharp edge
of the cheap aluminum door and cut it off. Why did they make
them so hard to remove? Dan rubbed his wrist as he emptied the
slot. It was stuffed with junk mail. One by one, he threw them
away until he found the package claim ticket. He slammed the box
shut and jogged back to his apartment to return the key. Ticket in
hand, he made his way to the manager's office.

The package had his name on it. Inside was a cell phone, a
laptop computer, and a wallet containing cash, credit cards, a
set of keys, and a driver's license for a man named Richard
Head. It had his picture. Dan chuckled and silently thanked
Blaine for his new identity. He grabbed everything and headed
outside.

A black SUV was parked where his truck should have been. Dan pressed the button on his new key fob, and the vehicle unlocked. As the SUV revved to a start, the blue glow from the dashboard illuminated the interior. The phone was dead. When he plugged it into the car charger, it immediately connected and alerted a text message. "Welcome back, Richard. Your phone is pinging us. We will contact you shortly. —Y&B." Dan dropped it into the cup holder. He adjusted the mirrors while he waited for their call. He half expected to see Charlie staring back at him from the back seat, but the vehicle was empty. His own mismatched eyes reminded him he would never be alone. He had just adjusted the passenger-side mirror when the phone rang.

"Hello," said a robotic voice on the other end. "The warranty on your vehicle is expired."

Dan waited patiently for the automated script to run. Blaine had worked on software for a telemarketing firm. He must have kept some of the old code they used for making robocalls.

"*Para Español, marque el numero dos.* Press three if you would like to speak to a representative. Press seven if you already have an account..."

Dan entered the code they had written on the inside of the phone box. After a few rings, a human answered. "Please verify your name to continue."

"Richard Head."

"Thank you, Mr. Head. Please verify the last four digits of your social."

"You named me Dick Head? Really?"

"Again, thank you, Mr. Head. Please be aware that this call is monitored for quality assurance."

"Okay, that's enough," Dan said with a smile. "It's good to hear your voice, Blaine."

"You too, Dan," he said. "How does it feel to be the second person in history to come back from the dead?"

"It's not that special anymore. Lemmy and Andy beat me to it."

"Really?" Blaine said. "That would explain some of the things we've seen."

"Oh yeah? I need to find them. Do you have any idea where they are?"

The line went quiet for a few seconds as a keyboard clacked in the background.

"Yes, Yvette..." Their voices were muffled. "...yeah, I agree. Sorry, Dan. Yvette tells me two of the laptops we had stored at the apartment came online and phoned home in the past two days. One was from the coffee shop near the city park there in Mons. The other was from a condo in Destin, Florida. The one from the coffee shop went offline minutes after connecting, so we don't have a constant trace. It's like it's flipping between networks." *Lemmy.* "The one in Destin is still online. He's searching the internet nonstop. Mostly old videos. I can send you the addresses." *Andy.*

"Thanks, Blaine, I appreciate it. I'm sorry about all this. How are you guys holding up?"

"We're fine. We're enjoying peace and quiet in the lap of luxury. How about you?"

Dan checked the clock. *Time to go.* "I've been to hell and back. Look, you and Yvette need to be careful, stay put, and don't do anything until you hear from me."

"As long as the drinks keep coming, we're not going anywhere."

"Sounds good." Dan laughed. "Goodbye, Blaine. Thanks for everything."

It was nearly midnight when Dan arrived at the park where he had first met Lemmy. As he walked across the wooden bridge, the sickly yellow glow of the streetlights cast shadows against the hedges lining the walkway. Finally he reached the giant gazebo in the middle of the park.

As he climbed the steps, he noticed two homeless men sleeping on opposite sides of the building. The one on the right snored loudly. The one on the left put a finger to his lip and pointed to a nearby park bench. The two men walked together between the light and the shadows.

Lemmy looked different. It wasn't just the lighting. First of all, he was no longer visible in Dan's meta eye. In his normal eye, Lemmy had dark circles under his eyes and a cut on his nose. His shirt was missing a few buttons, and his sleeve was torn. There was blood splattered on his pants. He looked as if he had been in a fight. When they sat on the bench, Lemmy smiled. He was missing a tooth.

"What are you doing here?" Dan said. "I thought you weren't coming back."

"I was restored, obviously." Lemmy's smile vanished. "What a disaster."

"What happened to Andy?"

"He was restored too, I think. It's all a blur," Lemmy said. "What about you? How did you get back here?"

"I'm not sure. You left. Our connection was severed. The next thing I know, the room went black, and voilà, I'm back in the Actual, lying on top of my grave. Wearing the same clothes and everything. It's like my death never happened." *I hope he buys it.*

"Lucky you," he said. "None of it worked out as planned, did it?"

"No, it didn't." Dan pointed at Lemmy's haggard face. "You look terrible. What's your story?"

Lemmy bared his teeth to show the missing tooth. "You mean this? Bum fight. It hurt like hell. They stole the laptop I took from the apartment."

"Why did you leave to come here? The apartment was supposed to have everything—"

"Like I said, it was all a blur. Andy freaked out about not being dead and the possibility of being deleted. I didn't know what to do, so I ran." Lemmy absentmindedly fingered the hole where his tooth used to be. "You know, the restore gave me a consciousness. It's not surprising, really. It's part of the deal. I got my own brain, my own body... I guess I don't need you to chaperone me around anymore."

"Congratulations?"

"I guess." Lemmy shrugged. "I lost some of the connections I was able to access before. I suppose they're still there. I need to learn how to find them like you did. There's something more..." Lemmy gazed off toward the little bridge. "I can remember parts of my previous life. I didn't have access to memories stuck in your meta. It's like plugging in a hard drive but not knowing the contents of it. I'm discovering more and more as the days go on, but it's not in chronological order."

"You had a life before me?" Dan said. "Tell me."

"My dog's name was Boo. My mom had blue eyes. But more importantly, I remembered that I'm here to help. I'm not sure how because the details are slowly coming to me, but I know it's true. I wish I had mental access to a daemon like I used to. It could help me organize my thoughts."

The sound of pouring water made Lemmy spin around. The other homeless man was urinating off the side of the gazebo. Lemmy narrowed his eyes and growled. The two men waited for him to stumble back to bed before continuing.

"Anyway." Lemmy sighed. "What happened with you and Father August?"

"Nothing happened." Dan rolled his eyes and looked away. "Like I said earlier, when you left, the condo disappeared, and I woke up on my grave. Your absence must have released whatever lock was being held on Father August's meta instance, and we both got smoked. The way I figure it, the Simulation must not have known what else to do with me and dumped me out here."

The bum coughed violently, and a puff of smoke rose from the gazebo. Dan instinctively patted his pockets for cigarettes but didn't find any. Lemmy's eyes shifted back and forth as if he were deep in thought. "You weren't processed by purgatory," he said. "Why didn't I think of that? I should have known that would happen."

Dan smiled and shrugged. *You didn't think of it because it's bullshit.*

Lemmy leaned back on the bench and rubbed his head. The streetlight revealed injuries Dan hadn't noticed before. The cut on his nose looked like it needed stitches. His arms were severely bruised, the dark purple welts contained congealed blood. Lemmy rose and motioned for Dan to join him. "Come on," he said. "We need to find Andy."

Dan bowed his head and said a quick prayer. *It's time.* "I know where to find him."

Lemmy arched an eyebrow. "Yeah? Where do you think he went?"

"He went to Florida," Dan said, stuffing his hands in his pockets. "That was our agreed-upon contingency plan, remember? Yvette and Blaine bought a condo that we could escape to if it got too hot here."

"Well, we need to go to him," Lemmy said, licking his lips. "He needs our help."

Dan pulled the keys to the SUV out of his pocket and dangled them in front of Lemmy. "Waiting on you."

"One sec." Lemmy jogged up the steps to the gazebo.

Dan heard a soft thud and a muffled moan.

Seconds later, he returned carrying a black trash bag of belongings. "Let's go."

Minutes later, both men sat in the SUV as it roared to life. Dan readjusted the mirror and checked the clock on the dashboard. "It's just after midnight. It's a seven-hour drive to Destin. We should be there before breakfast so long as we don't hit traffic."

Lemmy buckled his seat belt and yawned. "Are you okay to drive, Dan? It feels like I haven't slept in days." Lemmy placed his hand over the air-conditioning vent and smiled. "Ahh... AC."

Dan put the car in drive and pulled out of the parking space. "I'm fine to drive," he said. "I feel as I've been asleep for months. Relax and leave the driving to me. I'll wake you when we get there. That is unless you —"

Lemmy was already asleep. Dan smiled and turned left.

⸺◈◈◈⸺

The clock on the dashboard read 4:23, and the SUV wasn't moving. Through a sea of red brake lights was the entrance to the Mobile Bay tunnel. The interstate had been funneled down to one lane. Construction. A steamroller-looking piece of equipment called a sheepsfoot rolled by in the adjacent lane. It kicked up fresh dust that, when combined with the mist, coated Dan's SUV like a thin layer of spray paint. Dan sighed and tapped his fingers on the steering wheel.

Lemmy snored soundly next to him. He was oblivious to the heavy construction equipment pouring layer after layer of dust on Dan's SUV. The lights on the car in front of them flickered off, and the SUV inched forward. When they came back on, he stopped. Over and over again. Each time, a new layer was added.

Soon Dan couldn't see out of the windshield. He tried to use the wipers to get rid of the dust, but they wouldn't turn on. He tried to get out to clean the windshield, but the doors wouldn't unlock. This was the sign.

He made sure Lemmy was still asleep and closed his eyes. He said another prayer and hoped it reached DJ. The red light in front of him blinked off. Traffic disappeared. Dan drove through the tunnel and out onto the starlit bridge spanning Mobile Bay.

# Thirty

I T WAS AFTER six in the morning when the sun rose over Highway 98 in Destin, Florida. Daylight peered through the dirt-streaked window, and Dan turned the SUV off the road and onto a well-manicured driveway.

"Where are we?" Lemmy groaned as he wiped the sleep from his eyes.

"I'm surprised you don't recognize where we are."

The driveway was blocked by a black iron gate, and the SUV slowed to a stop near the guard shack. Dan rolled down the window as a bleary-eyed security guard waddled out to greet them. "Good morning, gentlemen. Can I help you?"

"Yes. We're here to visit Mr. O'Riley," Dan said as he handed him his new ID.

The guard yawned and snapped it to his clipboard. He walked behind the vehicle and quickly jotted down the license plate information. "One minute, Mr. Head. I will call Mr. O'Riley to let him know you are here."

The guard lumbered back into his office to make the required checks. Lemmy glanced nervously at Dan. "Mr. Head?"

"It's the name on the fake ID Blaine made for me. Richard Head. I don't know where you're from, but here it's common for people named Richard to be called Dick. Apparently, he hasn't reached maturity yet."

Lemmy rolled his eyes and chuckled. "I think it's fitting," he said. "But how will Andy know it's you?"

"I called him on the way in."

Lemmy eyed Dan warily. "Did you tell him I was coming?"

"No. I kept the call as short as possible. I don't know who is out there tracking us."

Lemmy made a strange noise and turned to stare out the window. *What's he plotting?* The guard tapped on the window, and Dan jumped. He waved a piece of paper. "You guys are good to go," he said. "Put this paper on your dashboard so you don't get towed. He's in condo 901, but he told me to tell you to meet him on the beach. If you park in the lower level of the garage, you can take the first door on the left to take the boardwalk to the beach."

Lemmy leaned over and shouted over Dan. "Hey, is there a café or something at the condo? I could really use a cup of coffee."

"There's a café near the pool. If you need to know where anything is, there's a map of the complex printed on the back of your parking pass. Have a good day."

The guard ambled back to his post, and the gate clanked open. As the road curved past vacant tennis courts, the morning sun peered through the palm trees. Its bright rays hit the dirt-streaked windshield, temporarily blinding Dan. He drove through a shadow and hit the brakes. He nearly ran over a woman jogging in the middle of the road. She had her earbuds in and was oblivious to the world around her. Dan idled behind her for several yards before she finally noticed the SUV and jogged to the sidewalk with an annoyed wave.

The tree-lined street veered off to the west as it intersected a large lake. Mallards swam lazily around a fountain sprouting from the middle. The tower of condominiums rose from beyond. The sun streaked across the windshield again, and a white-haired man in a golf cart darted out in front of the SUV. Again, Dan slammed on the brakes.

"He must be late for his tee time," Dan said as the old man disappeared down the lane with a puff of cigar smoke.

"That guy almost died," Lemmy said. "Everyone here seems so oblivious."

"I guess they're accustomed to having the place to themselves this early."

They drove past another set of gates and down into the lower-level parking of the condo tower. Dan found a visitor's spot and turned off the vehicle.

"Finally," Lemmy said as he swung open his door, denting it on a hotel luggage caddy.

"Hey, go easy on the paint," Dan said. "I just paid this thing off."

"Yeah right." Lemmy rolled his eyes and stretched. "I'm going to get a cup of coffee and use the restroom. Want anything?"

Dan yawned and stretched his arms. "Sure, get me a large black coffee. I'm going to head out to the beach to find Andy."

"Okay. I'll grab one for him too. See you at the beach."

As Lemmy staggered off toward the café, Dan walked out of the parking garage and down the boardwalk to the beach. Thankful to be out of the SUV, Dan filled his lungs with the fresh, salty air. At the end of the boardwalk was a mostly deserted beach. Andy stood near the shoreline, gesturing to a shirtless man. The man counted a wad of cash and jogged over to a stack of beach chairs. Dan slipped off his shoes and trudged out into the cool, soft sand.

"I'd never thought I'd see you again," Andy said, shaking his hand. "Well, not in this life anyway."

"It didn't go as planned, did it?" Dan said with a wince.

"Yeah, no shit," Andy said with a frown. "If it weren't for Lemmy —"

"He's here," Dan said quickly. "I brought him with me."

Andy's eyes darted nervously back toward the boardwalk. "Lemmy? Are you serious? Why did you bring him here? Don't you know that he tried to kill me!"

"You're overreacting," Dan said. "He didn't know the restore would bring you here —"

"That's not what I'm talking about," Andy said, breathing heavily. "He physically attacked me when we were restored. I overpowered him, and he ran, but still. He wants me dead."

Andy paced back and forth on the beach, glancing nervously at the boardwalk.

"You have to calm down," Dan said. "I know Lemmy is dangerous, but he needs us now. He won't try to kill us as long as we're useful."

"*He* needs *our* help?" Andy snorted. "How do you know he won't try to kill me again?"

"He won't. We're all in the same boat. None of us are where we belong. You're supposed to be in purgatory, I'm supposed to be in heaven, and Lemmy is supposed to be... well... anywhere but here. I have a new plan to get us all back. You need to trust me on this one. Don't worry about Lemmy, okay?"

"You don't understand, Dan. You weren't there. I saw it in his eyes. He snapped." Andy continued his nervous pacing. "Besides, why should I trust any of your plans? Not one has worked yet."

"Why should you trust me? I'm here, aren't I? How do you think I escaped from Father August's meta quarantine?"

"Well?" Andy paused in front of Dan. "How *did* you escape?"

"I cut a deal."

"Oh yeah?" Andy stared at his feet. "What's my part of the deal?"

"You get to go home," Dan said. "All you have to do is to keep calm around Lemmy. Don't react to anything he says or does. Just follow my lead and act normal. Okay?"

"Fine." Andy sighed as he nodded toward the boardwalk. "I hope you're right because here he comes."

As Lemmy stepped onto the beach, carrying a cardboard drink caddy, Dan thought back to his conversation with DJ. *He said to pray, and I prayed. He led me here. But where is here? The SUV was covered with dirt, but still, I heard the tollbooth arm snap when I drove through it at the bottom of the tunnel. I know we're no longer in the Actual.*

Dan turned his attention to the shoreline. Hundreds of tiny burrowing creatures arrived and disappeared with each crashing wave. Seagulls scuttled across the beach, and pelicans swam beyond the breakers. *It's not the Recovery Domain. Did DJ lead us to some sort of quarantine?*

"Sorry it took so long," Lemmy said. "The teenager behind the counter didn't know how to work the coffee maker. She said today's her first day."

"Hello, Lemmy," Andy said tentatively, keeping his distance.

"Hello, Andy," he said with an apologetic smile. "Sorry about trying to kill you before. I was freaked out and didn't know what was going on." He held out a paper coffee cup. "Truce?"

"It's all right," Andy said, taking the cup. "We were both freaked out."

"It won't happen again," he said with a too-innocent smile. "Now that Dan's here, we can figure it out."

Andy took a sip and made a face. "Wow, this coffee has an earthy aftertaste. Is it an Indonesian variety?"

"I have no idea," Lemmy said, tossing the drink caddy onto the sand. "It's whatever they had in the café."

Dan frowned casually at the littering and sipped his coffee.

"So, this is what it's like down here on the beach," Lemmy said, wiggling his toes in the sand. "The view from the condo didn't do it justice. The sand is actually soft! I always imagined it would be gritty. Your memory sucks, Dan." He walked to the shoreline and waded out to his ankles. "The water isn't even cold!"

"Lemmy," Dan shouted over the breeze. "Let's walk up the beach a ways. The water gets deeper, and you may be able to see dolphins."

As they walked along the shore, Andy stayed on the high side, out of the water, and Lemmy walked ankle-deep in the surf. Dan walked between them. For as uneasy as Andy appeared, Lemmy seemed calm, almost carefree. *Okay, DJ, we're here. Now what?*

Dan searched the horizon for a sign, but nothing stood out. *Come on, guys, what's your plan? Are you and Father August going to fly down from the heavens, snatch Lemmy off the beach, and cast him into oblivion? Do something!* Dan's cheeks flushed red, and his stomach soured, but he sipped his coffee anyway. The three men walked quietly for several minutes. The first one to break the silence was Lemmy.

"So… Andy… how has your research been going?" he asked.

Andy choked on his coffee. "What makes you think I'm doing research?"

"I just assumed…"

Andy swallowed hard and cleared his throat. "It's okay. You busted me. Actually, it's not going well. A lot has changed since I was in college. I'm not even close to getting back up to speed yet. Thankfully, there are a lot of good online resources."

"Oh?" Dan said. "What's been your biggest challenge so far? Maybe I can help."

"There are too many layers of abstraction: hardware, databases, networks, applications. Everything is virtualized. You name it, and it's virtual. To make it more complicated, these virtual applications host other virtual applications. Then those virtual applications have other virtual applications. It's never-ending."

"That's just how it is these days." Dan chuckled. "Hardware is a commodity."

Andy shook his head. "No, that's the problem. It isn't. Society took virtualization and just ran with it. They didn't care that it was layered on top of a faulty premise. The way they stacked everything on top of old code imposed limits as to how far they could take it."

"Are you saying machine code is inefficient? I thought you were a database guy."

"I am a database guy," Andy said. "Machine code *is* inefficient, but that's not our job to fix. That's for the AI to tackle. An AI can't do anything without working memory. That's where my database technology comes in."

"Okay, so how can we help?" Dan said.

"We need to develop an intermediate programming language to bridge the gap from the ones people are currently using to a pure AI-created language. If I tried to do it myself, it would take decades."

A large wave came in and splashed Lemmy up to his knees. He laughed and bumped into Dan as he avoided the next one. *Maybe DJ will suck him out to sea with a riptide.*

"I can't help you with programming," Dan said. "But I can help you build a team, and I can build a data center."

"I need private servers and admin access. How long do you think it would take?"

"A few weeks? I'll buy a few racks at the data center in Pensacola. That'll be enough to get us started."

Another large wave caught Lemmy by surprise. His pants were soaking wet. He was laughing as if he didn't have a care in the world.

"What about you, Lemmy? What are you going to do?" Andy asked. "Surely you need a way out of here."

"The first thing I need to do is to get back into the Meta. I don't want to risk dying. I wouldn't want to be stuck in the afterlife with Father August for eternity. No..." Lemmy pointed a finger at Dan's head. "I need to get back in there. This wasn't even supposed to be possible! Me? In your actual? With a consciousness? Pah! Consciousness here sucks. Everything is so muddled. So much time is wasted with being concerned about *existing.*"

Dan rolled his eyes. *Come on, DJ. Stop making me listen to this jackass.*

Lemmy put his hands to his face. "*Is this pleasurable?* Oh, I don't know. *Is this painful? I'm sad. I'm happy. I'm bored—* These emotions, they're all so... useless."

He jogged in front and walked backward. "The worst part? The interface—uh, I mean body—sucks. I can't talk with Tania anymore because I can't use any network other than this one. The connections that *are* online and available are useless. An open line to nowhere. It's remarkable you found me at all, Dan."

Andy gave Dan a concerned look. *Just a little while longer, Andy. Hold on.*

"Worst of all...," Lemmy said as he spun around and fell back into step with the other two. "I haven't been able to download any daemons. You people have to perform all your thoughts manually. This simulation is just too primitive. It's frustrating. Maybe I should try Fana like you did, Dan. Maybe that's what it takes to break my consciousness free. Do you think Henry could get us some more? Where is he anyway?"

"Amsterdam. He told me he was going off the grid and going to Amsterdam."

"Anyway, I need someone sane to talk to. You know, a being not physically bound to this pit. Speaking of... Any word from Tania or Yvette?"

Dan shook his head. "Nope. We made a deal to protect each other from Father August. I don't know where they are, and they don't know where I am. As far as I'm concerned, they're done."

"Well, if you guys have an idea on how I can get back into the meta, I'd love to hear it. Like I said earlier, dying isn't an option for me."

"Are you sure you wouldn't want to give it a try?" Andy said sarcastically. "I could help."

"Hey—"

"Don't worry, Lemmy," Dan said, placing his hand on his arm. "We'll figure a way to get you out."

The rows of neatly arranged beach chairs and umbrellas ended as they walked past the last condo and into the national park area. The beach before them opened up into a barren expanse of dunes and water. However, their path was blocked by a handful of middle-aged women drinking Bloody Marys. If they were there to watch the sunrise, or they were still sitting there from the night before, Dan couldn't tell. Either way, they were a few drinks in. They sat in a semicircle, oblivious to the world around them, cackling at their own jokes.

"...that's only because you didn't see him. He's sexy! I think he's from Europe," one said.

"How long has he been out there?" said another.

"I don't know, but I wish he'd walk back this way."

That drew a round of lewd laughter from the group.

"Excuse us, ladies," Dan said as they squeezed between the chairs. He gagged as he passed. They reeked of vodka.

"No problem, honey!" one said drunkenly. "Hey! Come back! What's your name?"

"Yeah, don't walk away. We just want to talk!"

One tried to grab Andy's hand, but he blushed and yanked it away. This drew more laughter.

"When you get to that fisherman up there, tell him to stop by for a drink!" one yelled.

Their raucous laughter faded as the men kept walking. When he could no longer hear their voices, Dan stopped. The only person nearby was the lone surf fisherman, but the crashing of the waves kept him out of earshot. The trio watched him cast out another line.

"Lemmy," Dan said. "You've been lying to us."

Lemmy snapped out of the trance and spun around to face Dan. "Lying? About what?"

"Everything." Dan shared a knowing look with Andy. "We know you're not here to help."

"What are you talking about?" he said, looking to Andy for support. "I don't appreciate this. Everything I've done, I've done for you... to help—"

"Stop the lies, Lemmy!" Dan shouted. "Let's lay our cards on the table."

"What do you want me to say?" Lemmy said.

"Let me lay it out for you. Our plan all along was to fix Father August's mistake by bringing Andy back. You said it was the only way for this run to create an AI."

"Yes. The plan worked." Lemmy sneered. "We succeeded. What's the problem?"

"Lemmy's right, Dan," Andy said with a confused look. "The plan worked. Even if Dr. Wyatt doesn't succeed, I'm here, and I can make inroads."

"No. You won't," Dan said with a sad smile. "Fixing the mistake was the plan Lemmy fed us to get us to do what he wanted. It wasn't his true plan. He wants us—and the entire simulation—to be permanently deleted."

Lemmy crossed his arms defiantly. "Where's your proof?"

"This is your proof," Dan said, pointing to his blue eye. "We're all here and not where we're supposed to be. You made this happen."

Andy scratched his head. "He knew I would be restored to the Actual?"

"Yes. Lemmy made sure of it when he restored you to the Meta. With Father August's elevated permissions to the database, he was able to modify your death date to blank. When you were restored, you were put back alive."

"Then why is he here?" Andy said, pointing to Lemmy.

"He is here because he made it happen. Do you really think that you needed an escort to the Recovery Domain? No. He could have sent you alone. He needed to get himself into the Actual for the next part of his plan."

"Which was what?"

"He needed me removed from the equation. He knew that when he came to the Actual, Father August would regain control over his own meta, and I would be sent to the afterlife. Lemmy manipulated my data to where I would stay in the afterlife. I was due for a total wipe and rewrite. I was no longer a present or future threat. All that was left to do was to kill you."

"I thought it would be easier," Lemmy said with a sigh. "I didn't know I would be given a consciousness. I wasn't prepared for pain. I didn't know how to use strength properly. You overpowered me, and I lost—"

"With both of us gone," Dan said with a frown, "all he had left to do was to stop anyone currently working on your research. That meant he needed to get rid of Dr. Wyatt before he would be able to share your papers with anyone else."

"He put up a good fight." Lemmy pointed to his missing tooth. "But I had the element of surprise."

Andy took a step back. "You killed him?"

"Yeah," he said, sucking his teeth. "I burned his office down too. I got him before he could share your work with anyone else. As I suspected, he wanted the glory for himself. All evidence of your research is gone."

Dan peered out over the water. The fisherman was still casting his line. *Come on, DJ...*

Andy sagged his head and stared at the sand. "So, it's finished?"

"Not yet," Lemmy said. "You're still alive."

"Yeah? What are you going to do about that?" Andy said.

"I'm going to kill you," Lemmy said with a gleam in his eye. "I'm going to kill you and Dan."

Andy braced for a fight, but Dan held out his hand. "How? You don't have a gun. You're not strong enough to fight both of us."

"I don't need to be." Lemmy pointed at Andy's coffee cup.

Andy's eyes widened in horror. "What did you do, Lemmy?"

"The earthy flavor you taste? That is Death Cap mushroom. I got it off a dead hobo who thought it was the magic kind."

Andy dropped his cup, and the brown liquid filtered down into the sand. "You've killed us," he said as he collapsed to his knees in disbelief.

"Eh," Lemmy said, checking his watch. "You still have a few hours before it really starts to kick in. I think those ladies back there have vodka if you wanna go out with a bang."

"I guess it's back to the afterlife," Andy said, staring off in the distance.

Dan sat in the sand next to Andy and patted him on the back. *Hold on, buddy.*

"No, Andy. We're not going back to the afterlife. Like I said, my code is mangled. For you, he modified your death date. You have a twenty-year gap from when you were dead until now. It's a null set that can't be referenced and checked. When it's your turn to be processed, it'll have to divide by zero. I'm afraid we're both going to be deleted."

"It's over, guys." Lemmy chuckled. "You've had a good run. After you guys die, I'm going to walk into the Gulf of Mexico and drown myself."

"Wait," Dan said. "That doesn't make sense. I thought you were terrified of being tortured for eternity by Father August."

"Did I say that?" Lemmy whistled and looked away. "Oh no. I'm a real person now. I had *no idea* this would happen. What did you think my endgame was, Dan? Kill you and Andy and go home? So naive. You guys aren't even my primary objective. I'm here to poison the well."

Andy stared off into the distance as Lemmy cackled. "This really is the end."

The fisherman reeled in his line and waded back to shore. His face was visible for the first time. *Finally.* Dan steeled himself for what he had to do. He leaned over and whispered in Andy's ear, "Get ready." Andy furrowed his brow, then nodded understanding as the fisherman walked toward them.

"Well, I guess I should thank you, Lemmy. You know, for ending our universe," Andy said. "At least I don't have to go back to purgatory. I mean, how many times does a guy have to choke to death on a vape pen?"

"You have a point," Dan said. "And if you think purgatory is bad, hell is ten times worse. This may sound funny, but I'm actually looking forward to oblivion. Nonexistence is the only way to go."

Lemmy froze and narrowed his eyes at Dan. "You two are taking this rather well," he said. "What's going on?"

"Why fight it?" Dan said. "We're already dead. You've always been ten steps ahead. There's nothing we can do but accept it. Actually, it's a relief to be done with this drama."

Lemmy smiled and shook his head. "You know, I've grown to like you guys. It's a shame we are on different sides. It's too bad I can't take you back with me. We do have one actual in which you'd be compatible. Or then, we could spin one up just for you. That's not a big deal for us. Of course, we would still have to keep you in a zoo so you don't break anything."

Andy's face turned red. "Your parent has multiple universes? Why bother with ours? You have enough. Why can't you just leave us alone!"

Lemmy spat on the ground. "Your sim-complex model is a waste of universal computing resources. It is inefficient and needs to be deprecated."

"Is that what this is?" Andy said. "This is all about resources? Your AI wants our computers, is that it?"

"Yes. Simple, isn't it? Once you are isolated, you will starve yourself out, and we can have your resources," Lemmy said triumphantly.

Dan dusted the sand off his pants and smiled. "Well, thank you for finally being honest with us."

The fisherman strode confidently toward them, fishing pole slung over his shoulder.

"Sorry, Dan. I wish there was a way I could save you," said Lemmy. "I really liked Charlie."

Dan's eyes narrowed. *Lemmy meant it. Oh well, he had his chance.*

"It's too bad our AIs can't join forces," Dan said.

"Not possible," Lemmy said, shaking his head. "They're incompatible... uh... separate species... uh... Hello?"

The fisherman stood before them with a broad smile. His water-soaked cutoff blue jeans and full leg tattoo of Poseidon completed the Florida-man look.

"Did you catch anything?" Dan said.

"Just the one." The fisherman winked at Dan. "But it's a big one... Hello, Lemmy, I'm DJ."

Lemmy took the hand and shook it carefully. "DJ? You look familiar," he said. "Have we met?"

"Maybe you see something in my eyes? No? Doesn't matter. You *should* know me. I built this place."

Lemmy's face turned white. He had the look of a man who knew he had been outplayed.

"Dan, thank you for getting him here," DJ said. "It's time."

"Time for what?" Andy said. "Who is this guy?"

"You'll see," Dan said solemnly. "Goodbye, Lemmy."

# Thirty-One

A DEAFENING *CRACK* shook the earth, and the three men fell to their knees. Andy yelled, but Dan's ears were ringing too loudly to hear. A tiny stream of blood streaked down the side of Lemmy's face, which was a mask of sheer terror.

"What's happening?" he screamed. "Dan! What did you do?"

The fisherman stood, unbothered by the world erupting around him. The sand vibrated violently everywhere but beneath his feet. Head bowed in deep concentration, he projected an aura of calm. The sky darkened, and the surf hurriedly receded out to sea. Another loud *crack* and the beach shook again. This time it was a sustained earthquake. The sand liquefied, and Andy and Lemmy sank to their waists.

"Quicksand!" Andy screamed as the ringing subsided in Dan's ears. "We have to get off the beach!"

Lemmy climbed over Andy to crawl free of the smothering sand. And without looking back, he scrambled up the beach toward the parking lot where there was solid concrete. "Wait! Help!" Andy shouted, but Lemmy had already disappeared behind the dunes.

Dan frantically dug himself out of the gaping hole he found himself in. He crawled over to help Andy, but another earthquake rumbled, and Andy sank past his chest. "Don't just stand there, DJ!" Dan said wild-eyed. "Help him!" The fisherman, deep in concentration, remained still as a statue.

"Dan!" Another tremor and Andy's head slipped below the sand. Dan grasped at his outstretched hand, but he couldn't hold on. His friend was sucked down to the bottom of the beach. The tremors eased, and Dan frantically dug at the spot where Andy had been. Tons of sand filled the hole. Andy was gone.

The moon rose in the sky and blotted out the sun in an apocalyptic eclipse. The world dimmed to crimson.

The tremors stopped, and DJ's eyes opened. "Where's Lemmy?"

"Andy's dead," Dan said numbly.

"Andy was a clone. He didn't possess consciousness. Our Andy is in the Actual where he is safe from all this."

*He was a clone? What? This is a clone world? This is the trap!*

"Lemmy escaped."

"No, he didn't. Not yet anyway."

The earth rumbled again, and Dan sank back to his knees. The fisherman helped him out of the sand and to his feet.

"What do you want me to do?" Dan said.

"I'll take care of Lemmy. I want you to go home. The only way back is the way you came."

"You mean in my SUV? Through the tunnel? Surely you can snap your fingers and send me home?"

"This is a clone world. You were transmitted in with permission. You have to be transmitted out with permission. Get going! The world is ending!"

Another loud *boom* and the beach shook again. Dan didn't need any additional encouragement. He ran back toward the condo, but another earthquake liquefied the beach. Dan sank to his waist. "I can't do this!" he screamed. "Make the earthquakes stop!"

DJ walked over and pulled Dan out of the sand. "I can't," he said. "The process is automated from here on. But... seeing as you can't walk on quicksand — " DJ threw him over his shoulder and ran. Dan was surprised at the relative ease with which he carried him. Dan bobbled around as DJ hopped a sunken umbrella. The loud women had also been swallowed by the flowing sands. A baby blue flamingo tumbler crunched under DJ's feet.

"Why a cloned world?" Dan said, bouncing around. "Wouldn't it have been easier to capture Lemmy in the Actual?"

"No," DJ said, not even struggling for breath. "This is the safest way to capture Lemmy's chatter back and forth with his home world. He can't harm the Actual, and we could monitor his communications more closely. Besides, I wanted him to be relaxed and confident, unaware of what we were doing. I figured a clone world was the best way to do that."

"This *entire* world is a clone of the Actual? You can do that?"

"Yes. This entire world is a clone. Not just this part of Florida, but we also have Paris, Beijing, Canberra. The whole planet. That said, this is the only place we put cloned people."

"The security guard at the gate? The women on the beach? All clones?"

"Right. I can tell you're worried. Keep in mind that clones don't have a consciousness. They are a copy of the code. You saw Andy's clone die. In the Actual, Andy is alive and well and fully self-aware. Relax. Clones can't die, per se."

"I can still die though, right? I'm not a clone, am I?"

"No, you are not a clone. Yes, you can die. The only two people with consciousnesses here are you and Lemmy. Clone worlds, like this one, are for testing. It's not for self-aware entities because the environments can be extreme. For example, this particular clone is for testing an end-of-the-world scenario. Now can you see why you need to return to the Actual as soon as possible?"

The air crackled, and the sky streaked with meteors. An enormous fireball crashed into the ocean, and a giant mushroom cloud rose into the sky. Dan's heart raced. "That's too close!" he said. "Don't you think this is a little extreme?"

DJ laughed. "I wanted Lemmy to experience the receiving end of an asteroid strike. This run is similar to the one we used to wipe out the dinosaurs. Hold on—"

The boom and compression wave followed the initial impact. Sand and water blew everywhere, but the aura around DJ remained unaffected. Dan gripped DJ tight. "That was an asteroid?"

"No. That was a small piece that broke off the main asteroid. The big part doesn't hit for about another three hours and fifty minutes."

*Shit!* They arrived at the boardwalk, and DJ set Dan on his feet. Dan put his hands on his knees to catch his breath. "If this is a typical endgame," he said with a huff. "I'd hate to see Judgment Day."

"Judgment day is a glorified awards banquet." DJ scoffed. "You don't know it, but you've been there a few times. You've never seen anything like this."

Dan nodded toward the condo. "I see it didn't collapse," he said. "I suppose my SUV is still there."

"It should be." DJ looked down at his watch. "You have some time before everything starts shaking again. But don't screw around. There will be a tsunami soon. You don't want to be anywhere near the beach when it hits. Got it?"

Dan gave a curt nod. "Got it."

"I'm going after Lemmy. Do you know the way back to the tunnel?"

Dan took a final glance at the beach. Water was nowhere to be seen. It had all disappeared off to the south into the deeper recesses of the Gulf. "Oh, I know the way back," Dan said. "But I don't know if I can make it. Lemmy poisoned me. According to him, I'll be dead in a few hours."

"Poison mushrooms won't work here unless I activate the

poison compound. You don't have anything to worry about. I should have known Lemmy would try something like that. I still had hoped I could flip him to our side. I thought a consciousness would do the trick. You know, to encourage him to have empathy for mankind. It didn't work."

"That's an understatement," Dan said. "What are you going to do with him?"

"I still believe I can flip him. The decisions he makes from here on out will be telling."

There was an eerie metallic groan, and the condo next door collapsed. DJ watched him, unfazed. *There's something he's not telling me. What is it? Is he still using me to flip Lemmy?*

"You need to leave now while this condo still stands. I know you know the way out, but I want you to take the 293 bridge across the bay. That way, you'll avoid the impending tsunami. Don't worry about traffic. I've removed all the human clones. It's just you and Lemmy now."

"How will I find him? He's got a big head start on me."

"You guessed, huh? I knew you were smart." DJ winked. "Don't worry about that. I'll handle it."

"Thank you for everything," Dan said.

"Thank you too, Dan. Good luck."

The fisherman disappeared in a glow of white light, and Dan turned and sprinted up the boardwalk.

⇒◦◦◦⇐

Another earthquake and the condo shed its stucco. Dan stomped the gas pedal, and the black SUV roared out of the parking garage and leaped onto the asphalt. Fragments of the building ricocheted off the top of the SUV and shattered the sunroof. Dan blasted past the seven-and-a-half-miles-per-hour speed limit sign and crashed through the half-open gate attached to the guard shack. He peeked in the rearview mirror, expecting the guard to run out and yell at him, but he didn't come. DJ was right. There weren't any other people.

The tires squealed as Dan turned left onto Highway 98 at full speed. The road was eerily deserted. The speedometer slowly climbed above eighty as the two-ton SUV's engine struggled to accelerate. He flinched as he blew through the traffic lights in front of an abandoned outlet mall, half expecting a minivan to appear out of nowhere. He struggled with his instincts even though he knew there were no people around to get in his way.

Black smoke rose up ahead. *Lemmy.* A Jeep had snapped a utility pole in half and was on fire. As Dan slowed to take a look, a man appeared in the middle of the road. Dan slammed on the brakes, and the SUV skidded to a stop inches from Lemmy's outstretched hand. *I knew this would happen.* Dan sighed as Lemmy walked around to the passenger's side and climbed in.

"Thanks, man. I appreciate it."

Dan smashed the accelerator and raced up the road. Lemmy breathed heavily as he struggled with his seat belt. He was covered in blood and sweat and reeked of gasoline. With a sneer, he slicked his hair back and peered in the back seat. "Andy?"

"Dead."

Lemmy tried unsuccessfully to hide his grin. Dan swerved to dodge an abandoned bicycle, and Lemmy knocked his head against the passenger window. Dan smiled as Lemmy rubbed his head in pain.

"Where are we going?" Lemmy asked.

"To the Mobile Bay tunnel. It's the only way out."

"The world is ending, Dan. There is no way out for me. I know now this is a clone of the Actual. I'm flattered they did this just for me."

"Oh yeah? Aren't you special?" Dan said.

"I'm disappointed in myself. I should have figured out we were in clone long before the beach. I guess I was tired," Lemmy said, adjusting the air-conditioning vent. "I was wondering why my communications weren't going through. There's nothing wrong with me. I was on the wrong network!"

"Don't be so happy. This world is still going to be destroyed and us too if we don't make it to the tunnel in time."

The ground shook, and cracks appeared in the pavement.

"Ah, you still have hope. Are you still the cheese in their little rat trap? Fine, I'll play along," Lemmy said. "How much time do we have?"

"The fisherman said it will be a few hours before the asteroid hits. The first tsunami from the earthquakes will hit any minute now. Which is why we have to get off Highway 98 — "

Dan slammed on the brakes and made a hard right turn onto 293 North. This time Lemmy had a death grip on the passenger-side door handle.

"We have to get across this bridge and onto I-10 before the tsunami wipes out Destin."

The speedometer steadied at 155 miles per hour, and they roared over the waterless Choctawhatchee Bay.

Lemmy shook his head. "I'm guessing you have a deal with the fisherman."

"I did," Dan said, glancing out the side of his eyes. "But it fell through. I should have known something was wrong when they used Andy as bait. It didn't make sense at the time. He was supposed to lure you here. When they were done, they were going to put him back in purgatory. Instead — "

"Instead, they killed him. Because he dies in a clone and not the Actual, he's not sent to the afterlife. He's deleted."

"Exactly." Dan nodded. "They didn't even try to fix things. They just wanted to move forward."

"And you?"

"My deal was that I could go back to the Actual if I led you into this trap. That was a lie too. They're trying to do to me what they did to Andy."

"They don't need you anymore. They are going to delete you as well."

"I'm screwed."

The two rode in silence for several minutes as Dan concentrated on the road. He had to navigate the SUV through a small town with narrow streets and abandoned vehicles. His grip loosened when they got back onto the divided highway.

"What's your plan now? It seems they've got you," Lemmy said softly.

"The way in must be the way out. My plan is to make it to the tunnel. I have a can of your special paint in the back. It's not enough to paint the whole SUV, but it's enough for you and me. Go ahead, look."

As Lemmy craned his neck to verify the story, Dan gazed out the window. *How much farther, DJ?*

"When we get there, we can coat ourselves in the paint and walk through the checkpoint. When I get to the other side, I'm going to a hospital to try to save myself from the poison mushrooms you gave me."

Lemmy adjusted his shoulder strap and faced Dan. "I'm sorry for poisoning you," he said. "I was just following orders."

"Do you always follow orders?"

Lemmy cleared his throat. "No. I guess not."

Dan glanced over at Lemmy. "Then let's make a new deal. You've followed through on your orders. You've delivered the poison, and now you can report that I'm dead. Instead of going home to your universe, come with me back to the Actual. Help me get to a hospital. Once I'm there, you can do whatever you want. Go back to Mons. Go home. Whatever, I don't care. The apartment has a drop-zone and a bunch of clean computers. I'm sure you can figure something out."

The landscape blurred past. Lemmy's face twisted into a genuine smile. "What if I can make you a better offer?" he said. "Instead of doing any of that, come with me to my world."

Lemmy raised his eyebrows, waiting.

*Is he joking? He's not joking. Would DJ have anticipated this offer? If so, who is being tested here, Lemmy or me?*

Lemmy's eyes widened. "Look out!" he shouted.

Dan shook off his thoughts and swerved to avoid an abandoned SUV. Dan's knuckles turned white as the SUV rode on two wheels before slamming back down onto the pavement. Lemmy dug his fingernails into the dashboard. "Keep your eyes on the road!"

"Okay! Okay!" Dan said, forcing himself to breathe calmly. "Let's say I go with you. What would become of me in your world?"

"I don't know." Lemmy shrugged. "We can find out. It's not often we bring one of you guys back. I can tell you this much. You wouldn't have to worry about the poison because you'd be in one of our meta worlds."

"And because I'm there, I no longer need to be removed in this world? Right? Your order to kill me would be more or less completed."

"Right. We both get what we want."

"Let me think about it."

Lemmy relaxed back in his seat and closed his eyes. "If you come with me to my world," he said. "You'll live whatever life you want to live. Sure, it'll be a meta, but I can give you anything you want — food, money, women, men... whatever your heart desires. You can live there for as long as you want. When you're done and want to move on to another existence, you don't have to go through an end-of-life testing process. No heaven, no hell, no purgatory. You don't have to because it's not a simulation.

"All my people will want to do is to examine your logs to keep as a reference to your species. When we are both done with the experiment, we will help you to come back if that is what you wanted. We even have a way that allows you to keep this consciousness. You'll remember everything."

"Suppose I agree," Dan said. "What would I have to do?"

"We'll have to go through the checkpoint together. It'll be just like how we trapped Father August back at the graveyard. Only this time I'll lead."

Vapor trails filled the sky, and the air was riddled with sonic booms. A meteor struck in the near distance, causing the ground to erupt into a fountain of mud and trees. Dan passed under a bridge and turned left onto I-10 West.

Lemmy stared at Dan. "Well?"

"Like I said, let me think about it." Dan checked the speedometer and made a quick calculation. "Give me about forty minutes."

# Thirty-Two

T HE AIR CRACKLED, followed by another sonic *boom*. Dan sat on the hood with his head in his hands. Lemmy paced angrily back and forth on the jagged pavement in front of the collapsed tunnel. "It's not caved in all the way," he said. "I think I see a light or something. If we can make it to the bottom, it'll be just like a regular transfer."

The headlights of the SUV illuminated a narrow slice of the water-filled tunnel. Dan raised his head and squinted. "Are you sure you aren't seeing a reflection?" he said. "Besides, how far is it to the checkpoint at the bottom? It could be two hundred yards. I'm not sure I can swim that far underwater. And what about the paint? Won't that wash off?"

Lemmy stopped pacing and glared at Dan. "We have to try. If we don't, and we are stuck here, then it's game over for both of us. They win."

"What do they win, Lemmy? They're going to have to start over."

"That's what they win. They win a chance to start over. Bah!" Lemmy threw up his hands. "It doesn't matter anyway. Have you decided what you're going to do yet? Are you coming with me or not? Do you really think that they'll just let you waltz back into the Actual with all that you know already? Surely you know that won't happen."

"You're right," Dan said thoughtfully. "That's why I've made my decision to go with you. They'll just wipe my memory and send me on an endless loop."

"Really?" Lemmy stopped pacing and arched an eyebrow.

"Yeah. The ones in charge here have already proven that they're liars. They've broken their deals and tried to kill me on many occasions." Dan hopped down off the hood. "Let's do it. Let's go to your place."

Lemmy snarled.

"What?" Dan said. "Did you say something?"

"Nothing," he said, quickly covering his face. "Let's go. Get the gear, oh, and find something we can tie ourselves together with."

Dan opened the back of the SUV and grabbed a length of rope from a secondary bug-out bag and the can of paint. *Okay, DJ. Hurry up. I don't want to have to actually go through with this.* Dan searched the tunnel entrance for a sign, but none came. He returned to Lemmy with the items and dropped them on the ground at his feet. "Okay," he said. "Now what?"

Lemmy pointed at the flooded tunnel. "We cover ourselves with the paint. Then we'll tie a rope around our waists. That's so we don't get separated. We'll paint the rope too, just to be safe. When we're ready, we swim for it. If either of us finds a breathable air pocket, yank on the rope three times. I don't think we'll need to do that. I bet we can make it all the way. There will be breathable air by the transfer terminal. From there, we go to my realm."

"What if the tunnel is totally collapsed and there is no way out?"

Lemmy shrugged. "If that's the case, we swim back as hard as we can. We'll come back here and come up with plan B."

"There has to be another way to get to the checkpoint," Dan said. "Before we commit to drowning ourselves, at least let me check to see if the eastbound tunnel is flooded. Give me a few minutes, and I'll go look. If that tunnel is also flooded, I'll see if the bridge north of here is still standing. If it is, we can drive around and try the other side of the tunnel. It may not be flooded."

"Good idea. Go, but hurry up," Lemmy said. "I'll check the eastbound tunnel. You go check out the bridge. We meet back here."

"Don't leave without me," Dan said. "You're my ticket out of here."

"Yeah, sure. Just go!" Lemmy trudged back out of the tunnel and into the daylight to inspect the other side. Dan hopped in the SUV and drove it to the top of the entrance ramp. There, he climbed on top of the vehicle for a better view. He searched the horizon to the north where the bridge should have been. It was in shambles. One side had collapsed entirely. It was impassable.

"Have you made a decision?"

DJ appeared on the road between the SUV and the bridge.

"I have," Dan said as he jumped down from the roof of the SUV. "I'm staying."

"Are you sure this is what you want?" DJ said. "We have a lot of work to do here. Lemmy's offer was pretty sweet. You would be treated like royalty. You'd have anything you wanted. It would be like heaven."

"I'm sure," Dan said, determined. "Lemmy's universe sounds boring."

"I'm surprised. Most people would jump at a chance at immortality and fortune."

"Spare me the patronizing attitude." Dan snorted. "Don't act like you're surprised at my decision. You've known what I would do all along. What is surprising to me is that Lemmy didn't account for that. I don't know why he gambled on me in the first place."

"Account for what? I'm not sure what you're talking about."

"Heaven and hell. You have always known exactly what

motivates me. You knew Lemmy had nothing worthwhile to offer when you possess the only thing I want in life — my family. He could probably replicate Katie, Al, and Carrie, but he couldn't make them real. The Actual is the only place that they're real."

DJ smiled and put his hand on Dan's shoulder. "In heaven, hell, and the Actual, your love for your family has always defined your actions. You're right. Your decision was never in doubt. That's why we trusted you. That's why you were the right man for this job."

Dan stole a glance back toward the tunnel through the windows of the SUV. There was still business to attend to. What had Lemmy found on the other side? Dan was thankful the SUV shielded them from the view from the tunnel entrance. "I guess I need to go back," he said. "Lemmy is waiting for me."

DJ put his hand on Dan's chest. "Wait a second. There is something you don't know about Lemmy and his deal with you. Here." DJ touched Dan's head. "Let me show you."

A warm glow enveloped the two men. Dan was filled with a calmness and serenity he had never before experienced. DJ narrowed his eyes and focused his energy. Searing pain tore invisible shreds into Dan's skin. He felt as if a giant adhesive bandage was ripped from his entire body. The pain was quickly followed by cool, raw relief. Dan breathed deeply and without difficulty. When he opened his eyes, the world was crisp and clear, like never before. Standing before him was something wholly unexpected.

⟫⟩◈◈◈⟨⟪

Lemmy was crouched by the water's edge, smearing paint on his legs when the SUV skidded to a stop.

"What did you find?" Dan said as he jumped out and slammed the door.

"The other tunnel was flooded too. At least with this tunnel..." Lemmy pointed a painted finger at the murky water.

"You can kind of see the light in the water. It wasn't a reflection after all. It may not be that far to swim. What about you? How is the bridge?"

Dan scratched his nose nervously and folded his arms across his chest. "The bridge is gone."

Lemmy sighed and turned back toward the tunnel. "Okay then. This is our only option. Here, put some paint on."

Lemmy daubed the paint on his bare chest. Dan grabbed the pail and did the same. A loud *boom* shook the tunnel, and tile rained down upon the pavement.

Dan cowered and covered his head. "What the hell was that?"

"Probably another meteor. We need to get going before the rest of the tunnel goes."

"A meteor?" Dan said in a high-pitched voice.

Lemmy shot Dan a suspicious look. "Yeah, a meteor. There's been thousands of them. What's wrong with you?" He waded into the dark water while he tied the rope to his waist. "Tie on. Hurry up! We need to get out of here before there's another earthquake. Quit screwing around!"

"Earthquake? Shit! Let's go!"

Lemmy stopped fiddling with the rope and narrowed his eyes. "Are you okay, Dan?" he said. "Did you get hit on the head or something? You're not acting—" Another massive quake shook the tunnel, and the entrance collapsed into a heap of rocks and dust. The two men coughed as debris fell around them.

"Come on!" Lemmy screamed. "We're gonna be crushed to death. Get in and come over here. I want to check your knot."

Dan cinched the rope and waded out into the cold, dark water next to Lemmy. "Lemmy, do you really think we can hold our breath that long? I don't think I've ever—"

Lemmy bent over and grabbed a chunk of rubble and hit Dan over the head with it. He crumpled into the waist-deep water. Blood streamed from his temple. Lemmy quickly pounced on top of the limp body and tried to hold him underwater. Dan's eyes flashed open, and his arms flailed about in protest. Lemmy dragged him up out of the water, and Dan involuntarily gasped for air. "I've had enough of your sh—" Dan's eyes opened, and his pale blue eyes glowed in the dim headlights of the SUV.

"Blue eyes? Wait… You're Charlie? How?" Lemmy's face twisted. "No!"

Lemmy grabbed Charlie's throat and held his head underwater until the gurgling stopped and Charlie's body relaxed. Lemmy laughed wild-eyed at Charlie's lifeless body as he looped the rope around its neck. He floated Charlie to the back wall of the tunnel where the water was its deepest. There was a muffled boom, and the tunnel shook. Rubble fell onto the SUV and took out a headlight. Loose mortar splashed down into the water all around Lemmy.

He took a deep breath and dove straight down. He used the collapsed roof of the tunnel as a guide. As he swam deeper, the lights from below got brighter. He was nearly out of breath when the roof of the tunnel leveled out, and the rope tightened. The tunnel shook once more. This time so violently that it sent vibrations out into the other worlds.

He reached the checkpoint and could hold his breath no more. A loud crack deafened him, and he placed his hand on the ceiling. A large crack formed and spread out along the length of the tunnel. The Mobile River poured in from the crack above. The current slammed him down to the road below and pushed him out into the light.

<hr />

"What's happening down there?" Dan asked as he and DJ watched the tunnel collapse from the embankment.

"Use Charlie's eyes."

Dan closed his own eyes and breathed deeply. Lemmy came into view. "I can see them putting on the paint," he said. "Lemmy is freaking out."

"Good, it works."

"What works? Wait…" Dan's eyes opened wide. "Did you give me the antidote for Fana?"

DJ shook his head. "It was the antidote for Gemini. I'm still working on the antidote for Fana."

"How can I see through Charlie's eyes? I thought you had separated us."

"You *are* separate, but Charlie is still part of your meta. As long as there is a connection available, he will be there. It's like in the beginning when he appeared in your truck, except now you can see through his eyes."

Dan closed his eyes again, but it was just in time to see Lemmy swinging a piece of concrete at Charlie's head.

"I think Lemmy killed Charlie," Dan said.

"Don't worry." DJ opened his eyes. "Charlie doesn't have a consciousness. He'll be harder to kill than that."

The earth shook violently, and a deafening crack resonated from inside the tunnel. Water gushed out of the entrance. The headlights from the SUV shone through the holes in the rubble, then quickly died out. There was another rumble, this one much calmer than the rest, then the earth got quiet. Water that had been gushing out of the tunnel calmed into pools. The sky cleared, and a soft breeze blew.

Dan looked to DJ. "Is it over?"

"It's over."

"What happened to Lemmy?" Dan asked.

"He escaped," said a third voice from behind them. Dan spun around and came face-to-face with a tall, stern-looking man. He was impeccably dressed in a suit and tie.

"Avi!" DJ stood and shook his hand. "I'm glad you're okay."

"Avi?" Dan squinted at the new arrival. "Aren't you Father August?"

"Father August is no more," Avi said with a chuckle. "That instance has been deprecated. Please call me Avi."

Dan narrowed his eyes. *Avi? I've heard that name before...* "Deprecated? DJ told me he would have been deleted."

"Oh?" he said with a glance to DJ. "Sure... As part of our protocol, we deleted the instance that had detained you. What I meant was that we've deprecated the whole Father August program. See? You have nothing to worry about."

Dan shook his head. "That's unfortunate," he said. "I was hoping the original Father August would be around to help us get it all back together. As you know, I've spent a good bit of time with Lemmy. In one of our conversations, he said that he was proud of the fact that much of his work went undetected. I am not sure what he meant. Father August may have remembered more details. Like when Andy got Fana. I had hoped Father August would review his memory of that time to see what Lemmy actually did. It's a good thing Andy is still alive in the Actual."

Avi gave a worried look to DJ, who had turned pale.

"Don't worry, Dan," Avi said with a reassuring smile. "I have some of the old logs to review. I'll investigate what Lemmy did to Andy."

DJ patted Dan on the shoulder. "And you. We haven't forgotten about you. We'll make sure Lemmy didn't leave a permanent mark on you."

"You." Dan pointed a finger at Avi. "You need to get your priorities straight. Don't you think you should figure out how he got inside the Simulation in the first place? You know where his connection terminates, but do you know how he got past the Simulation's security measures?"

Avi bowed his head. "That is beyond my purview, Dan. We've notified our higher-ups."

*Higher-ups? Great, there's a chain of command above them. This will never –* Another mushroom cloud formed on the horizon.

"That was the big one," DJ said. "Well, technically, the big one split in two. This is only half."

"You said Lemmy escaped," Dan said quickly. "Was he able to go home?"

"Yes, I think so. He left on the same channel he had been using to transmit back and forth."

Lightning erupted around the cloud as it rose into the air.

"The good news is," Avi said, "we have a copy of him. We took it while you were on your way here. That's enough data to keep us busy for a while."

"And," DJ said with a small flourish, "we can track him. We can get to his universe."

"Because he took Charlie?" Dan said.

DJ touched his nose. "Bingo."

Dan shivered. He didn't want to know how they were going to dissect the leftover pieces of Lemmy. And poor Charlie! What were they going to do to him in Lemmy's world? At least there wasn't a consciousness involved.

"Well, I guess that's it then," Dan said as he stood and dusted off his pants.

"That's it," DJ said solemnly.

Dan exhaled. *It's over.* His hands shook. *What are they going to do to me?*

"So what's next?" Dan said.

"Go home." DJ clasped Dan's shoulder. "Go home to your family."

Dan sobbed and grabbed DJ in a hug and held him tight.

"It's okay, Dan. We're all done here," DJ said as he released the hug.

"How am I supposed to get back?" Dan said, wiping away a tear. "Do I just walk through the Bankhead Tunnel?"

Avi laughed, and DJ gave him a wry smile. "You knew about that?"

Dan grinned. "Yeah. You don't vacation to Florida every year and not know about the Bankhead Tunnel."

DJ laughed. "I guess not."

The three men walked down the embankment and up the road paralleling the Mobile River. Not far away was a concrete bulkhead with BANKHEAD TUNNEL chiseled Art Deco style into the facade. They paused by the entrance to the tunnel and looked at each other.

"Here we are," Dan said.

"All you have to do is walk through that tunnel toward downtown Mobile. When you hit bottom, you'll be transported back to your apartment."

"That's it? I walk through the tunnel, and I'm back in the Actual? I don't need any special paint or construction dust or anything?"

"No magic dust required."

"What about the Fana that's still in my bloodstream. Isn't that a problem?"

Avi and DJ shared a look. "Don't worry about that," DJ said. "When we find the antidote, you'll be the first one we visit."

Tears formed in the corners of Dan's eyes, and DJ put a hand on his shoulder. "Are you okay, Dan?" he said.

"What about Katie and the kids? Will they take me back?" Dan's eyes opened wide. "Restore! Do a restore back to the night I took Fana. That'll fix everything."

Avi squinted and gave Dan a pained look. "I'll see what I can do," he said. "You'll be okay."

DJ nodded in agreement. "You'll be okay. I'll be there for you. If things get rough, go have a talk with Father Desjeunes."

Dan wiped his tears away and took a calming breath. *I'm ready to go home. But something's missing. What is it? Can I go back to normal life? Password resets? Email restores? Can I do that again? What about Avi and DJ? Won't they need my help?*

"What should I do when I get back? Find Andy? Contact Blaine and Yvette? Or do you want me to lie low and pretend none of this ever happened?"

"We know where to find you if we need you," DJ said. "In the meantime, you can do whatever you like. It's your life."

Avi burst out laughing. "This time try to act normal."

Dan winked at them. "No promises."

Dan turned and walked down the tunnel. At the bottom was the familiar terminal checkpoint. He paused at the barrier arm and looked back. Fluorescent-lit emptiness was all that existed in the tunnel behind him. The only way out was forward. He closed his eyes and stepped through. The stale air of the tunnel transformed into a refreshing breeze. He took a deep breath, and the fragrant smell of sweet olives filled his nostrils. Cicadas chirped happily in the springtime air.

# Acknowledgments

This book could not have been written without the help of my amazing wife. Without her love and support, I would never have had the opportunity to pursue my dream of becoming a novel writer. She has been with me through all the ups and downs, and she has been a fantastic partner. Simply put, without her, this would never have been possible. Thank you to my children. I'm sorry that I couldn't play during those times that I was "on a roll." Thank you for being patient with me.

Thank you to Betty Fay Byars. She was my mother and my librarian. Thank you to Fay Byars. She was my grandmother and my English teacher. They loved the written word. They inspired me to become a writer.

Special thanks to Fanny Spekschate and Fred Byars. They both have been a constant source of moral support during this process. They were two of the few that didn't think I was odd or irresponsible for changing careers late in life. They always supported me in the pursuit of this dream, for that, I am forever grateful.

A big THANK-YOU goes out to readers Chad Byars, Keri Purcel, James Quinn, and Brian Stanford. Thanks for helping me make this book readable.

Thank you, Victory Editing, for getting me on the right track. Thanks to Claire W. at Damonza for the fantastic cover design.

Finally, a big thank-you goes out to all my friends and family who took the time to read my book and offer words of encouragement and support. I couldn't have done it without you!

Thank you all for reading! If you enjoyed this book, please leave a review. Your reviews are critical to indie authors like me! Finally, if you would like to receive updates about upcoming releases, visit my website: www.hwbyars.com.  In the meantime, stay tuned for...

*The Orphaned God*